Blood and Sand

The Collected Stories of Ramsbolt

Jennifer M. Lane

Cover design by Alia Hess – cultofsasha.com

Copyright © 2019

Published by Pen and Key Publishing

jennifermlanewrites.com

ISBN: 978-1-7334068-1-9

ACKNOWLEDGEMENTS

Thank you to Sunyi Dean, Shelly Campbell, Essa Hansen, John MacAdam, Meghan LaSalle, Leigh M. Morrow, and Cheryl Murphy.

Special thanks to Alia Hess.

CHAPTER ONE

Logan Cole had never been on a bus in her life. As she stretched her legs and stumbled onto the sidewalk at the tip of Maine, she cursed the eight-hour learning experience and swore never to do it again.

The last stop before the border was less like a terminal and more like a dead end. No benches, no depot, no ticketing window. And no taxis. Just a little yellow house with leaning porch surrounded by scruffy blueberry shrubs. At least it wasn't sweltering out.

She yanked her black Rimowa suitcase, one of the few things the FBI let her keep, from the bottom of the bus. She gave the driver a wry smile and thanked him for the trip. It wasn't his fault a woman coughed and crinkled candy wrappers the whole way, and that guy with his earbuds in behind her never learned to sing.

"Six hundred miles better be far enough." She mumbled to herself as she dragged the suitcase down the sidewalk, fumbling for her phone in her purse. It was a habit she still hadn't broken, opening apps to fill a void, but she'd deleted Twitter, Facebook, and the rest of them when the threats started pouring in. Eight months, four court cases, a thousand stories in the news, and she still hadn't gotten used to being without social media. Being disconnected was better than scrolling through contempt, though.

"Battery's almost dead. Map won't load. Damn it." She walked back the way she'd come, past quaint little houses and blueberry bushes, back to the bar she'd seen a mile or so before. It was across from a cheap motel with moldy siding and mildewed plastic chairs. The bar itself was windowless and brick. Definitely not the kind of place where someone would look for one of the wealthiest people in the country. Or someone who used to be.

She paused at an intersection and started a text to her mom, a quick note to say she was far from the gossip and rumors, safe from tabloid headlines squawking about a Cole Curse, and nowhere near the internet trolls who flooded her notifications with threats, saying they knew where to find her and what they would do to her when they did. All because of her father.

She waited among the cigarette butts and rusted beer caps while her text bounced its way to France.

Delivered. Three dots appeared. Her mother's reply came slow.

Good luck. Lay low. I'll send money if I can. Try to blend in.

Logan sent back a smiley face and a greeting for her aunt and uncle.

Letting her phone fall back in her purse, she swallowed hard and tugged hem of her T-shirt down over her jeans. Her heart pounded so loud she wouldn't be able to hear traffic if there'd been any. But the intersection was dead. The only other animate object in that town was the little orange hand blinking on the stop light, telling her not to walk.

The light changed and a little white man blinked, urging her to cross the street before it was too late. By the look of the town nothing was urgent. The only signs of life were two cars in the bar's parking lot. They could be abandoned for all she knew.

A countdown timer marked off the seconds. Eleven. Ten.

Left to the motel. Straight to the bar. Neither option looked all that inviting.

For the first time since she left New York, rage, hot as the surface of the sun, boiled within her. She was supposed to be in an air-conditioned office somewhere, running a foundation. Sipping a latte that came from cart. Logan kicked a beer cap into the street, and it skittered into a pothole.

Five. Four.

The little man on the pedestrian signal had his whole life together. He had purpose and goals and a job. He had an identity, and everyone knew who he was. Logan had all of that until her father screwed up, and the government charged him with money laundering and took it all away. All she had left were some comfy pants shoved in a suitcase and a cell phone plan she couldn't afford. She squeezed the handle of her suitcase so tight her knuckles turned white.

Two. One.

The Do Not Walk signal blinked, and she crossed the street defiant.

The sidewalk rippled. Uneven slabs of concrete were mere islands, broken by the freeze and thaw of ice, lost in a sea of weeds and road dirt. She faced the bar.

When she opened that door, she would find herself in a whole new world. There would be questions. What was her name? Where did she come from? Maybe they would recognize her right away from the newspapers, the tabloids, Twitter. She wasn't prepared for any of it, and she never would be. She didn't even know how to fill out a job application. What was she supposed to say? I'm a Yale graduate with a degree in Art History, the daughter of a felon, and I've come to scrub your bathroom?

The sun would set in a few hours, and that motel did not look hospitable. The keys to a job and a cheap apartment were somewhere in that bar.

Taking in a shaky breath of Maine air, she held it in until her lungs soaked it up, then let out a steady stream of all she had left.

"Get in there and prove your mother wrong. You are still a Cole and Coles do not give up. We don't stand on the sidewalk and talk to ourselves, either."

Her whole future lay ahead of her. She just had to get by until her dad set it right. Shoulders back, head up, she opened the door.

CHAPTER TWO

A hollow-core door, crooked in its frame, stood between Logan and the bar. Textured yellow glass nested in a window at eye level. But the window was no more level than the door, and the security bars were useless. Other than a small flag outside the gas station that moved in the breeze, Ramsbolt, Maine didn't see enough action to warrant protection anyway.

Logan turned the knob and pushed, stepping into a wall of stale cigarette smoke, an acrid and nauseating blend of chemicals recycled through the lungs of the lonely. She closed the door behind her and wiped her hand on her jeans, leaving behind the faint smear of gritty residue. The vestibule was long and narrow, paneled walls with cheap plastic coat hooks, yellowed and brittle, cracked and held in place with rusting screws. The carpet was bubbled up, thin and worn, its dark-brown threads faded from heavy boots and weary shoes. Ahead, an old cigarette vending machine, a wooden case with aged brass knobs and a coin slot, declared through an advertising banner as old as the bar that this was Marlboro Country. Logan smirked. She'd figured that out on her own, by the state of the parking lot and the overfilled pot of sand by the door.

It would have been easy to judge the bar by its lobby. Vestibules were supposed to give the best first impression. Under the dim light of what this place had to offer, she lowered her expectations. Helen's Tavern didn't have the luxury of putting its best foot forward. This was a utilitarian space. A buffer from the cold and wet.

Beside the door leading to the bar were wire magazine racks. Shopping guides and cars for sale. A dusty stack of apartment listings caught her eye, and she tugged one from the bottom as the outside door flew open. The lobby flooded with light, and a mailman stopped short of walking into her.

"Ah, sorry. Almost tripped over ya there. Stocking up that rack?" The man's attention was fixed on his envelopes, small stacks bundled with rubber bands that he shuffled into some kind of order. "Don't think anyone's refilled it in a year. More than that. Think that car's been for sale since I was in high school."

"No, sorry." Logan pulled on her suitcase, tugging it out of his path to the door.

The mailman considered her like a new animal species. "Are you lost?"

Lost. That was subjective. She had no idea where she was going. Where she would sleep. Who she was going to be when she stepped into that bar? Pride bristled, a need to hide her weakness as ingrained as drinking through a straw, and she cloaked it with a smile. She'd need all the help she could get. "I guess you could say that. Looking for a place. And a job."

He stepped past her, pushed open the door to the bar, and Logan followed. She lifted her suitcase a few inches from the floor, eager to avoid attention.

The bar was dark and empty, but for one man in a far corner under a dim lamp. No one tended to him. She took a seat at the bar, her suitcase at her feet, and placed her hands in her lap. No one sought her drink order. Nothing about the place looked inviting or worth the health risk of touching. The mail fell beside her, and the man who delivered it, slender and in his forties, dug through his bag. He dug out a scanner, scanned the stack, and pressed buttons on the machine, focused on his task.

"Helen. You got a visitor," he called out, without looking up. "Helen!"

Behind the dark bar were rows of shelves cluttered with dusty bottles. They framed a door papered in notes and licenses, sketches and pictures, curled and cracked, yellowed with age and the ghosts of the last cigarettes to pass through the bar before the smoking ban. The door swung open, and a stout older woman creaked toward to the bar, her knees a disadvantage. Helen braced herself against a cooler behind the bar and squinted at Logan through the dim lighting.

"It's so dark in here. One second." She reached over for switches behind a collection of Jim Beam bottles and lights flickered in the faux Tiffany lamps overhead. A million miles away from everything Logan had ever known, and many hours away from her mother landing in France, she couldn't help but think that her mother would be mortified. With the turn of a dial, Helen turned up the radio, and Coldplay offered a "Hymn for The Weekend." The last time she'd seen Coldplay, she'd arrived by private jet. It was a spontaneous trip, a maiden voyage for its new tan leather seats and new dark blue carpet. It had smelled like upholstery glue and given her a headache, so she had sent it home empty and bought a first-class ticket to Rome.

"I don't bother turning all this on when it's just me in here." Helen rested her weight with her palms on a cooler lid. "Saves electricity."

"But there's a man over there." The man across the bar could have been a wax figure in a museum for all the movement he made. The fastest thing in Maine so far was the mailman, but he was motivated by the daily deadline. The man at the end of the bar turned the page of a newspaper. Logan hoped it was a story about a cat in a tree or a good day for a lobster, and nothing to do with her father.

Following Logan's gaze, Helen dismissed him with a shake of her head. "That's Arvil. He's always here. Not always drinking. Doesn't get busy in here until the after-work crowd falls in the door, looking for the opposite of whatever bothered their day. What can I getcha?"

She hadn't thought about it. After twenty some years of a bottomless bank account, a meager ten thousand would go pretty fast. She spent more than twice that in one day in Rome. Her thirst for a cocktail quenched itself. "Soda, please. Diet."

Helen raised a glass from a tray and filled it with a soda gun. "That all you here for? We don't serve food no more."

Tapping the cover of the apartment guide, Logan had an easy excuse. More than an excuse, a necessity. "Research. I need a place to stay and a job, if you know of anything. You don't happen to have a pen I can borrow, do you?"

"I do." An old blue ink pen with a chewed cap landed on the bar. "If I were you, I'd go down to the newsstand and talk to Warren. He owns the place. He has a bunch of apartments up there."

"Place above the post office is empty." The mailman leaned against the bar, eating beef jerky out of his bag. "Can I get a cup of coffee to go while you're out here?"

"Don't have any made. Can you wait?"

"I can wait."

Helen fussed with the coffee maker. "She don't want to live above that old post office. That place smells like cats."

"Good enough for you, wasn't it?"

"I was divorced, and I would have lived in a refrigerator at the edge of the dump if it'd saved me some money." Helen emptied a foil packet of grounds into a filter and started the machine with the press of a button. Coffee sputtered into a carafe.

Logan turned to the mailman. "Wait, maybe I do wanna live above the post office. What kind of cats are we talking about?"

The mailman's jaw worked against a strip of jerky. "The urinating kind. You don't look like the kind of girl who wants to live in a place with peeling paint and metal kitchen cabinets. Fancy suitcase. Nice shoes. Where'd you come from anyway?"

The soles of her shoes were clean for their age. She tucked them under her stool. "These aren't nice shoes. They're at least five years old."

"They don't walk much. Stick to plush carpet, huh?"

"Certainly not." It wasn't a lie. Half the house had hardwood floors.

Helen dropped a paper cup and lid in front of the mailman. "Riley Groves, leave her alone. You're making my place inhospitable."

"I'm just messing with her. Seems to me like the opposite of what usually happens. Some city girl moving to the country to strike it poor."

Something in his smile was disarming. Logan returned it. "Good point. Truth is, I'm not here for the economics. I'm here for the geography. All those people and all that noise gets annoying after a while. I decided I'd prefer to live in an episode of *Northern Exposure* than to keep living in *Sex and the City*."

The coffee wasn't finished, but it paused when Helen lifted the carafe. She filled Riley's cup. "Wrong side of the country for that. *Northern Exposure* was in Alaska."

"But that bus trip was too long." Logan sipped her soda and returned to the apartment guide, eyes peeled for a place that was free and didn't smell like cats. Maybe it was an old copy, but there had to be an apartment complex with a vacancy somewhere.

"Good luck on your search, city girl. I gotta get this mail to people or the town will go feral. Way out here, the mail delivery is the only thing we get out of bed for."

Helen swatted him with a bar rag, collected two bills he'd dropped on the counter, and wiped beneath them as he made his way out the door.

Logan pulled her phone from her back pocket and brought the screen to life, but no icon called to her. No portal to the rest of the world. She'd let her fake friends fade into the distance as the court cases dragged on. In a willful disconnect, she'd deleted her social media accounts and removed the apps from her phone. The aftermath of her father's downfall and the death threats that followed had taught her that the comments on news stories left a lot to be desired. The reception was terrible, there was no Wi-Fi, and her battery was dying. And the apartment guide, like Riley warned, offered little by way of direction.

"Thanks for the tip about the guy at the newsstand."

Helen flipped a switch on the coffee maker, and the orange light on the machine went dark. She dumped the used coffee grounds into an overfilled trash can and started to lift the bag but let it fall back. She rubbed one hand with the other.

"How much do I owe you for the soda?"

"That depends."

Did they haggle for soft drinks in Maine? "On what?"

"You running from somebody?"

"No, ma'am. I'm not a convict or a felon. I just need a change of pace. I need a place to start over. You know how life goes sometimes. And I hope you don't take it the wrong way or think I'm insulting you or this place, but if I'm not mistaken, maybe you could use some help here."

Helen rested her weight against the cooler again. Everything about her looked pained and tired.

Logan took a chance. "I know how to make coffee, and I don't have arthritis. I've got nothing else going on, and I'm willing to work hard for honest pay."

Helen rubbed at a water spot on the stainless steel cooler door. "Perceptive."

Logan was smart enough to know she lacked knowledge—how to do the job, what hard work meant. But she was also smart enough to seize the opportunity, to get what she could from this place until her father got out of jail and fixed all this, or she moved on to something bigger. This little room with no windows seemed as good a place to start as any.

"Being perceptive is a good skill to have at a bar, right?"

Helen leaned back in her seat, scrutinizing her with a hint of amusement. "It's imperative. My body won't let me be as prideful as I once was. I looked to hire somebody a while ago."

"Consider me for it. Please. Give me a chance." How hard could it be? Fill a glass, empty it, put it in a dishwasher, make some coffee for the mailman. What was his name? Riley. Arvil the Statue sat in the corner and didn't ask for much. He'd been staring at the same newspaper page since she walked in the door. There was no evidence that anyone ordered any drinks by the dust that collected on everything. And by the looks of the trash Helen couldn't lift, this was a beer place.

Helen raised her chin and nudged open the door to her office. Light spilled out around her. "Come on in here."

Logan slipped behind the bar, holding her suitcase above the puddle, careful not to coat the wheels in whatever glazed the floor.

Helen closed the office door behind her, trapping her in a fog of dust and humidity. An old metal fan clicked in the corner, pushing stale air around and rustling the papers tacked to the wood-paneled walls. Helen used the bulky metal desk for leverage and made her way around to her chair.

"There's another chair over there. You can move those folders to the floor."

A stack of green hanging file folders was piled on a padded folding chair, with no filing cabinet in sight. No laptop. No window to the outside world. She expected a chair like her father's, some high-backed leather thing with a comfortable seat and wheels. Not a folding chair across the desk from a woman in a mumu in a dusty old bar. Helen's office was a monumental departure from the one she thought she'd be working in as the head of her family's foundation. Cold. Isolating. It would take some getting used to.

"I had two kids in mind once. There's a kid in town who used to sweep up in here. And my friend Colleen has a son who wanted a job. But one is heading out of town for college, and the other is just leaving town. Like everybody else who grows up here, they leave and won't be back. Why would they when there are cities out there and the television makes everywhere else look so appealing?"

"I never watch it."

"Smart girl. What did you say your name was?"

Her name. She should have changed it legally. Should have asked her father to include it in the plea agreement after he said he didn't want to see her anymore, back when he told her not to visit but before the world came crashing down. But the deal had been done. She could lie, but she'd only look worse if they asked for her social security number. She could say she goes by an alias. Make some excuse. But the part of her heart that told the truth blurted it out before her brain could stop her.

"Logan Cole. No relation."

"No relation to who?"

"Never mind."

"Do you have any experience?"

Making coffee? Yes. Pouring a drink? You bet. Tending a bar or cleaning up or taking money? Nope. Taking orders from people? Definitely not. "Sure. It was a while ago, and the place is closed now, but I worked at a friend's bar for a little while. Small place in New York." She kicked herself for lying. And for not saying Boston.

"Do you have any references I can call?"

"No, not anymore. The bar closed, and I wouldn't know who to call."

"But you said it was a friend's bar."

"Well, sure. But we're not friends anymore."

"You left New York with a fancy suitcase after having one job at a bar that failed and you have no friends or connections to use as a reference?"

"This isn't going well, is it?"

Helen pushed papers around on the blotter. The woman really seemed to like paper. "You can't blame me for being curious. A homeless woman walks in from somewhere and begs for a job? How do I know someone isn't after you?"

Thousands of people had wished Logan ill. The *hope you get cancer* messages and the *you should just hang yourself* advice could be dismissed, as much as one could ignore such vile comments. But the ones that kept her up at night were the *watch your back* texts. The *people are coming for you* emails. And the photoshopped pictures, however crude, of her figure beheaded like an ISIS victim in the middle of Times Square. It was hard to judge the credible from the moral and social outrage, so she reported them all to the FBI like the lawyer told her to and never heard about them again. Was anyone really after her? She didn't think so, but the lump in her throat didn't listen to reason.

"No one is after me. I didn't do anything wrong. I know it sounds strange, but it's the way it is. Life is like that, stranger than fiction. Sometimes people just pick up and leave because they want a whole new way of life. I'm a quiet person. Kinda private, really."

"And sometimes people pick up and leave because they have a mean man on their tail. I don't need trouble at this bar. I'm too old for that."

Logan could hear the ticking clock on her bank account. It was louder than Helen's hesitancy. The woman's eyes seemed to beg for her objections to be laid to waste, searching for a reason to trust. With the whole country thinking she deserved the worst that could happen, Logan wanted more than anything to find a place to settle and prove them all wrong. Plus, if someone really was looking for her, they would never think to look for her in Helen's dusty, humid bar. It was the perfect place to be when the tide rolled in again. She could pick up and leave at the end of all this, and no one would even care.

Logan clasped her hands like her father did when making a final offer.

"I totally understand if it's a bit of a leap. I'd be hesitant too. You could always give me a chance and see how it works out. Rest your hands and your knees and take it easy for a day or two? If it doesn't work out, I can move on. We both can."

Helen hunched over her desk, a smiling lump of a woman in a blue floral mumu. "Do you think you'd have a hard time working for a recovered Type A control freak?"

"As long as you don't mind if I clean the floor out there." She had no idea where to start, how to mop a floor. Marta used a mop and bucket with some kind of soap. How hard could it be?

"This bar was my baby. I opened this place more than fifty years ago. It's not what it used to be. I had a diner back here, but people didn't want that food anymore, and the old trucking company closed down, so nobody came around to buy sandwiches. Now it's just a bar. Busy enough and serves the town, but I'm a tired old woman. I do need someone I can trust to help me out around here, and I don't have much to pay because not much comes in, but I can probably pay you enough to get by on."

"Is that an offer?"

"I'm a good judge of character, and I can see you're motivated and got some drive in ya. I don't know why you're here or what you're looking for, but if you do a good job, I can pay you in cash at the end of each week, and you can keep your tips."

"There's paperwork, right?" Her father had stacks of them. W2s or I-9s or something.

"We can take care of it tomorrow. We don't open until one in the afternoon, but if you come by around eleven, I'll show you how to prep and get ready for the day."

Helen reached out her hand, and Logan shook it, lighter for having passed inspection. She offered her thanks, said her goodbye, and slipped out of the office.

Behind the bar, she took a last sip of her soda and poured the rest of it into the sink. Ice cubes skated on the stainless steel. She found a green tray of dirty glasses and left her empty cup there. Offering a nod to Arvil that went unnoticed, she slipped out the door, through the vestibule, and back onto the sidewalk.

The little man in white blinked at her, told her it was safe to cross, but she had no destination. She forgot to ask which way led to town and the newsstand. The map on her phone said it was a six-minute walk to the left, and she stepped into the street as the orange hand protested.

CHAPTER THREE

One-story houses lined the street, their roofs at steep pitches to keep heavy winter snows from piling on. New York saw plenty of snow, but nothing like what she'd face in Maine. She'd need a coat. A pair of boots.

The sound of Logan's suitcase wheels echoed off the brick houses, and no one was there to hear. No one stirred. No one tended a barbecue, no children played on swing sets. Row after row of tended lawn, yet no hint of human life. As if all of humanity suffered the same fate, torn from their roots and scattered in the winds.

Between the yards and on untended plots, prickly shrubs and blueberry bushes grew with wild abandon. Her mother would have paid a gardener a lot for that aesthetic, for such an elegant decay. But the peeling paint and patchwork shingles, old cars and oil-stained driveways spoke of neglect. Judging by the missing and broken shutters, Logan could tell the town rationed its resources. Something she would have to get used to. Any hope for stainless steel appliances and gym access at her new apartment faded.

Over a gentle hill and around a curve, the street widened, becoming more boulevard than country road. It opened to a turning circle that ringed a grassy park where scattered benches faced a memorial statue of a sailor. A fondness stirred within her. For a town so far from the coast, a sailor statue seemed as out of place as she was. His eyes were weary, but his jaw was strong, and the evening sun painted him pink, throwing his shadow long across the road. She stepped into the pool of his silhouette, taking a shortcut across the park, and paused for a passing truck. Small and clean, the park was inviting but empty. The way parks were when taken for granted. Logan was desperate to sit, to get her bearings about her future and the kind of life she would live in Ramsbolt, but rest would have to wait. Either for an apartment or a room in that cheap hotel that probably smelled of beer and cigarettes.

Narrow storefronts lined the street. Two- and three-story buildings that varied in height, a bar graph of hierarchy and competing affluence. The tallest buildings had names etched in stone, homages to businesses closed generations before. The shortest were more modest. Among them, she found the newsstand, a brightly lit, optimistic beacon with a window display of children's books. Logan pressed the lever of the brass door pull and tugged the door open.

The unmistakable smell of magazines, their ink and print and glossy paper, hit her as she stepped over the marble threshold. It reminded her of the *TV Guide* that came in the mail when she was a child. Over the faint country music that played overhead, two men at the counter complained about politics. A man on the other side, the man she'd come to see, nodded along.

"It's like this every two years. Some big company wants something, so they put a lobbyist in there to get it for them. Then a bunch of bleeding hearts funded by some billionaire rush in to complain about an endangered fly. It don't matter. None of it matters."

"These people should all go to jail. Right now. Forever. They appeal these cases, and it goes on and on and costs me all this money. I could feed myself for years if they'd stop paying judges and juries to do the same stuff over and over again. I want my taxes back. Should send *them* an invoice for all the crap I gotta read and hear."

Logan browsed a stack of magazines. Some glossy tabloid with her old Instagram profile picture, tiny and out of focus in the sidebar. *Cole Curse: Costly Divorces, House Fires, and Money Laundering. Will the curse take down Logan next?*

Christ. It wasn't the first time she'd seen a headline like that. Whose grandfather hadn't gotten a divorce? It was hardly a tragedy. And what house fire? Were they talking about the time a car caught on fire in their driveway, and the firemen came to put it out? There was no curse. She hadn't done anything wrong. She hadn't even been *accused* of doing anything wrong. Logan hid the magazine at the back of the shelf. It was months old anyway. Maybe people here talked more about scandals than they read about them.

The man behind the counter, who Logan assumed was the owner, waved a hand in dismissal. "These rich people are assholes. The real world doesn't care about them. They should put real issues on the cover. Put hungry farmers on the front page."

A small relief to Logan. At least she stood a chance at being a former asshole.

One of the customers shuffled toward the door. "I'm not arguing. No one in the real world has enough money to care about this shit."

The two men left, and a bit of Logan's concern went with them. The door clicked closed behind them. Logan wheeled her suitcase around the stacks, passing racks of cards for birthdays and holidays. What ever happened to them, to the ones she got as a child? Marta, her nanny, had always picked them out on her mother's behalf. She picked one up and flipped it over. Three dollars and change. Peanuts once. Seemed like extortion, now, for something so useless.

She took a bottle of water from a cooler by the register and focused on keeping her story straight. A new start. That's what she'd told Helen. The man behind the counter looked up from his cell phone when she dropped the bottle on the counter.

"This all? You find everything okay?"

"Almost everything." Logan dug her wallet from her purse. "I'm not sure who to ask. I got a job working for Helen at the bar, and she suggested I come here and ask the owner about an apartment. The mail guy, Robert?"

"Riley."

"Riley. Right. Sorry. He said that there are some upstairs apartments that might be available."

"It's good you caught me because I'm not usually here in the evenings." He punched keys into a register. It clicked and clanged. "A dollar twenty."

He stared a little too long, his eyes lingering. Did he recognize her? Surely he'd seen her face before. Logan unzipped her wallet, like she had a million times before. Her thumb found the edge of a metal credit card, her favorite one, now useless. Lifting it from its sleeve in her wallet was a habit hard to break. She pushed it down, out of sight, and found exact change, willing her hands steady.

"Thank you, ma'am." With the press of another key, the drawer slammed open into his stomach and change rattled. He dropped the coins in their slots and lifted the plastic cash tray, taking a set of keys from beneath it. "I have a few apartments you can see. Some are bigger than others."

"Anything furnished and, like, ready *now*?"

Sympathy creased the man's face. His forlorn smile was a relief. Maybe her mother was right; people were sympathetic to a young woman starting over with nothing but a suitcase. He rounded the counter, waving her to follow.

"Nothing fully furnished, but I've got a place above the post office. It's not much, but it's served a few people over the years. Been empty a while now. It'll be a bit dusty, and I'll have to get someone in there to straighten for ya. The power is on. And the water."

Power and water. Bills to pay. She'd be happy if it had a lamp and no bugs. Or cat urine smell. The man flipped a sign on the door from Open to Closed and crossed the street without looking. Logan and her suitcase scampered in his wake, barely keeping up with his long stride. His face and hands were lined by the sun, but the spring in his step said he was ten years younger than her father. An unmarked door, brick red with a brass knocker and mail slot, stood next to the post office door. It could have gone unnoticed. It opened to a flight of stairs, with a second locked door at the top.

"Name's Warren. I've been buying up these little apartments and things when I can. It's a nice way to make a little extra money." He stepped through the unlocked door and disappeared into a pool of darkness. "One second. I'll get the light here."

After a few heavy footsteps over creaking floorboards, the switch flipped, and an overhead light came on, painting the room with a blue tinge. "These new lightbulbs are terrible. Gotta warm up. Anyway, this place is cheap, and you can see why. It's not meant for more than one. The light switch is on the other side of the room, and the wiring is old, but it works fine. Just don't run too many big things at once, or you'll pop a fuse. Box is there by the door."

Big appliances. Logan couldn't afford a laptop, let alone a big screen television. It wouldn't fit, anyway. The apartment was smaller than her shoe closet back home. It consisted of two rooms, just one open living space and a bathroom. To her right, the kitchen counter hugged the corner, ending at a small, scuffed refrigerator. The narrow sink and small stove were more than sufficient for someone who'd never cooked a meal. To the left, a round table painted white, scuffed and dinged, was framed by two unmatching chairs. Behind it, the bathroom.

A mattress covered in plastic sat on a wire bed frame against the far wall. Against the peeling paint, it was a lot like the room she pictured her father living in. The kind of neglected place that either made you feel worse or pushed you a little harder. Her father was pushing against those walls; she knew it deep down. And she would push too.

But unlike her father's prison cell, the apartment was furnished, a small blessing in her exile. A small wooden night stand collected dust at the bedside. Dust she would have to clean on her own. A bare cable stuck out of the floor, behind the imprint of an old television stand. Things she couldn't afford. At the foot of the bed sat a plain dresser made of unfinished wood. She folded her arms against the chill, against the void. It was empty, unwelcoming. She couldn't picture herself there, her clothes in that dresser, but her heart swelled with gratitude all the same. To step off a bus, find a job and an apartment with furniture and not have to fight too hard for any of it was a miracle she didn't deserve.

"It's hard to tell right now, but there's plenty of sunlight." Warren nudged the door closed. He pointed to the window next to the bed. "The sun comes up over there." Logan went to it, pushed a tattered curtain aside, and peeked out to the street below. The sun was setting, making silhouettes of rooftops and trees and shading the street. Houses dotted the roads beyond Main Street, and in the day, she'd have a clear view of the sky. Dozens, hundreds of people, living in warm homes with family who loved them, and she was alone in a cage.

She turned her back on the town. The tan carpet was stained. The trim dinged, bare wood splintering through white paint. The whole thing seemed comical, like a glamping trip gone tragically wrong. Her mother would be horrified. Marta would be on her hands and knees scrubbing at stains. Logan could use some of Marta's magic. She needed too many things to care about the state of the carpet or the walls though. Dishes, cookware, towels, and a bath mat. Food for the fridge. How to do laundry. *Where* to do laundry.

"It's six hundred a month. You can pay by cash or check at the newsstand, or you can send it through the bill pay thingy on your phone there. First of the month, it's due."

She stepped away from the window. Yellow paint lifted from the wall when she pulled her hand away. Her money wouldn't last long.

"It gets humid up here," he said. "When it's all shut up. You may want to keep a window cracked. And I can have somebody paint before you move in."

"I can paint it. If you want. Can I move in today?" She prayed for no background check, no credit check. To keep her past to herself as long as she could. "I don't have any furniture or anything, and my savings account is kinda small. It would save me some money instead of getting a hotel room. I can give you the rent money now."

"First and last security. One-year lease." He opened a kitchen drawer and withdrew a small stack of papers, placing them on the counter. A year. Warren seemed nice enough, like he'd let her out of it when her father sorted everything out. By then, she'd be able to pay the cost of breaking the lease. Still, signing off on the commitment for an apartment required a new kind of independent fortitude. "You can paint it. Saves me some work. I can drop the supplies. We like this yellow color, my wife and I, 'cause it's sunny and neutral. Makes the place look bigger. You'll have to scrape a bit and put a primer on first."

What had once been the color of Marta's buttercream had darkened and cracked with age. She had no idea how to paint, but she had the internet, and she could look it up. Logan poked her head in the bathroom and reserved judgment on the stand-up shower, toilet, and sink. She sat on the edge of the bed. How many people had lived here before? Did her father get a new mattress on his first night in prison?

"Do you have any questions?"

How to cook food? Why did she feel so alone? "I don't even know what to ask."

"I usually do a credit and background check, but I know Helen, and if you're working for her, I'll let it slide. I know what it's like to start over. Our house burned down twenty years ago. We were young and worked hard to get what we had and losing it all was tough. I don't know what you got going on, but someday, these'll be the good old days." He patted the papers on the counter. "You fill these out and send me twelve hundred, and you'll be set as long as you follow the rules. Trash day is Tuesday. Electric and water are in the rent."

Electricity. Everything cost money. Even things she hadn't thought of. She dropped her purse on the bed and dug a pen from the bottom of the pit. She had no choice but to give the man her name, to let him think what he would about where she'd come from, hoping that if or when he looked at the paperwork, he didn't match her up to the headlines. She scrawled her name and social security number in their fields at the top of the page.

"Is there a store around here that sells used things? Like kitchen stuff and furniture?"

"A-yup. There's a second-hand shop of sorts that's got dishes and old pots and pans. Lots of old furniture. Stuff like that. Go right at the circle, up that street, past the bicycle shop. Give yourself enough time, though. It's crammed full."

"Thanks. I appreciate all of this." The words weren't enough to convey it all. The lightness of not being homeless and jobless. The weakness and wanting to slump to the floor, having crossed the finish line of a grueling race to arrive at an anonymous life. But the race wasn't over. It had only just begun.

With more than a tenth of her life savings spent, Logan accepted the keys, said goodbye to Warren, and closed the door behind him. Shutting herself away from the outside world, alone in a place of her own for the first time in her life. Cold in an impersonal space. Tired from the travel and the mental exercise of working out who she was supposed to be. Her mind weary of keeping up the story she hadn't had to tell. Money could buy security, distance from the rest of the world, and a comforting isolation from the perils of reality. Logan could afford none of those things. She needed food and money to pay her cell phone bill. She needed sheets for the bed and dishes to eat from. And she would need a raise if she hoped to break even on bills and cost of living.

Logan cursed her father for leaving her impoverished. She had no idea if he was guilty of the accusations they stacked against him or not. Whether the evidence was a chain of lies like he'd said, links of an elaborate shackle of revenge used to teach him a lesson he'd never learn. But either way, nothing he ever did was a mistake. His entire life had been a series of long games with big returns and small deft maneuvers that inched those plans along, selfish perhaps but expert in the execution. She'd witnessed the ebb and flow of money, the constantly churning tide of fortune, from the moment she was born. Anyone with wealth was at risk of destitution, and any means, even the spread of rumors and lies, would be used to wipe them clean. Her father would be back. Life would go back to normal. She was sure of it. In the meantime, all she had to do was survive his consequences. The infuriating consequences of his self-centered behavior driven a step too far.

CHAPTER FOUR

Six-year-old Logan Cole wobbled on her feet and wrinkled her nose in the floor-length mirror. Behind her, her mother tugged on a bow attached to the waist of her dress.

"Now, keep this dress clean. Don't kneel on the floor and tarnish the knees of your stockings." Her mother tied the bow tight.

"Yes, Petra."

"Appearance is everything, and the best of impressions should be made to even the closest of acquaintances. Shoes." Her mother dropped a pair of black patent leather shoes on the floor. "Elizabeth and her parents will be here at seven."

"I have to wear these all night?" Logan stepped into them. The most horrible thing in her closet, their buckles cut into her feet. "Can I watch cartoons?"

"That's a great idea. *Walk* down the hall and tell Marta to turn on the television in the playroom." Mom used her cranky voice when she said *walk*. Logan got the point. This was not a playdate. Even at six, she knew the difference between her father's work dinners and play dates. Not that she needed to be reminded; Elizabeth was hardly a friend. She was a brat who always wanted her way and never wanted to share. And her house was cold and uninviting. Logan stomped to the door in her too-tight shoes.

"Quietly," her mother hissed. "Your father is in the library, and he's in a mood."

"He's always in a mood anymore."

Logan expected a scolding, but her distracted mother focused on the floor-length mirror.

"Half of New York is biting at his heels. And that's just the lawyers."

"Is Dad in trouble?"

"No. But he has a lot to talk about with Alexander. That's why you have to play with Elizabeth after dinner and stay out of your father's way. Fingerprints all over this mirror. Tell Marta to go around with some cleaner. And keep your hands off things. Okay, dear?" Petra stood back and smoothed her hair.

"I don't want to play with Elizabeth."

"But Elizabeth is your best friend."

"No, she's not. Jill's my best friend."

Her mother moved past her into the hall. Logan knew better than to argue when her mother's focus was on adult things. "You'll have a wonderful time. Color. Draw. Have a tea party. Whatever the two of you do."

All of those things were for babies. "Can we have dessert up here and watch a movie?" At least she could avoid talking to Elizabeth *and* the adults. "I wanna watch Pee-wee Herman."

"That's fine. Let Marta know." Her mother was already on the stairs.

Logan ran down the hall of her wing of the house. Past the bathroom and her blue bedroom. Past Marta's bedroom with its peach walls and airy curtains. The playroom door was open, and Marta was on her knees, cleaning the baseboards with a rag.

"Marta." Logan used a soft voice, to avoid startling her nanny. "Mom said Elizabeth and I can watch cartoons before dinner, and we'll have dessert here too. Can you find the Pee-wee movie? And Petra asked if you could clean the windows and mirrors. But I can do it, if you want." Logan hated giving orders.

Marta set her rag aside. She leaned back against the wall, and in her Dominican accent said, "No, bug. I will clean it. I know you don't like Elizabeth. The last time she was here, the two of you argued."

Logan scrambled onto the leather sofa. "I call bullshit on this whole thing."

"You know you shouldn't talk like that." Marta's swatted the tip of Logan's shoe with the rag, her words playful. It was barely a scolding.

"It is, though. Petra said Elizabeth is coming over to play, and we should get along 'cause our fathers do business together, and we'll be glad one day that we have a friend we grew up with."

"She's not wrong." Marta ran the rag as far along the dustless baseboard.

"I *have* friends. I don't like Elizabeth. She's prissy." Prissy was Logan's new favorite word. She heard her mother use it to describe her dad's friend's wife.

"You just have to find some common ground with her. There must be something you have in common." Marta folded the rag into quarters. "It's hard to see at your age, but the world isn't like it is at school. We don't all wear uniforms and sit in the same classroom. It's not a level playing field. Adults like to put themselves in categories, and we don't move outside of them very often."

"Categories? I don't know what that means."

"You know how your dad hangs out with other lawyers and how your mom goes to lunch with their wives? Like that."

"But you hang out with me, and I'm a kid."

"I get paid to hang out with you." The sofa springs settled when Marta sat, jostling Logan to the side. "But I enjoy it. We have a lot of fun together. But if we were adults, and I didn't work here, you wouldn't give me the time of day. Not because you're mean or because you don't like me, but because people move in their own circles."

"Because I have extra rooms?"

Marta laughed and patted Logan's white-tighted knee. "Like extra rooms. And the power and influence that come with having extra rooms. Sometimes, people with extra rooms aren't so nice to people who have less. But you're not that way."

"That's why my parents want me to be friends with Elizabeth. Because she has extra rooms."

"They just want you to add Elizabeth to your list of friends, so when you grow up, you'll have other friends that have extra rooms."

"But I like Jill more." Jill didn't have patent leather shoes. She didn't have extra rooms or an assistant like Marta. But her mom had a tall Jeep that had windows with zippers, and they had an above ground swimming pool with a ladder. When she went to Jill's house, they ate hot dogs. At home, Logan had to speak softly and eat scones and fancy salads and sit like a lady while her parents socialized with people who wore suits. "My parents should eat more hot dogs."

Marta laughed. "I have no idea where that came from, but I can't picture your parents eating hot dogs."

"I'll be nice to Elizabeth. But if I want to stay friends with Jill when I grow up, do I have to give up my rooms?"

Marta patted the knee of Logan's white tights. "No, you don't have to give up anything. No matter how many rooms you have, you'll be okay. You'll make friends everywhere."

The sofa jostled Logan to the side again as Marta stood and turned on the television. That's where Logan sat, laughing with Pee-wee Herman, until the doorbell chimed, and her mother called her down to shake hands and have a dinner that was even colder than usual. Petra and Elizabeth's mother ate from dainty forks, their eyes never meeting. And the men exchanged glances, eating in silence. They hinted at something big, speaking in broken sentences that Logan didn't understand. It was like watching one of her mother's tennis lessons, trying to follow the ball. The more frustrated people got, the more entertaining it was to watch.

"Looking forward to seeing your ideas, Alexander," her father said.

"The options are narrowing, Lorne. There's only so much I can do if you insist on not taking my advice."

"I'm sure you've thought of something. It'll be a shame if you haven't. And quite unlike you not to cover all the bases."

The maid took their empty plates, and the men set off for the office, closing themselves behind the solid wood door, yet talking in voices loud enough to be heard. Something about putting money in the laundry. And racketeering, which could only mean hanging it up to dry when they were done.

Logan followed Marta, lured upstairs by a bowl of pudding, and Elizabeth rustled behind her in a cloud of wooshing taffeta. They sat on the leather sofa, Logan giggling at Pee-wee Herman and Elizabeth staring at the television with her mouth open. Poor Elizabeth was always confused. Logan hid her smile at her frenemy's sidelong glances. She felt bad for the girl who understood nothing and would never find pleasure in hot dogs or car windows with zippers.

"I am not going down on some RICO charges, Alexander!" Her father's voice boomed up the stairs, and Logan pressed pause on the remote.

"Lorne, you need to calm down." Elizabeth's father's voice followed. He was a big, important lawyer. Everybody was afraid of him. Everybody but Lorne Cole. "You're a persuasive man, but now is the time to be quiet. Patrick gave a lot of evidence that you were the one calling the shots. The money trail will go straight to you. Even if they can't find it all, they'll be able to prove you were pulling the strings. We have to work with what we have here. If you'd listened to me years ago, you wouldn't be in this situation."

"Then we will drag that man in court. Make it a *he said, he said* situation."

Her mother's voice followed, too quiet to hear, mere mumbles carried in the wake of her father's fury.

"Come on. And be quiet. Shh." Logan slipped to the floor without sound and motioned for Elizabeth to follow.

They moved down the hall to the stairs, where they sat on the landing, Logan's hands grasping her knees, and Elizabeth surrounded by her skirt in a mound.

"If you sue him, you will only give the investigators more reasons to look into you. And they could charge you with obstruction too." Alexander's voice edged on panic.

"Then Patrick will have to be reminded of his position so he stops talking."

The last of the summer sun streamed through the window at the top of the stairs, casting pink light on the wall above Logan. Whoever they were talking about had fewer rooms and fewer windows, and Logan's father was going to crush them. Logan wiggled her toes inside her shoes. The men must have been in the barroom, because the unmistakable sound of ice hitting the stainless steel sink filled the air, and Logan used the opportunity to shift her weight on the creaky landing.

"I can't stand these whiskey sours. This woman can't get it through her thick head." The clink of ice into a glass meant her father was pouring himself a new drink. "If she makes one more of these things, I'm sending her back to the Dominican Republic."

Beside her, Elizabeth shifted, swishing her skirt, fidgeting with the hem. Logan swatted at the distraction. Marta had been making the drinks since the older woman from the kitchen staff retired. Her mother couldn't let Marta go. She was Logan's friend, not theirs. Besides, Marta knew how to make the rum drinks her mother liked.

"The power and influence are in your court." Alexander sounded calm, but it was almost pleading. "Say nothing. Don't respond at all. It'll scare the shit out of him. He'll be so paranoid, he'll crawl into a corner."

"Patrick has to stop talking. Period. What if we go at him from the side and hit his partner? That man's whole life is lies. We can expose his tax evasion. They'll put him in jail, and Patrick will go bankrupt." Logan hugged her knees. It wasn't the drink her father was angry about. Her dad had done something that made somebody mad. She didn't know what, but she knew her dad would win. He always won. "They'll never tie it to us. Patrick will be reminded what I could do to him, and he'll keep his mouth shut."

"Patrick already knows what you could do to him. Trust me. He's probably drinking cheap scotch and crying into his Joseph A. Banks shirts, making up lies to tell the FBI. He doesn't move in our circles. He doesn't have anyone in his pocket with half your influence. He's unprotected."

A floorboard creaked beneath Elizabeth when she fidgeted with the hem of her dress. Logan swatted at her to be quiet. If their fathers weren't so upset and anxious, she'd be bored, too, by what she didn't understand. But her father only raised his voice when something interesting was going on, and she held on to every word, even the ones she couldn't understand.

"Shh," she whispered. "We'll get caught. This is important. I'm trying to hear."

"What's going on?" Elizabeth hissed.

"I'll tell you later."

Elizabeth rolled her eyes and fiddled with the buckle on her shoe.

"Alexander, social standing doesn't mean shit to a judge or a jury. I'm damned either way." She'd never heard her father so scared before. He sounded small. Defeated. But what about the plan? He'd sounded so sure just a moment before. "What if I get in front of the press before anything happens? Make sure I look like the good guy so I can get a fair trial? You saw how it went with Barney. The prosecution leaked like a faucet, and there wasn't a thing his lawyers could do." Her father's voice got louder. "You need to get in there and make sure they know there are consequences before this goes any further."

"Lorne, calm down before you have a stroke." At the sound of glass on glass and ice settling, Logan pictured them at the bar cart beneath the giant oil painting of her grandparents. Her grandfather looked scary in that painting. He would have fixed it. "With your money, you're untouchable. There's rich. There's superrich. Then there's Lorne Cole.

This will work out."

That wasn't what Marta said. She said there were consequences for everybody.

"No one's untouchable. Life is all about risk analysis. I can't just sit here and do nothing and expect it to all turn out okay."

Logan hugged her knees tighter. Dad was never scared about anything. He always won at everything, and he never forgot to buy her a toy when he went out of town on a trip. It had to be okay. It had to.

"Listen to me. There are forces at work in your favor. You will never step foot in a courtroom unless you're there to destroy an enemy. The kind of power you have will absolutely crush him, and you won't have to lift a finger."

The floor creaked behind them. Logan spun to find Marta at the top of the stairs, a stern look on her face.

"You two." Marta wagged her finger. "Up here."

The girls followed Marta up the stairs and into the playroom, careful not to make a sound.

Logan and Elizabeth never spoke of what they heard, and the topic never came up again. For all Logan knew, Elizabeth didn't understand a word of it, and Elizabeth's father had been right: Lorne Cole was too influential to be taken down in the courts. As she lay in bed under the swaying shadows of a backlit tree's branches, Marta's words began to make sense. Consequences belonged to people with fewer rooms in their houses. She and Elizabeth needed each other because someday, someone might want to take their rooms and all their windows, and they'd have to stick together. No one else would understand.

CHAPTER FIVE

The antique store was where Warren said it would be. A right at the turning circle and across the street, just past a bicycle shop, next to a toy store. Peering through the window into the darkened shop, Logan struggled to see potential. Stacks of dishes and shelves with pots and pans lined the walls. Rows of toys from her childhood and furniture stuffed with trinkets and home decor. Something moved within, and she jumped when it tapped on the door.

"Don't leave. I'm open." The woman's voice was muffled by the glass. "I just have to unlock this door. The key sticks in the lock." She fought with a key and pulled the door inward. "I'm sorry. Time got away from me. Come on in. Sorry it's so dark. I'll get the light on in a second, here. I'm Penny. Enjoy the browse and scream if I can help you find anything."

"Thanks. I wasn't even sure you'd be open on Sunday."

Penny was a fitting name for the flame-haired woman. Her cat-eye glasses framed bright green eyes. "Open seven days a week. Tourists stop on their way through town. Mostly for the bathroom, but a lot of them buy little trinkets and things."

The woman scampered from the door behind some cabinets and flicked on the light. It pooled on piles and careful stacks of dust-covered junk. Logan took a shopping basket and slinked past a desk littered with glass figurines. Sets of old dishes and broken place settings filled two lower shelves. The assortment was disappointing, aged florals and plastic plates from the eighties with cartoon characters. She chose one plate with yellow flowers, a bowl that didn't clash, and a white coffee cup, scratched on the inside but otherwise unstained. It was nothing like her mother's Spode. She swallowed back the disgust of eating off someone else's used dishes. Just a like a restaurant, she told herself.

In a milk crate beneath a record player, she found dozens of utensils and sifted through them to find the best of the oldest cooking tools to be abandoned in Ramsbolt, Maine. When she unloaded everything at the register, along with a warped baking sheet, a small skillet, and a saucepan, she startled the woman, who'd been resting on a steamer trunk behind the glass counter, reading a tattered romance novel.

"Is it any good?" Logan lowered her shopping basket to the floor.

"Not really." The woman straightened her jeans when she stood. Logan could almost feel her bank account draining as the woman rang up the dishes. Was this what buyer's remorse felt like? "I have a goal of reading everything in that bookcase over there."

The bookcase was grand, a fall front desk at the bottom topped by a tall secretary. The glass doors were old, the panes wavy, like the glass was giving up and flowing to the floor. The shelves inside were packed with paperbacks, two rows deep. The woman behind the counter was only a few years older than Logan, so if she planned to read them all, she had plenty of time to work on it. "How's it going so far?"

"Not well. They're pretty bad, as books go. Not my thing. You furnishing a giant dollhouse?"

"A what?"

"Just small talk. This place setting. It's random."

"Oh, no. I'm new here. Starting over, if you know what I mean. Just trying to get on my feet without spending a fortune." The starting over theme had worked so far, and it wasn't a lie.

The woman wrapped her dishes in paper. "Haven't been here that long myself. That's good of you, buying used instead of new. There's so much trash in the landfill, you know? We keep buying plastic, throwing it away, and replacing it. It never disappears. Our grandkids'll be swimming in junk." She slipped the items into two plastic bags and hit a key on the register. The price decreased by ten percent, and she gave Logan a wink. "First time customer discount."

"Thank you." She never thought she'd appreciate saving a dollar fifty. She didn't even know what to do with only a dollar fifty. She could buy another plate, but it seemed like such a waste. "This town is really nice. Everybody here."

"We take care of our own. We take care of newcomers, too. Not that we get a lot of 'em. It's a great place to live. Not a lot of jobs around here, but we all get by."

"Yeah, I...Yeah." She couldn't get too close. She couldn't afford to start being personable with people, to talk loosely and risk unleashing her past. She'd be run out of town and left with a lease to break before her father even found a way out of jail. She lifted the bags from the counter and returned the shopping basket to the stack by the door. "Thanks again for the discount. That's very kind of you."

"You got it. Come again."

"I will. I'll need the rest of this set one day."

Logan stepped out onto the street, the paper-wrapped dishes rustling in the plastic shopping bag. She unlocked her phone and skimmed her email. Nothing but spam and a notification from Amazon that they'd shipped her cheap queen-size unicorn sheets, and she could expect them on Monday. One more night on plastic.

She turned left at the circle and headed into an oncoming crowd. The church at the end of the street had let out. Men greeted each other, shaking hands, their voices booming off the brick storefronts. Women in slacks and dresses walked to their cars and fanned out through the streets to their little steep-roofed houses. With no place to hide, the urge to run washed over her. As if she were somewhere she shouldn't be. Somewhere she didn't belong. A woman in a long plaid skirt paused at a car door, nodded, and smiled. Her demeanor was pleasant, but her eyes lingered. And Logan was eight years old again, unable to meet her mother's eyes after some long forgotten crime, immobilized by the guilt of having sinned before she'd even been caught. There was a shame in not belonging, in not wanting to be known, that drove Logan faster, past the barbershop and the pet supply store, where a parrot squawked at her through the window. Past the market, where sweet potatoes cost fifty-nine cents per pound and a sad teenage boy bagged her groceries the day before, throwing canned vegetables on top of her loaf of bread. Past closed stores, she dodged people out for a Sunday stroll and ran up the stairs to unpack her dishes.

She sat on the foot of her bed, eating a peanut butter and jelly sandwich from a yellow plate with pink flowers. Fine china from someone else's life that once was a source of someone's pride in some other happy time. But none of this was hers. Not the walls or the windows or the view. And not the life of a woman who couldn't even afford a decent set of sheets. Through the window came the voices, happy voices of friends greeting on the street. People she would probably run into at the bar, where she'd have to navigate their questions. Get to know them well enough to serve them drinks and let them know her just enough to leave her alone.

The gold band around the edge of the plate blurred behind tears, and Logan wiped her nose on her sleeve. She would not cry. If she did, she would have to face what she'd lost and how far away her life was from the poor substitute she'd been dropped into. And there was no use crying about it. It was all just temporary. A grand adventure. No passport required.

* * *

She had no gaming system. No Wi-Fi. No car waiting to take her to the airport for a quick trip to London. Her mind wandered to the past, to the rush of music festivals and the exhilaration of a plane taking off for a new adventure. Her one-room apartment felt like another universe, and without distraction, her thoughts ran down a list of things she used to have. Bored, she packed her dollar-store duffel bag with a change of shoes and went to the bar early.

The chill in the air made it easy to rip off the Band-Aid, to plow into the bar and face the truth that working there meant being seen. All she had to do was keep her head above the water. She rubbed her hands together in the vestibule, praying for warmth. Inside the bar, it was sweltering. Helen sat on a stool, sweating, hunched over a cutting board like a weary patron over a beer.

"That you, Logan?" Helen didn't turn around.

"Yup. It's me. Can I help you with that?"

Helen dropped the knife to the bar and leaned back in her chair. She massaged the knuckles of her right hand. "It's all yours. My hands are slow and tired. You can start by prepping fruit for the day. For garnish. And making sure the coolers up here are stocked. I'll walk you through it all."

"Of course." At least she wouldn't have to figure it all out on her own.

Logan stepped behind the bar and took the cutting board and knife. Her first real task as a working girl, cutting fruit in a windowless brick room. It would be the perfect place to break down and have a good cry, if not for Helen. The woman was a comforting presence, though. No hint of judgment or air of criticism about her. Logan couldn't let her guard down, but she was grateful her first boss was a nice one so far. Nothing like her father. And all of it was temporary; just until things turned around.

Helen reached across the bar and pointed to a stack of empty pitchers. "Each morning, I cut up enough lemons and limes to fill two of these. Then I cut a few oranges. Put some in this tray here. These little cups get olives and cherries. Easier than picking them out of the jar. Don't forget to cut your fruit all different ways."

"What do you mean, all different ways?" She cringed when she said it, forgetting for a moment that she was supposed to have experience.

"Some wheels, some wedges."

Logan dropped four slices of lime into the bottom of a pitcher. The kind they served in gin and tonics. At this rate, it would take all day. "It looked really slow when I was in here before, do you really get enough customers to go through all of these?"

"It's not New York traffic, but we get plenty. People come in here when they get off work." Helen shuffled in her seat, and the squeak from the seat echoed in the room. With no carpeting, no windows, and brick all around, even the smallest sound bounced around the room. "I heard you found a place to live."

"Yeah, I did what you said. I went to the newsstand and met Warren. I'm renting the place above the post office."

"Did he fix that shower curtain rod? Used to fall down in the middle of the night and scare me half to death. Of course that was more than twenty years ago."

"It seemed fine. It could use a little paint." Logan stopped short of asking if the carpet had been just as stained when Helen lived there.

"Warren is good people. This town is full of good people. Mostly, they work hard and raise families. We don't get troublemakers here."

There was a hint of a question in Helen's voice. As if she were seeking reassurance.

"I'm definitely not a troublemaker." Unless the trouble followed her. But she couldn't take responsibility for the words and actions of an angry mob. "I know you're worried about me being followed here by somebody but—"

Helen reached a hand across the bar and patted Logan's arm. "I don't mean to sound like a worry wart. I'm too weary to fret over things. Though I do care about my bar and wouldn't want to see harm come to you or anyone else. I've had my fair share of friends who got out of sticky situations. I don't need to know your whole story, but I hope you'll be honest with me if it follows you here. What I meant was that the town doesn't get rowdy in the bar. People come to sit until they can see the bottom of a glass. Almost like there's joy in knowing it can be filled up again."

"I could use a little joy like that of my own right now." She hadn't chosen to start over. The only ray of light on her horizon was the day her father walked out of prison and rebuilt what they'd lost. She squeezed a handful of lime wedges in her fist hard enough for juice to find every little nick and cut she didn't know she had. She dropped them into the pitcher and switched to lemons for the change of pace.

"I've started over a time or two. Divorce takes a lot out of you. One gets the silverware and the other gets the towels. Jerry drove a truck delivering stuff from these farms to markets. Took them hundreds of miles. All around. But then these big box stores came to the suburbs, and they had their own trucks. They didn't need food from our farms anymore. The markets closed, and Jerry lost his job. It takes a toll on a marriage. The house was in his name, and I owned the bar, so I had a better income. Figured I had a better chance of getting back on my feet, and I moved out with nothing. I remember standing in the store trying to decide if I could afford to buy a lamp."

Helen made it sound so easy, laying it out like a story that belonged to the past. Maybe it would be that easy someday, to say where she'd come from and how far she had fallen. But all she'd achieved so far was a discounted plate from an antique store. Exile denied her even the catharsis of a friend. Even to hint at it, the lilt of her voice would give away how much she had lost.

"It takes a lot of bravery to start over with nothing." Logan dropped lemon wedges in the pitcher. "And a lot of kindness to let the other person keep the things you shared."

"We're a bigger club than you think, young lady. These will be the good old days someday."

She let Helen think what she wanted. A pitcher each of lemons and limes, the garnish tray filled, Logan cracked her knuckles. "What's next?" If she didn't keep moving, she might break.

"Take a look at any empty spots up here in the coolers and fill them up with more from the big fridge in the back. There's a handcart back there. And while you're there, peek in that stock room? There are wash rags and some pots and pans. The dishes are all gone, but there's lots of drinking glasses. Take home what you need. I'm too old to run a restaurant again, and no one ate here enough to pay the bills." The stool squeaked when Helen lowered herself to the ground with wincing effort. "If you need me, I'll be in the office with a bag of ice on my knee."

The door closed behind Helen, leaving Logan alone at a bar she didn't know how to man, with the lies she had to keep straight. She found a scrap of paper next to the register and made a list of the beers she needed to fill the coolers. The light in the back popped and crackled when she flipped the switch. The small room was made of concrete. Mortar oozed and dried from between each block. Shelves lined the walls, covered in dusty liquor bottles, jars and cans of fruit, and mixers, like a frat house bomb shelter. Not at all the kind of place she wanted to spend time in. She found the handcart tucked behind a stack of old liquor boxes and wheeled it into the walk-in cooler. She collected what she needed. Three coolers served the bar, two tucked under the counter with stainless steel lids that wouldn't close and one tall cooler with glass double doors that wouldn't stay open. A puddle of water oozed from beneath one, conveniently next to a mop. Her shoes slipped on the wet floor, and she dabbed at it with a mop on her way to return the cart to the stockroom. Cleaning the place had been her bargaining chip to get the job. Who was she kidding? She didn't even know how to dust.

She took a soda gun from its holster, running her thumb over the worn lettering. She held it over a glass and pressed buttons, sampling the contents to figure out what drink came from where. Syrupy cola a bit too flat and a bland water that could be tonic were all she identified before a mountain of a bearded man in a thin T-shirt dropped his tangled chain of keys on the bar and sat.

He didn't look her way or offer a greeting. He dug his wallet and a folded knife from his back pocket and picked at the knife until he dislodged his blade of choice. He ran it under a fingernail and wiped the blade on his stained jeans.

"Do you want a menu?" It seemed like something bartenders would say. Logan dumped the contents of her test glass into the sink and left the glass by the register.

He raised an eyebrow, but his eyes remained fixed on his nails. He scraped more dirt onto his pants. "You don't have menus."

"Right. Sorry. I'm new."

"I can see that."

"Do you want anything? I mean—" It was a bar, after all. Her mouth went dry. Maybe it was some kind of message? That no one wanted anything to do with her? Or maybe it was the kind of bar where people picked at their fingernails with a knife.

With the flick of a wrist, the blade closed. "Where's Helen?"

Logan glanced over her shoulder at the door to Helen's office. Orange light bled from beneath it, reflecting off the damp floor. "She hired me. I'm the bartender now. If you know what you want, I can—"

"Not until Bern gets here. We order at the same time."

Logan surrendered, her hands in the air. She took a step back. "Okay, that's fine. It's no big deal to me, though, to pour you a beer or whatever."

"I don't like to make Helen get up more than she has to."

"But Helen's in the back."

"I'll wait." The man scraped another blob of dirt from his nails and wiped the blade on his pants.

"Suit yourself. I'm just gonna keep cleaning up. Scream if you want anything." Logan slipped on the slick tiles, like a novice carhop on skates. She flailed and clutched the edge of the sink to catch her balance and inched along, then used the coolers for safety on her way to the far end of the bar. She couldn't even walk.

Shelves lined the wall around the register, and the office door, every inch covered with bottles and knicknacks, all covered in dust, stuck fast with a layer of oily residue. With a damp bar rag, she started at the bottom.

Behind her, the man cleared his throat. "Why?"

"Why what?"

"Why are you cleaning up? Is Helen selling the place?"

"Not that I know of. She didn't say anything like that to me. Sounded more like she can't move around as fast as she used to, and she'd like to slow down some."

"She never said she was hiring nobody. She never put up an ad or said nothing. Where'd she find you?"

She'd expected the questions. Where she'd come from. What she wanted from their town. Without convincing detail, rumors would fly, and they wouldn't be for her benefit. She wiped the dust from a bottle of Knob Creek and set it on the shelf, careful not to clank the bottles together. She stuck to her story. "I came here to start over. A woman has to do that sometimes."

The door blew open, shoved by someone who could only be Bern. Another person from town with the same set of questions. Pocket Knife

Man shifted and settled, pushing the chair next to him away to make room.

"Usual." The man who seemed to be Bern slapped his friend on the back and took a seat at a comfortable berth for Pocket Knife Man's expanded frame. The smell of cigarettes wafted in with him, and Logan shied away from the sour smell. She tucked the bar rag into her back pocket and walked toward the taps. Domestic beers were easy, their logos iconic, but she hadn't consumed a single one since her fifteenth birthday. They were bitter going down and worse coming up.

It was a stare down, Logan on one side, waiting for Bern to tell her what his usual was, and Bern on the other, demanding she read his mind.

"She don't know what you want, man." Pocket Knife Man pressed the dull side of the blade against the bar and closed the knife. "She's new. You gotta tell her."

"Why do I gotta do all the work?"

"You're not doing work. You're sitting on your fat rump. You'll get your drink a lot faster if you tell her what you want."

Bern glared, first at Pocket Knife Man, then at Logan. "Where's Helen?"

Logan tugged the rag from her back pocket and flung it on the counter. "She's in the back. If you'd like a drink, I can get it for you." She'd signed on to tend a bar, not heal the emotional rift of men who were happy to be waited on by Helen but not by her.

"Yuengling. It's the green tap."

"I know which one it is. Knife Guy? What would you like?"

"Name's Dan. A six pack of Bud. Regular Bud, not that light stuff. To go."

Logan placed a glass below the tap, holding it at an angle so the beer wouldn't foam in the glass. The way they did on television. She let the head settle while she unfolded a paper six pack holder.

Dan cleared his throat, and Logan stopped, one foot in a puddle and one hand in the cooler beneath the bar. "Not from up here. From the big cooler back there. By the register. The one with the two doors."

Of course. It made sense to make six packs from the cooler to keep beers for customers closer at hand. A blast of cold air gave her goosebumps when she opened the door to the tall refrigerator. She slipped the beers into a paper bag and dropped it on the counter by the register. She found prices and instructions to run the register on laminated pages dangling from a thumbtack behind the register, as if Helen were forgetful enough to need the reference tools.

"Five fifty-eight." She turned to Dan and pushed the bag down the counter, then topped off Bern's beer.

She made change for both men, proud of herself for completing a sale, but her hands were sticky and her shoes wet from the growing pond on the floor. She dropped coins into Dan's hand, and he didn't push away from the bar as she expected. Instead, he took a beer from the bag, removed the cap, and placed the rest at his feet.

"I thought you wanted those to go?" Logan second guessed herself. "You did say six. To go. Right?"

"I did."

"Then why are you drinking them here?"

"You'll figure it out on your own."

In New York, Logan had friends who only ate raw food, wore only clothes designed by women, and who crossed the city for just the right pizza. The people of Ramsbolt were just as entitled to their quirks. Logan washed the beer from her hands and returned to the task of smearing greasy dust from the liquor bottles. Among them she found corks, receipts so old their blue numbers had faded, pictures, the tchotchke collections that come from decades of inside jokes, and enough pocket change to pay for a few rounds of beer. She collected the change in an old empty bottle by the register. Her hands were coated in residue so sticky her fingers turned to prunes while she scrubbed it off. No shower would be long enough to get the sour stench of the bar from her hair and feel of it from her skin. It was a punishment for a sin not committed. Like the stale and acrid vestiges of a house party that went on too long, got too out of hand, and in the light of day was nothing but broken glass and the musty, putrid scent of what went unconsumed. It made her stomach churn.

"Can I get a refill?" Bern's voice drifted across the bar, but it didn't reach Logan's ears, her attention taken by water in the sink and grime under her nails. "Hello? Anybody home in there? Refill time."

Dan cleared his throat and the room shuddered.

Logan turned off the tap and dried her hands on a rag. "What can I get you?"

Dan looked at Bern. "You wanna try again?"

"Not really but I guess I have to. Refill."

A group of men came through the door, bringing cold air with them. She lifted her chin, acknowledging their presence, and took another glass from the cooler. She turned to Bern and paused at the row of taps, her memory blank. Was it the green one or the blue? "Refresh my memory?"

"Yuengling." Bern's face lined with impatience and his voice edged with ire.

Logan filled his glass as another group came through the door. More people to please in a game she'd never learned to play. The night wore on, Logan serving beer and cleaning the shelves while people from town scattered along the bar, asking for beers and glasses of wine. A woman asked for an old-fashioned. Any claim Logan would make to being experienced behind a bar would prove a lie if she looked it up in a book. She snuck into the back room and looked it up on her phone. She was slow and messy and used too much simple syrup, but it looked like the picture when she handed it across the bar. The customer was either too nice to complain or had a serious sweet tooth. Logan couldn't count it as a victory, but at least she didn't have to add it to her list of failures for the night.

By the time Helen emerged from the office, the old wooden bar was clean, but the counter beneath was covered in dirty rags and the remnants of fruit. A broken glass lay in the sink. The floor was wet, and the puddle beneath the cooler had become a small lake. Beer streaked her hair where she'd run her hands through it and sweat dripped down the back of her neck. There was no hiding her defeat, no covering up for the lie she told. Helen would know. She'd be fired. Sent back to where she'd come from. She would lose her security deposit if she couldn't find another job and had to leave this place in search of something else. She'd been pressing her luck already. Logan only knew business to be run with an iron fist. People like Helen were few and far between. She may have gotten the job the wrong way, but she was determined to be good enough to deserve it.

At the sight of Helen, several patrons erupted into an angry mob, demanding Helen's attention. All the pride Logan had repressed flamed hot within her. She'd never been spoken to with such disdain, treated as a servant, or condescended to with such disregard. The last time someone spilled beer on her in a bar, the man she was with yelled "Don't you know who she is?" Now she was soaked from serving it to ungrateful people who didn't tip. She plucked glass from the sink and tossed it into the trash. The night had been a failure, and there was nothing left to salvage of it. But there would be another. She had to plead her case.

Helen ignored the crowd and stepped next to Logan, her feet in the dirty water. "I'm just checking on you. Everything okay out here?"

It wasn't. Logan couldn't keep up. She'd tried to take two orders at once but got them confused. Everyone looked the same to her, the woman by the door in the gray tank top and the other woman ten years her senior on the other side of the room. She didn't know how to muddle a sugar cube or where to find a bar spoon. But she couldn't let Helen know any of that, and she couldn't give up. She straightened her shirt and cracked her neck.

"Typical first day stuff. I'm finding my way around." She rinsed the last of the tiny glass shards down the drain, grabbed a dirty rag from the bar and turned, angling Helen toward the door, away from the mess.

Helen rested a hand on the counter. "These folks can be demanding. They're not used to change. They'll get used to you."

"No one likes change, right?" Logan offered a weak smile. She wasn't handling it well herself. "We'll all get along fine. You can go, if you want. I can figure it out from here. Except I can't lock up."

"And you don't know what to do with the register. Why don't I come back and help you close at the end of the night. If you're sure?"

"I'm sure. Go. Rest."

Logan returned to the mob of reaching hands and angry faces. She started at one end of the bar, pouring beers and trying to keep the people and voices straight, until she reached the other. Her goal was a quiet crowd. Her dream was a happy one. One that would give her better tips.

She accepted every collection of coins with a nod, swallowing the shame of taking coins from strangers. She scattered apologies for delays and the temperature of the drinks. It was all she could do to hold the bar together.

An older man, a shadowed form behind the taps, his nose and forehead creased by years of sun and his fingers hooked with arthritis, made so little movement she almost missed him. She peered around the taps. "I'm sorry. I didn't see you. I hope I didn't miss you." She knew she had. She could see it in his eyes.

"You'll have to do better than that."

She raised an eyebrow. How dare he? "Excuse me? Can I get you something?"

"This place is a mess. I'll have a seven and seven. You can't possibly destroy that."

She managed to hold her retort. As if groveling for tips wasn't low enough. "You got it."

Logan slipped into the back room to consult her phone. Two to one, Seagram's 7 and 7UP. But by the time she got to the bar, she'd forgotten the ratio and made a drink possibly too strong in probably the wrong type of glass.

The curmudgeon leaned over the bar and dumped the drink into the sink. "Do it again." He reached an arm across the bar and pointed at a woman's drink. "That glass. The short one."

Logan measured, two to one. An ounce and a half of whiskey. Three ounces of soda from a can. She topped it with ice and placed it in front of the man with so much gentle deliberation the ice didn't move in the glass. If that didn't please him, nothing would.

He didn't lean forward to accept the drink or uncross his arms. He didn't look at the glass or at the bill she placed in front of him. His eyes locked on hers, narrowing in disgust. "You'd better get it together."

Logan said goodbye to another tip and nudged the bill. "Three fifty. When you get a chance." She may be new, but she wouldn't be pushed around.

People faded from the bar one at a time. Some angry, most in silence. She didn't notice when the older man left, but he'd paid his bill in coins left by the tap, next to his untouched drink. She dumped it into the sink and dropped his glass into a dishwasher tray with the rest of them.

She had a new appreciation for Marta, the nanny she'd considered a second mother. How had Marta looked after her for so long while her father treated her like a servant, issuing demands that made no sense? Maybe the sting of wounded pride numbed over time.

Stripped of all of the power that came with being a Cole, ripped from the mansion and all its windows, Logan had less now than Marta ever did and none of Marta's skills.

Logan soaked the pond of water off the floor, furious at her father for not protecting her, for not giving her the means to live as she was accustomed to. Ten thousand dollars barely covered a weekend. How could she get by on that in a world that expected her to carry her name like a shameful scar? If her mother had taught her some life skills, she wouldn't have to look online to learn how to turn on the dishwasher. Where was the pride in that?

Every inch of distance she could put between herself and being a Cole cost money she didn't have. And there was no one to talk to. Not even a cold and distant lawyer.

CHAPTER SIX

"I hope this goes better than yesterday." Bern slid into the barstool next to Dan. "For everybody's sake."

Logan had spent a restless night blaming herself for her failures. Soaked in all that disappointment, she didn't try to hide the sigh. But she had to draw a line somewhere. "Bern, you know I was busy yesterday, and you're lucky I remember your name. What is your usual?"

"Dammit, girl."

"Just tell me. Cursing at me isn't going to make me move any faster." Standing up to him, speaking his language, had to count for something.

Bern softened. He rolled his eyes. "Yuengling."

"Got it." She swallowed back a scream. Not because he didn't know her place in the world and not for her wounded pride. She wanted to beg and plead for patience and pity for all she had lost. But cries for help would only lay her bare, and she needed anonymity more than compassion.

Beer fell into the glass, and she recoiled when it spilled over, flicking it into the sink when it streamed down the side and onto her hand. She belonged on the other side of a different bar, a sleek and modern place where people dressed in haute couture, and she could sulk, heavy-lidded in a corner, wishing she were in yoga pants.

On her way to Bern, beer dripped on her sneakers, shoes she once wore in her private home gym. Everything else was ruined. She might as well ruin her good trainers too. At least Dan's order was memorable. Getting it right might win her some support.

"Regular for you, Dan?"

He nodded his consent and returned to picking dirt from his nails, an uncouth ritual, but at least he wasn't rude. Logan pulled six bottles from the fridge and dropped them in the box, then into the paper bag, beginning her second night as the bartender at Helen's Tavern.

Just as disorganized as the night before, with only a dash less ire, she tended to impatient patrons and Arvil, that bitter old man who demanded drinks he didn't consume. When the night came to a close, she was no less tired than the night before, and the bar was no cleaner. Rags covered the counter. Spilled beer coated the floor. Helen came in to help close the bar, and a handful of patrons remained, the old man among them. He grabbed Helen's arm as she walked past, knocking her off balance and bringing Dan to his feet in her defense.

"You made a mistake with this careless woman. She doesn't have the best interest of this bar at heart." The man spit his words at Helen, who swatted him away.

"Arvil, you have to calm down. It's just a little change. It's not easy back there. It takes a bit to get yourself on your feet. I know. I remember."

"You're wrong. She's bad at this. She doesn't even know the basics."

Helen patted his arm and slipped to the other side of the bar. "Everyone starts somewhere, Arvil. You were new once too."

Leaving his untouched drink on the bar, he walked toward the door, planting one foot at a time in a solitary stampede. Pausing, he wagged a finger at Logan. "You'd better get it together, or you'll destroy this place."

She did her best to put his rant aside, to ignore it as the machinations of a fragile mind, but he wasn't wrong. She needed to improve, if not for Helen's sake, to save herself the risk of a wounded outburst.

She saved face by standing at the register, ringing up the remaining tabs with her back to the crowd. Tucked under the register, one corner peeking out, was a slip of register paper. A tab she'd missed or forgotten to hand off. How could so be so careless? Another waste of money. But it wasn't a tab. It was just a scrap of paper, two columns of faded black ink, one column of names and another of drinks. It was Helen's own cheat sheet. The realization washed over her that even someone so loved by their customers needed a helping hand once in a while.

She thumbed through the papers and junk mail and bills that Helen stashed between the register and the wall and found a composition notebook. On the cover, Helen had colored in some of the white rivers with ink, but the pages within were blank, the perfect place for Logan to start lists of her own. A new list of regulars and their favorite drinks, the things she got wrong, and what she needed to learn. Her bank account wasn't big enough for her to blow this chance, and with nowhere else to go until her old world called her home, she would have to work if she didn't want to sink.

* * *

"This is the worst one yet." Arvil stretched across the bar and held his drink in the air. There was no way he could know that he was over the sink when he turned the glass upside down. Logan got lucky when the contents splashed into the stainless steel tub.

Next to him, a woman raised a pink cosmo. "Mine is perfect. I think she's a natural."

The lines on Arvil's face deepened with his scowl. "She's a natural terror."

Logan closed her customer log. "For the love of God, if you don't want it, don't dump it behind the bar. Please." Her diary of customer complaints had helped her survive for a week. Having calmed half the irate customers, Logan had enough energy to snap back through gritted teeth at him. It gave her a small satisfaction. "If it gets on the floor back here, and I fall, I will absolutely make you clean it up."

"Give me a beer instead." He folded his arms like a toddler facing a plate of vegetables. "Can't screw that up."

Logan dropped his empty glass in the tray with the others. "You're gonna have to be more specific." She cocked her head to the side, an intentional, impatient expression she knew would anger the man. She'd seen enough of her father's old dogs learn new tricks to believe that he was capable of offering honey instead of vinegar.

"Bottle of Oxbow."

Fixing her expression in an emotionless gaze, she paused for a moment, long enough to give him alarm. He could read into it what he wanted. She knocked her fist against the edge of the cooler handle, slid the door open, popped the cap off the beer, and placed it on the bar before him.

"Two fifty."

Arvil sipped the beer, his eyes pinched tight. "Warm!"

His voice grated like gravel against her nerves. "It's not warm."

"It's warm. It's not cold. You put it in the wrong place, and it's warm."

"Do you want something else or are you done for the night?" When Helen told her the place had no troublemakers, she must have forgotten about Arvil.

"Whiskey sour." The corner of the man's eye twitched.

"I don't have any eggs, and you hate the mix. We did this yesterday."

"Then you should have got eggs for today." Arvil pounded a fist on the bar, rattling glasses. Heads turned in his direction and hands steadied drinks. Next to him, Bern leaned away and gave him side-eye, but Arvil was focused on Logan, pointing his finger, his face red with heated accusation. "You are going to destroy this bar and run it into the ground. How can you expect this place to make a profit if you can't even serve a cold beer?"

Logan's face seared hot, and she clenched her teeth, holding back a rage she couldn't dare let loose. What could this man possibly know about profit that wasn't encoded in her DNA? She refused to give into the fighting instinct, rinsing dirty glasses instead and adding them to the tray. Her life had become an endless stream of dirty glasses, giving her a new appreciation for Marta and every cook and cleaner who'd made it look so easy in her past.

Arvil continued his tirade, wagging his finger over the bar. "You shouldn't have taken this job if you didn't know what you were doing. You're gonna ruin this place and take the whole damn town with it. You need to go to the library and get a book and learn how to make a basic cocktail. Better yet, why don't you go back where you came from?"

She'd give anything to go back to where she came from. She'd give up her apartment, her dollar-store duffle bag, and her chipped dinner plate. Anything to go back to a predictable life of leisure and not have to spend one more minute on aching feet in a pool of water, her hands sticky with beer, her sense of self-worth called into question by a man who did nothing but sit on a barstool all day and complain while her lower back ached.

"Calm down, Arvil." Dan's hands were fixed around his third bottle of Budweiser. "I work all day, and I don't want to listen to you carry on when I'm trying to relax."

"See what I mean? People don't want to deal with this shit." Arvil sank back in his chair, his face red and strained.

Logan took Arvil's full bottle of beer and dumped it in the sink. He was right. It wasn't cold. She tugged the bar rag from her back pocket and wiped the bar in front of him, taking the opportunity to get close and level with him in the quietest voice that would cross the bar. "The cooler must be broken. That's not my fault. If there's something else I can get for you, let me know. Otherwise, stop screaming in the bar. It's unbecoming."

"Unbecoming? Get a pint glass."

"Excuse me?" Logan tossed the bar rag over her shoulder.

Arvil folded his arms again, back in defiant toddler mode. "Pick up a clean and empty pint glass and put ice in it."

"Are you seriously giving me instructions for ice water?"

"No, I'm trying to get a drink fit for consumption."

She could either continue to fight Arvil in a staring contest or give him what he wanted. And only one of those options stood a chance at keeping him quiet and out of her way. She slammed a glass on the bar and added ice.

"Two ounces of rye," he barked.

"Which kind?"

"Rittenhouse."

She found the bottle on the third shelf and poured two ounces on top of the ice.

"Sweet vermouth. One ounce."

Scanning the shelves, she tried to recall the label. Before she made it along the top row, Arvil groaned. "It's in the fridge. Every bartender knows that vermouth goes bad, so you keep it in the fridge. You would know that, if you were a bartender. And two dashes of bitters. The white label Angostura. Not the orange. Now stir it. Until it's cold."

Manhattan. Logan knew the smell of it. Her father used to drink them. At home, he'd put them in a short glass. A rocks glass. But when they were at the club, they came in that old-style champagne glass. The bar book she found in the back room called it a coupe glass. She scanned beneath the bar for one. Placing it before Arvil, she strained the manhattan into it, tossed a maraschino cherry on top, and dumped the ice, stained pink, into the sink. If that old-style glass was good enough for her father, it was too good for Arvil.

"Five twenty-five."

"What makes you think this is worth five twenty-five?"

"That's what it costs. And that's how I know this is a profitable bar. That beer was the last free drink you waste tonight."

Logan locked eyes with Arvil and matched his glare. Without looking away, he slid the glass down the bar to Bern.

"What am I supposed to do with it?" Bern shrank back, away from the drink.

"Taste it."

"You taste it. You wanted it."

Arvil took the drink back, reached over the bar, and dumped it in the sink. Logan clenched her molars, and the muscle in her jaw twitched as the drink splashed in the basin. She held in a breath to keep the words in and let it all out in a slow exhale. It was Helen's bar. No matter how inclined Logan was to toss Arvil onto the street, she had to find a way to cope with this ungrateful and rude man.

He laid two quarters on a five-dollar bill and walked out of the bar.

Logan let out a slow sigh and raised her hands in thanks to the bartending gods. She tucked one quarter in her front pocket and put the rest in the register. *The man is not going to make me quit this job.*

But Arvil had a point. The beer was warm, and the drinks were mediocre at best. They were too sweet or too strong, and the customers were too kind to point it out. She knew it. Maybe they appreciated her progress, that drinks arrived faster, and the bar was cleaner than it had been in years. Five minutes before closing, she raised the lights a little. The harshness, Helen had told her, would drive them out into the shadows. It may have been cleaner at the end of the night than it was a week before, but in the bright lighting, Logan could see fruit juice on the counters and sticky beer on the floors. Cleanliness had become an aspiration.

Two men remained, nursing what was left of the day. One of them was Bern. He pushed his glass as close to Logan as he could and shoved away from the bar.

"It wasn't so bad in here today. Arvil's just an old grump. He's at that age, you know? Where everything has to be just so. Don't let him upset you."

Bern must have mistaken the physical pain on Logan's face for emotional turmoil. Her ankles throbbed from pounding on the hard tile floor, and the exhaustion had set in on a cellular level. Even her fingernails hurt. The physical torture outweighed the emotional toll, but his words rang true. Arvil had upset her, though she'd deny it with her last breath. "I'm not upset. It'll take more than that to run me out of here."

Bern wore his sympathy out the door. It was quiet enough to hear the outside door open and a gust of autumn air push against the door to the bar. She went back to cleaning, to the running commentary she kept in her mind like a mantra. This would all be over soon. Her father would call, and it would all work out. In the silence, her ears rang from hours of assault by patrons shouting over each other, the dishwasher, and the radio. Until he cleared his throat, she forgot one last patron remained.

One guy, a few years older than her. Wavy dark hair pouring from beneath his beanie cap. A long-sleeve T-shirt, the wrist stained with something silver. He wore no watch, no ring. Things she noticed out of habit. And his glass was almost empty. An observation she was glad to make.

"Can I get you anything before we close?" She said *we* like she had help. It had been days since Helen came by before closing. All the better for Logan, who appreciated one less person to please.

"Nah. I'm good." He took another sip of his beer. "You know, there's a trick to those coolers."

"Yeah, what's that?"

"One of them is on its last legs. You've been keeping beer in it. If you put the beers you think you'll serve in this one over here and in that tall fridge, they'll be cold when you serve them."

The pond of water. Of course. "That's why Helen had glasses in here. I wondered why she had the beer so far from most of the customers."

"Right. Well, now you know." He downed the last of his beer, slid the empty glass to the edge of the bar, and stood, tugging his coat from the back of the stool.

"How'd you know that?"

"I'm the HVAC guy. I'm the only one in town who knows how to fix them." He laid cash on the bar and wiggled his wallet into his back pocket.

"Can you fix that one?"

"Unfortunately, no. I mean, I'm capable. But Helen can't afford it. I'm willing to bet that if you put the beers in this cooler over here, though, and keep serving strong drinks, she'd be able to afford it before too long."

It was hard to be offended by a guy who didn't look like he wanted to push her into traffic. She extended a hand across the bar. "I'm Logan."

"Grey. Like the color." Lines formed at the corners of his dark brown eyes when he smiled. He shook her hand, shrugged into his coat, and moved to the door. Logan rinsed his glass, dropped it in the tray with the last of the night's dirty dishes. Her shoulders ached as she lifted a full tray to take it to the back room, to the dishwasher, but Grey lingered by the door, his hand on the knob. "You know, if you want, I could teach you something else tomorrow."

She had no witty comeback. No snappy retort. Logan hadn't learned the tricks to dealing with misogynistic men because she'd never met a man dumb enough to talk down to a Cole. She let the tray of dirty glasses fall back to the counter, glasses threatening to break, and reminded herself, just in time, that he could be the only person in town who could keep the coolers working. Maybe he was lying about that, but she couldn't take a chance.

"I didn't mean to offend you. I'm sorry. Look, Helen said you knew what you were doing, but I can tell you lied to get the job. We all can. Thing is, nobody cares as long as they get their drinks. I wasn't trying to be mean, I just meant that I could show you some tricks behind the bar. Like when to shake a drink and when to stir it. Stuff like that."

She'd inherited her fuse from her father, but she also inherited his self-control. Being mean to the nicest guy in the bar and the only person trying to help her wouldn't be the kind of lying low that would help her blend into town and go unnoticed. At the end of a long day, she had to admit the possibility that she was too raw to judge his intent.

"Thanks. I wasn't sure what you meant. Sorry I took it the wrong way. I'm exhausted."

"I bet. There aren't a lot of us in this town, but when we're thirsty, we're like vultures."

"Why is that, anyway? Why shake some drinks and stir others?" It was risky, showing her hand, letting one person inch closer to the truth. But there wasn't a game worth playing that didn't benefit from an alliance. Even a weak one could be bent to her favor.

"It's about what you're mixing. Drinks with ingredients that have different consistencies, like eggs and fruit preserves, those get shaken to emulsify it. You stir when you're mixing alcohols and stuff that's the same, like when you're just trying to chill it." Grey did a little dance and pushed the door open. "Secret's safe with me."

"Thanks," Logan called after him, but he was already gone, and she was alone in the bar.

She locked the door behind him, grateful for at least one person she wouldn't hate to see across the bar, but that's where he'd have to stay. The only way to keep her past to herself was to stay distant, to move through town without being noticed or standing out. If Ramsbolt made room for men like Arvil, it would certainly make room for an introverted transplant from a big city who just wanted a little peace and quiet.

CHAPTER SEVEN

The first sign that something was wrong came with heavy footsteps on the stairs. The Marchesa gown she wore to someone's stupid retirement party was still in a puddle on the floor. The maid would wag her finger at her for not leaving it in her dressing room where it belonged. Her TV glowed a faint purple, still on from the game she was playing before she fell asleep.

The footsteps grew louder. It sounded like her old dormitory at Yale. She hadn't heard that much racket since graduation. No one stomped in the Cole house and certainly not at five in the morning. The petite woman at Logan's bedroom door introduced herself as Meredith, with federal investigators from somewhere or other. The FBI? She asked nicely if she could come in and take a look around.

A man with a gentle countenance asked her if there was a place they could talk, and she led him down the hall to her old play room. It had been converted to a gaming room, where she sat next to him on an old leather sofa and answered his questions. Logan hadn't paid enough attention to what her father did to understand their questions. No, she hadn't seen signs of money laundering, bank fraud, wire fraud, or racketeering. She really hadn't. She didn't even know they had a fax machine. Her father did a bunch of stuff that had something to do with international public relations, and he did a lot with real estate. And he kept her at a distance. With money enough to drive her distraction, she simply never bothered to see the answers to all their questions.

The people in black jackets were kind and tidy. They showed her a warrant and tossed her bedroom, her blue bathroom, her dressing room, and the old playroom, where she spent all her time since she graduated from Yale. They let her have a cup of coffee, but they took her computer, her cell phone, and gaming systems, cutting her off from the rest of the world. But not before the text messages began to roll in, asking about the big black SUVs in the driveway. An old friend from high school who worked for a cable news station begged for a scoop. Her social media apps lit up with thousands of notifications as strangers commented on photos and tagged her in posts. Hoping she'd die of cancer in jail. Be pulled to pieces by dogs. The last thing she saw before she handed over her phone was a photoshopped image of her whole family, beheaded in Times Square. Logan yearned for the easy days, for Pee-wee Herman and cookies on the sofa. For the days before Marta was fired and someone could help her make sense of the world's complexities.

The house fell quiet in the days after. Her father bumped apologetically into Logan, and her mother in the hallways and kitchen, but offered no explanations to the questions they were afraid to ask. Logan was too nauseated by what she'd read—by the detailed threats to kidnap her and throw her off the George Washington Bridge or leave her body to decay in the reeds of Fire Island—to ask for explanation. The questions simmered in an angry stew, but she wouldn't let them reach a rolling boil. The Coles locked themselves in separate rooms, living silent and separate lives.

From her bedroom, she heard the coming and going of lawyers, but none departed with a laugh or toast. Not the way they used to. Every entrance felt like bad news Logan wasn't allowed to know, and every exit brought more gravity to the silence.

One early morning on a biting March day, a lawyer returned her electronics. Useless, since she'd bought all new. He warned her that they were likely bugged, not to discuss the case or anything she heard near them. Logan didn't know enough about what was going on to relay anything of value anyway and her social circle had diminished to the point that it was as tiny as a period at the end of her social sentence. Jill hadn't been by for years. Elizabeth and the rest of the debutant dolts avoided the house. Even the guy she'd been sleeping with dropped off the face of the earth, afraid to catch the plague that had fallen on the family. She dumped the electronics in the trash can in the kitchen, happy to have a new, unlisted number.

More charges were filed, and her father was deemed a flight risk. From her bedroom window, Logan watched as he was taken from the house in handcuffs. He'd shaved for the occasion, a clean ending to weeks of gradual collapse. Everything was falling apart except her insides. There was no way, as busy as her father was, as many friends as he had and opponents he'd overcome, that any of it was true.

It's just for a few days, she told herself. *Someone will file some paperwork, and he'll be back. This will all be over in no time.*

But the lawyers stopped coming. They visited her father in prison instead, leaving Logan and her mother in the dark. Alexander stopped by and gave them the high points, and they scoured the news for the rest. He said things like, "Don't worry your pretty heads over all this." Logan's mother accepted the reassurance, but Logan could have spit nails. She demanded the truth from him, the real story of what her father had done. How a real estate developer and public relations guy could possibly have committed all those crimes and what the accusations really meant. But he brushed her off. Told her not to worry. She believed him.

She visited her father again, demanding answers, and he insisted she never visit again. It was an embarrassment, he said, for her to see him that way. To pick up the paper the next day and see her pictures in the press as she visited him in prison. The optics were bad. And he lamented what the other inmates said about her. It was only for a little while, he said. Until they could get it straightened out. And then he'd be home, and it would all be back to normal. Her heart broke as she walked away.

Nothing had been normal. There was no desk at her father's office. No foundation to run like he'd promised. The bank accounts were frozen, and the money was running out. And her father had no answers. No plan. Just a promise it would all go back to the way it used to be. Soon.

Logan clung to it. She had no reason to doubt him. When you run an empire, someone's always trying to scale the castle walls, he'd said. Life had always been a stream of minor lawsuits from people who tripped on curbs and slammed their fingers in doors, and he'd always come out unscathed.

Logan and her mother received a list of court dates. They practiced their poker faces and wore them into court, past protesters carrying signs that called for her father to fry. Someone threw food at her. They called her names. Cameras followed them from the house to the parking garage and into the courthouse day after day. During a recess, Logan convinced her mother to walk to a sandwich shop, and the woman who held the door for her whispered in her ear as she passed that she should kill herself and save the taxpayers money.

Logan cried in the bathroom, reapplied her mascara, and smiled for the cameras on the way back to court.

They judged what she wore, how she walked, the color of her hair. They hunted her ex-boyfriends and classmates for quotes. They judged how close she stood to her mother, picking at every loose thread of their family. Were they close? Was there family conflict? Were they complacent or guilty? Logan held her breath and rushed past the crowds, like riding in a car through a tunnel. It would be over soon. But it was worse than that. It was violating. It breached the fortress walls and dragged her into the public light. No one had cared about her on the red carpet at the Tony Awards. She wasn't a media darling. And now they wanted to poke and prod and examine her for bruises and leave a few in the process.

On the day her father signed a plea agreement, the clock began to tick on their personal security. Ten thousand dollars was placed in her bank account, part of her father's negotiated plea to provide for his family. Then, officers and moving companies packed everything the government deemed valuable in trucks and drove it all away. Even the diamond Mouawad clutch her father gave her for her eighteenth birthday that the rude FBI man said was worth two million dollars. He'd laughed when he said it would cover the cost of the investigation. The joke was on him. Logan found it heavy, impractical, and she didn't really care. All she wanted was her life back. Some kind of future. Something that felt like home.

A week after that, they stood in the driveway, mother and daughter, and said their goodbyes.

"I wish you'd come with me to France." Logan's mother stood by a long black sedan, its door held open by a suited driver. The one-way trip to the airport was a parting gift from her father's lawyer, Alexander. "It's not a *farm,* as you call it. It's a gorgeous estate. Your uncle Patrick has plenty of space. I should have plenty of money to get by on."

"How, Mom? How do you have money? They took everything."

"Creative investments. I can't say." Her mother's eyes said there was plenty to the story, but nothing she would say in front of a driver. Her mother had always been fond of offshore accounting. If she had money that hadn't been declared, touching it wouldn't bring her father back any sooner.

"I don't want to live in Europe. There's nothing in France for me. Uncle Patrick talks about cars all the time, like he never retired from that mechanic job. And Aunt Jeanette runs around feeding chickens. I don't speak French, and I don't like French food. And no offense, but I can't imagine living in a cottage with my mother for the rest of my life. We are two very different people." The thought alone made Logan want to run.

"Your uncle ran a multibillion-dollar car company. He wasn't a mechanic. My sister eats organic food, so she keeps her own chickens. Seriously. Ten thousand dollars won't get you far. What about security? What about a job?"

"I haven't gotten a death threat in almost twenty-four hours. And I guess I'll have to get a job, won't I?"

"Don't be smart, Logan. I'm serious. The life you used to live is gone. You can't come back here if things get hard. Where are you going to work? Doing what? I really think you need to come with me. You'll have to figure out—"

"Stop. We don't want the same things." Petra Cole always got her way, but not this time. All of the emotions boiled within Logan, and she let them spill out in the driveway. "Marking time until death comes and drinking milk straight from the cow may be fine for you, but I have my whole life ahead of me, and all of this is going to blow over. We just have to wait it out. All I want is my life back. It can't be that hard to get a job until Dad sorts this out."

"You're not going to get your old life back by sitting in some apartment while your money drains away. And you can't expect lawyers to help you anymore. They're not on retainer." Her mother shot a glance at the driver standing by the idling sedan. "It's not going to blow over, Logan."

"I don't need lawyers, Mother. And maybe I don't want to live that kind of life anymore."

"What kind of life do you want? I mean, you say you think this will go back to normal, and you're going to wait it out in some fast food restaurant somewhere, and then you say you don't want this life. What is it that you want?"

"I want everything to go back to normal, okay? I want people to listen to me. I want my bedroom back and all my shit, and I want to run a foundation like Dad said I would, but the government took the building, and my father's in prison, and I've never even filled out a job application before, but I am not living in a cottage on a farm with you. So please! Stop."

She fixed her eyes on the front bumper of the town car sent by her father's former lawyer to take her to the bus station. It was easier to look at than her mother's wounds.

"It *will* blow over," Logan said, her voice soft but firm. "People will forget. They'll move on. I just have to lay low until this all smooths itself out. How many lawsuits has he been through? You know what he said.

Power and influence are like a bank account. It's always there, and all you gotta do is live off the interest. He'll be back. Maybe I'll house-sit and watch cats or something."

Her mother pulled her into a rare hug, awkward in its execution and uncomfortable in its release.

"Where will you go?" Petra Cole dug through her monogrammed purse, perhaps for a tissue or as a distraction. Logan had seen that purse hanging on countless chairs at fundraisers and from her mother's shoulder at charity events. She wondered how out of place it would look on a kitchen table in the south of France. "How will you get there?"

Her mother's tears breached Logan's floodgates, and a few of her own threatened to fall.

"I dunno. I'm taking a bus to somewhere small. Quiet. Some little town where people have bigger problems, and no one cares about this shit. As long as it doesn't follow me, I'll be fine. Small towns don't seem half as scary as all this noise in New York. Can I have a tissue?" Logan wiped the tears from her eyes with her sleeve. Why was being on her own so hard?

"Here." Her mother handed her a tissue and a fifty-dollar bill. "It's all the cash I have on me. Be careful telling people about your past. Even saying you went to Yale. They could look into your background, and the next thing you know, there's an angry mob at your door. And don't sit with strangers. Look for people who might have sympathy for a young woman traveling alone."

"I'm twenty-six."

"That's young. And try to be believable. Genuine. You know, small town-like."

"Mom, stop. Thanks for the cash." Logan wiped her nose. "Call me when you land."

"And visit your father. He'll need the company."

"He won't let me." She hadn't told her mother about her visit, about how he sat stone-faced on the other side of that thick glass and told her not to come again. Logan gripped the handle of her suitcase tighter. Once her mother left, she'd have no one. "He said he doesn't like what the men in prison say about me. He doesn't want to put me in that situation. He doesn't want to see me there, for me to see him that way. He said he doesn't want me mixed up in any of it."

"He'll change his mind. It's just his pride."

"I don't think so. He sounded serious." Logan didn't want to climb into the waiting car, to watch her life get smaller in the back window with no idea when she'd see it again. But she wouldn't be caught dead with tears in her eyes over it. She would find a place to lay low, a place where no one cared who she was. She'd get an apartment, and she'd be just fine. She shoved the tissue in her front pocket. "This is all temporary. They'll straighten it out."

Logan's mother turned and paused at the open car door. "This is so stupid, Logan. You should come with me."

"I can't. I have to figure this out on my own." Logan lifted her chin. "I don't need all this. Name brands and all that travel. I wanna be part of the world for a while. I wanna make my own place in it."

"Just like your father. The harder something pushes against you, the harder you push back."

With the shake of her head, her mother was gone. Swallowed by a giant black whale of an automobile and whisked down the driveway. The car turned left at the gate, toward the airport and a wasted life, waiting for it all to end in a field somewhere in France.

Logan filled her lungs with a full breath of estate air. The scent of tended plants from the botanical garden drifted across the driveway. She wouldn't mourn over the spot where she played with a stray dog until Marta read the tag on its collar and called the relieved owner. She wouldn't let her eyes wander to the gentle divot in the lawn where a giant maple tree once stood until it succumbed to disease and was felled by a landscaper. And she wouldn't look up at the windows and wish for the life that once dwelled behind them. It would all be hers again one day.

She turned to the driver, thanked him, and stepped into the waiting car. She would go north. Somewhere cold and inhospitable where no one would think to look for her. After a forty-minute drive in dense city traffic to the bus depot, she stepped onto a curb and walked through steam that smelled like food and urine, suspicious yet brave, like a child afraid of the dark in search of a midnight glass of water. Yet unlike young and fearful Logan, adult Logan knew real dangers lurked in the shadows beyond her bedroom walls. Did her father have enemies? Were the text messages and emails and memes nothing more than empty threats?

Logan avoided eye contact as she bought a bus ticket for the furthest point in Maine she could find on her mapping app. When she arrived, she would have enough left for a deposit on an apartment and a few months' rent, some food, and her cell phone bill. But there wasn't enough to buy the kind of power and influence that should have sustained her throughout her life. It had been transferred to the government with everything else.

CHAPTER EIGHT

The thin dollar-store duffle bag caught on the handrail in the narrow stairway, and Logan almost missed a step on her way out of her apartment. Her hands on the walls, she caught her balance and let her racing heart slow. The last thing she needed was to break her leg. At the bottom of the stairs, she fought the deadbolt open and the door out of the jamb.

Her cell phone gave out a muffled ring, and she felt her back pocket for it but came up empty. It had to be in the duffle bag with her shoes and apron and the spare shirt she brought in case she made a mess out of her clothes. She clutched the bag, partly for warmth and to keep it from swinging while she locked the door. Her work shoes weighed it down. She spun on her heel and stepped onto the sidewalk, stepping right into Riley's path.

"I'm so sorry." She grabbed the postman's arm to steady herself, and he grabbed her shoulder. "I can't get it together today."

"No problem. You good?"

Her phone rang again. She held up a finger. "One second." She found it in the front pocket of her hoodie.

"My mother." The call went to voicemail. "I'll call her back when I get to the bar. Sorry I ran into you."

"It's all good. I'm not usually around at this time. Behind schedule today. Cold out. Blood gets thick."

Logan's phone rang again. She held it up. "I guess I gotta take this. Come by for coffee!"

Slinging her bag over her shoulder, she hopped a few steps to get up to speed and made her way to the bar.

"What's up, Mom?"

"Have you seen the news?"

"I try not to. Why? Am I in it?" Logan hoisted the strap of her bag higher on her shoulder.

"No, your father. More charges are coming. It may extend his sentence, and Alexander said it may put the plea deal at risk." Her mother's words slurred. She was drinking and frantic. France was six hours ahead, so it had to be just before dinner there. Drinking on an empty stomach always made her mother overdramatic, but that didn't mean the threat wasn't real. She couldn't afford for her father to suffer any more setbacks. Or to think about him suffering at all, sitting in a tiny cell counting down the days as they increased in number.

"I thought you said we didn't have Alexander or any lawyers anymore. And what does that mean? Are they taking my money away? Because I've already spent some of it on this apartment, and I can't find any place smaller than this."

"No, no. You'll be able to keep the money. They would add time onto the sentence they agreed to. Are you poor? Of course, you are. Do you have a job? You said you'd call. It's been more than a week, and I haven't heard from you since you found that shed to live in."

"It's not a shed, it's an apartment. And, yes. I haven't called because I'm always at work. Christ, it's actually work doing work." A bitter blast of cold air stung her cheek as she crossed the circle. She needed a winter coat. "I'm a bartender."

"A bartender. You've never even poured your own water. Have you?"

"I had to do something. This came up, and it almost pays the bills."

"I guess you have to start somewhere. The money in your account won't last forever. Your father and that horrible plea deal. I don't think Alexander did the best he could, if you ask me. Ten thousand dollars? That doesn't last a week."

"Tell me about it. I got everything I need for the bathroom and blankets and sheets and stuff from Amazon. I had to walk half an hour to a dollar store on the edge of town for everything else. I got a decent pair of work shoes that cost a fortune. Almost a hundred dollars." A blast of cool air found its way through every seam of her sweatshirt. "And I still need a coat. Why didn't I ever buy a winter coat, Mom?"

"Because pretty coats aren't meant to keep you warm, and we don't walk around the streets of New York in the winter. It's full of tourists and angry drivers. We'd take a limo. Took a limo."

"Right." Logan gulped against the biting wind that took her breath away.

"I wish you'd come to France. I can help you get here if you want."

"No way. I don't want my uncle's money. I don't want to owe anybody anything."

"It's not his money, Logan."

"And I don't want yours." Logan picked up the pace for warmth. She knew her mother would never answer over the phone, but her anger at going without and living the right way while her Mom pulled more shady crap wasn't making her feel better about needing a winter coat.

"It was just a little nest egg I set aside for myself years ago."

"Don't bullshit me, Mom. If you had access to money while you were in the US, you'd have stayed here or given me a big fat check. Or you'd be offering to send me some. This has something to do with Dad, doesn't it? He was supposed to turn it all over and—"

"Logan Marie Cole. Watch what you say." Petra Cole's words spit through the phone. "Come to France. Just for a week. For Christmas."

Her mother's desire to maintain her lifestyle was strong. She'd been the last woman in their circle to give up fur coats, fighting against it with the last shred of her dignity. Her affection for her way of life was stronger than her desire to keep her nose clean. At some point, money doesn't have to buy a reputation. It *is* the reputation. Logan had her whole life ahead of her, and she was more motivated to live it than to end up on the dark side of another scandal or indebted to someone else.

"I appreciate the loving offer, but I gotta let things play out here. I have to make my own way, and there's nothing in France for me. All of this is going to blow over anyway." It had to. He promised.

"Don't be delusional, Logan. Things are not going back to the way they were. I hope you don't think that."

"Don't be so negative. I gotta keep my head above the water here. I'm not joining you on your anxiety attack today. Don't you understand? He's coming back. Period." She fumbled the keys into the bar's door and pushed against it with her hip. Yellow glass rattled in its frame when the door swung open. "I have to go. I'm at work, and I have to get started." She didn't wait for the goodbye before ending the call. Things couldn't fall apart anymore. She couldn't carry the burden of her mother's negativity while trying to keep her head above the rising tide.

Logan dropped her bag to the floor and changed into shoes with grippy soles. She zipped her sneakers and hoodie inside and unlocked the door that opened to the bar. Dark and musty, the room smelled like Simple Green and disinfectant. She left her bag in the back, turned on the lights and the radio, and prepped lemons for the night. They'd wasted so much fruit that Logan only cut half of what Helen suggested. In the time it took the radio station to get through two songs of an Elton John marathon, she'd filled the trays and put the rest in the fridge beneath the bar. She carried the fruit she hadn't cut to the back room and emptied the dishwasher, bringing up one plastic tray of glasses at a time. On her last trip to the bar with beer for the coolers, movement in the corner of her eye made her jump.

"Helen. You scared the crap out of me." Her heart raced. A nervous laugh was all she could muster.

"Sorry about that, dear." Helen laid the morning paper on the bar, pulled herself onto a stool, and propped her elbows on the curved wood edge. The newspaper. She hated that thing. Nothing good was ever in it.

Logan wheeled the cart to the far end of the bar and pulled bottles of beer from the boxes, pushing the new ones to the back of the cooler. "Thanks for getting the paper. I was on the phone with my mother and walked right past it. Can I get you something? Water or a soda?"

"No, I'm just here to chat."

From the corner of her eye, Logan searched the woman's face for a hint. Her eyes were lowered, fixed on her hands, and her slouch was more sullen than usual. Helen hadn't brought great news, and Logan couldn't take any more of the bad. She closed the cooler door harder than she should have and grabbed a rag to wipe condensation from her hands. Is this what being fired felt like? Like being dumped by the world's worst boyfriend, being rejected from a bar that barely paid the bills. But she didn't really belong there. She'd lied to get the job. She had no way of knowing how much she cost the bar by being slow, but Arvil's drink orders were a definitive loss. Being honest with Grey and letting him think she had no experience instead of saving her own hide could have been her undoing. Or it could be Arvil, running a social campaign to have her removed from town? What if that sulking lump of a miserable man had found out who she was?

Helen sat, staring down the crooked fingers of her aging hands, offering nothing. Logan would have to drag it out of her. She should have taken her father's advice and never shown her weaknesses. Now she had to beg someone to tell her she'd been fired.

"Is this about Arvil?"

"Arvil?" Helen stretched an arm along the edge of the bar and leaned back in mock surprise. "What's happened with Arvil? Did you put us all out of our misery and kill him?"

"No. No one's killed him. I may have come close. He is really hard to please. Is he like a secret shopper sent to test me?"

Helen reached across the bar and squeezed her hand. "No, not a secret shopper. Not a spy, either. He's just picky about everything. When you get to be our age, you like things just so."

Logan felt some of the tension fall from her shoulders and offered Helen a smile. It was a small relief, but Arvil wasn't the only reason she could lose her job. "That's what Bern said." By the time she got to be that age, she hoped she'd learn to accept that nothing would ever be just so. "He's a handful. I'll just ignore him."

"Do I need to say something to him?"

"No. Please, don't. I just have to find a way to keep him happy so he doesn't upset everyone else. I thought Dan was going to kick him out."

"Dan's good people, but he's got a temper when it comes to uproar. He just wants to drink in peace."

"So am I being fired? Because I'm really trying, it's just hard getting on my feet and—"

"Fired?" Helen folded her hands. It looked like a last resort in a tough negotiation. "No. I'm here to ask for something bigger than your absence. I'm hoping you would be willing to put in more work. I'll make it worth your while."

For most of the world, more work would mean more pay, but Logan barely survived each shift as it was, and she'd already cost the bar more than she'd given it. No matter how badly she needed a winter coat, she didn't deserve a raise. Besides, if Helen couldn't afford to fix a broken cooler, Logan couldn't expect more pay.

"I thought money was tight. What kind of work?"

"Money is tight." Helen twisted her fingers together and held them close to her chest. She looked like a vulnerable child protecting a treasure. "I'm not bankrupt, but it's not good. I do pinch pennies. I own the building here, and it's paid for, but I'm a bit behind on the lot rent and insurance on a bar is expensive. This place is old, and it's in bad shape. You should have seen it years ago, though, how great it was."

Logan slid open the door to the broken cooler. She took clean glasses one at a time from the tray and stacked them inside. They wouldn't get cold, but they'd cool down enough to keep Bern from complaining about warm draft beers. She wished she had something to offer Helen, some skill she'd learned or a trick she'd picked up from her time at Yale, but nothing in her art history classes prepared her for working at a failing bar.

"I don't know what I could do to make it better. I mean, you could refinance the mortgage or renegotiate your lease. Maybe fix it up a little and add some paint. We could charge a tiny bit more and save up for improvements."

"Who would pay it? Nobody in this town wants to spend more than they have to. Kindness feeds people here, not raising prices. This town has so little to give that it can't bear any more weight."

"And I'm extra weight." As much as Logan needed the money, she couldn't justify the greed. Bleeding the bar dry for her own benefit would only bring her short-term relief. She turned her back on Helen and slipped six Budweiser bottles into a carrier for Dan, then tucked them onto the bottom shelf of the fridge.

"You're not extra weight to me. I need you to take over more of the business with this bar. I can't stand behind this bar anymore. I can't cut one more piece of fruit or open another jar of cherries. I'd hoped a young person from town would want to learn to run this place, but they leave as fast as they can get a driver's license, and who can blame them. You coming by here asking for a job answered fifty of my prayers."

Logan let go of the cooler door, and it closed on its own. "I don't know the business of running a bar. I've never done that kind of thing before. And you can't afford to pay me more."

"I need a knee replacement someday. It hurts to drive, and God knows I can't walk across town to get here. I put a lot of responsibility on you already, and I'm sorry for that. It just kinda happened, and you haven't complained. It's not hard stuff, just ordering supplies and accepting deliveries. I'd pay you for the extra work. I'd find a way. I know you can't live on what you're making."

Logan stacked empty boxes on the handcart. Its handle was still cool from sitting overnight in the unheated back room. It wasn't much, these brick walls, but they'd answered some of her prayers, too. "It'd be stupid to say no. I don't want to put you out, though."

"It's no trouble. Even if I have to tighten the belt a little in other areas. It's a mutually beneficial thing."

"What kind of raise are we talking about?" Was it enough to buy a winter coat and cover her cell phone bill?

"I can get you up to eight dollars an hour, which is about what bar managers make in this neck of the woods. Plus your tips. I'd have to watch my pennies, and we'd have to see what we can do to bring costs down here. Is that okay with you?"

Eight dollars an hour. Sixteen thousand a year before taxes. She used to spend that in two weeks. Her allowance at eleven years of age had been bigger than that. If she had saved it instead of wasting it away, she'd have more money now than her father. With eight dollars an hour, she could pay for her cell phone. She could even afford a few more plates from the antique store. Whether or not Helen could afford to give it to her, she couldn't afford to pass it up. "It sounds great. It's a deal."

"Excellent." Helen slapped the edge of the bar and shimmied down from the stool. She took a key from her keyring and laid it on the bar, along with a twenty-dollar bill. "Not that you have any free time, but feel free to clean up the office and make it yours. I'm embarrassed by the state it's in. There was a time you could smoke in places like this, and for years, I'd keep a lit one back there. Everything is covered in ick. You're going to need some cleaning supplies, and if that twenty doesn't cover it, I'll reimburse you. Just bring me the receipts."

Logan tucked the twenty in her pocket and placed the key with the others on her keyring. Sixteen thousand to clean a mess like that would have been a deal breaker two weeks ago. And she still had to paint her apartment. She had no idea what her father paid Marta, but it had to be more than sixteen thousand a year. No one in their right mind would do this much cleaning for so little. "I'll chip away at it. It'll be done in no time."

Helen patted her hand and waved off Logan's offer of help as she hobbled out the door and to her car, leaving Logan alone with her diary of the town. Bern came in late on Thursdays, so Dan would be drinking alone. The couple who owned the hotel across the street would be in late, after the office closed, looking for a beer. They liked cold, frosty glasses. She slipped a few pint glasses into the back of the working cooler for them, proud of herself for knowing that.

For the first time, the stillness of the empty bar didn't feel ominous. A coming storm didn't seem inevitable. The small cooler clicked on, and the condenser whirred. Giving one last mop to the ever-growing puddle beneath the broken cooler, it dawned on her that it had become a habit. It was progress. Learning to make drinks and finding the best places to store the beer weren't going to make her happy or even keep her afloat. She would have to be a different person if she was going to get along and succeed here. She couldn't let pride stand in the way of serving customers.

She slipped the rubber band from the newspaper and let it fall back on her wrist. It would come in handy later, when she lost her hair tie. The paper unfurled, and she left it at the far end of the bar, where Arvil would read it when he began his day of ordering nothing. The headline read like one of her father's planted stories. *Cole Appeal on State Charges Pushes Forward Despite Plea Deal.* He must have been restoring his connections, calling in old favors and staging a public relations comeback to flex what little influence he had left. Appeals were a good thing. They meant her father was still fighting, even if her mother had given up.

She had to hand it to him, his perseverance was extraordinary. It spoke to his innocence, even if the evidence in court had been compelling to the jury. As for Logan, she didn't know enough about the law to know one way or the other. But she'd seen enough of the world to know that what people deserved and what they received were rarely the same thing. She took the news as a sign of good things to come.

She left the newspaper in front of Arvil's seat. She couldn't manage his expectations or control his temper, but she could give him the paper to keep him occupied for an hour or two. She had to learn to make one drink he wouldn't complain about and figure out how to stand up to him when he got out of hand.

She stacked the last of the empty boxes on the handcart and tipped it back just as the door opened, and the first visitor arrived. Arvil shuffled to his seat.

* * *

The bar was dead for a Thursday night. It was dead for any night. By the time nine o'clock rolled around, five patrons had stumbled through the door, and none of them made much noise. Arvil sat in his usual seat, staring down the finer print of the newspaper's local news section. A couple sat by the taps, celebrating the twenty-second anniversary of their first date at Helen's Diner in the hushed tones of a couple familiar enough with each other to have nothing to say. Dan hunched over his beer, the remains of a six pack in a paper bag at his feet. Logan tried not to take it personally, but she could help wondering if she was destroying the bar, driving the regulars away.

"No Bern tonight?" Logan wiped at nonexistent filth on the bar. "I know he said he'd be late, but it's almost closing. Nobody's here. What gives?"

"Football's on."

"So it's not me then. I figured it was me."

"No television." Dan nodded to an invisible point above the bar. "Can't see the game here."

Logan threw the rag over her shoulder. "You don't do football?"

"I don't care if sports are on or not. I'd rather enjoy the quiet before I head home, though. I don't have time for games."

"A lot of people enjoy the escape. It's something to look forward to anyway. Not you, huh?"

"Real life is far more interesting."

The couple at the corner got Logan's attention and waved for another round. She pulled two chilled glasses from the cooler and slid one beneath a tap. "I wouldn't mind having a television in here," she said to Dan. "But if I had a choice, I'd rather have a window. I miss the sun sometimes. Especially now that it's coming up later. I see a lot less of it."

"At least you miss it going down earlier. Can't tell in a windowless bar."

"That's the truth." She placed a full beer in front of the lady and poured a second glass for her husband.

"Arvil, you okay down there?" It was a constant battle between being too attentive and ignoring him too much.

His head snapped up from the newspaper, his eyes like fire. "Stop being so clingy. It's all about validation with you, isn't it? I'll let you know if I want something."

She placed the beer in front of the friendly couple and returned the smile the husband offered. Avoiding Arvil was easy, but biting her tongue was harder than dealing with internet trolls. At least she could mute and block them. She couldn't delete Arvil, so she turned to face the register, her back to the bar and her customers, and resorted to the habit that served her in the past. She unlocked her phone, started a new note, and typed a response she wouldn't send. At the bottom she jotted down a reminder to ask Helen about getting a television, stopping short when Dan's grunt got her attention.

While her back was turned, a woman had entered and taken a seat. A fancy woman from outside of town. She wore an expensive Barbour coat, one of those dark green outdoorsy things with a brown corduroy collar. It was a size too big. The woman didn't fit. An energy came off her that made Logan recoil. Was she a journalist? Some private investigator sent by an internet troll to drag her down? Plenty of people had lost their jobs when her father went to prison. They lost investments and had axes to grind. Logan offered no pleasantries. The woman scowled back.

"Whatcha havin'?" She wouldn't meet the woman's eye. She wouldn't give the enemy that much of her attention.

"Surprise me."

Logan reached into the cooler, into the warmest corner, and withdrew a Corona. She dropped the hot beer on the bar and gave the woman a cold look. Short enough to go unnoticed by a casual customer, if she was one, but long enough to be understood if she was intent on starting trouble. Turning back to the register, she tilted her phone to take a picture, but there was no way to do it without seeming obvious. Her hands were shaking anyway. So she memorized the woman's features and typed a description in a note in her phone. Long brown hair, brown eyes. The Barbour coat. She'd come too far to lose it all now. She'd found this town, this little bar, these people. She had a job and was making something of herself. Whatever this woman wanted from her, she wasn't giving it up without a fight. Maybe she could get Dan's attention and ask him not to leave. But how would she do it without sounding unreasonably afraid of a random bar patron?

Logan kept an ear fixed on the woman's conversation with Dan. She claimed to be traveling, lonely in her own right.

Lonely.

It was a concrete status from a wayward spirit, in search of her place in the world. The woman picked at a broken brooch, a pin she'd found on the street as a tourist in some little town. Dan fixed it with his pocket tool. Then the woman took his advice, ordered a six pack from the cooler, and made her way back across the street to the motel. Just another woman seeking solace. She was no more a threat to Logan than anyone else who found themselves at the little crossroads. Logan wiped down the bar, ashamed that she hadn't been more welcoming. Helen had worked hard to build a place where people could come to escape the world on their own terms. Unchecked, Logan's fear could destroy it.

CHAPTER NINE

The Ramsbolt public library was crammed into an old house, behind a notice-covered door with a hand-painted sign. The porch was covered in chalk scribbles, remnants of an autumn children's book festival, judging by a flyer taped to the door. Just inside, a woman guarded the vestibule from behind her tablet reader, her desk bare but for a few event flyers, complimentary bookmarks, and another hand-painted sign that declared the rules of the library in tiny letters. It smelled like old books, like glue and ink and yellowed paper.

"The door sticks. If you don't mind, just give it an extra shove to keep the heat in." With the press of a button, she closed her tablet and extended a hand. "So you're the new resident. I don't think we've met."

Logan reached for her hand. "Sorry about the cold hand. I'm Logan."

"Nice to meet you. I'm Sandy. It's your first time here." It was more declaration than observation. Sandy offered her a welcoming smile. It had been a while since someone in Ramsbolt didn't hate her just for showing up. "I guess you'll need a library card."

Logan took a tight grip of her purse strap. Her name would be printed on that card. Her name in a database. They'd find out about the book she forgot to return in high school. And worse, they'd know where to find her. Was the library a ruthless institution? Logan hadn't been a star pupil, but she'd learned enough to know that no one was safe from the wrath of a librarian, especially a Yale librarian. Even the ones who preferred tablets over books. "Do I need a library card to do some research if I don't borrow anything? I'd be happy to save you a step."

"Nope. Happy to save a piece of plastic if you're not gonna use the card. Feel free to browse." Sandy rescinded the paper, returned it to the folder, and dropped the folder back into the drawer. "If you change your mind, I'll be right here." She patted her tablet reader.

Many librarians had impressed upon her the sanctity of a library's stillness. Not wanting to disturb it, she tiptoed past the desk and into the library proper. The walls that made up the old house had been removed, leaving behind painted lines, scrapes, and gouges. It was impossible to make out the life the old building had lived before its present incarnation, but in this one, the wood floor creaked. Old fireplaces at opposite sides of the room were blocked off, their mantels covered in children's books. Tall shelves lined the room, stuffed with books. Shorter shelves in the middle held even more.

It was the smallest library she'd ever seen. A thousand of them would fit in her library at Yale. But it was quaint and wore the same smell as every reading room she'd ever known. Stepping into it wrapped her in comfort. And she felt less alone, surrounded by a million stories more tragic than her own.

Clusters of chairs and small coffee tables covered in magazines were scattered about the shelves. Logan chose a seat at random and dropped her purse onto a table. She browsed the card catalog, thumbing through book titles until she found what she needed. The Ramsbolt Library had plenty of books about liquor to skim.

She piled armfuls of books onto the coffee table and flipped through them one by one. With a scrap of paper and a small pencil from a tray on the windowsill, she wrote down recipes from a book about cocktails. In a book about bar safety she discovered the three sink system of cleaning and sanitation. How did Helen get past the health inspectors without it? She learned what the metal rack in front of the sink was for and the proper order to stock liquors in it. She learned that the empty space next to the sink was called a jockey box, and it wasn't for stacks of clean rags, the way Helen used it. It was for juices and mixers and there was a proper order for storing them that opened a whole new set of questions for Logan about what Helen had been getting wrong.

Next was a book about absinthe. She'd heard about its hypnotic properties and its history of turning artists crazy, so she'd been too timid to try it, even in the poshest bars of Europe, for fear she'd turn into the woman in the famous Degas painting, lifeless and withdrawn. Sucked into the history of wormwood, anise, and fennel, she didn't hear Sandy enter the room. But she felt Sandy's presence when the lithe librarian slipped into the seat across from her.

"Need any help?"

Logan lowered the book. "I'm good. Thanks, though. Just doing some research."

"Food and drink, huh? Are you writing a book about cocktails?"

"Never. I'm no writer. I work for Helen, at the bar across from the hotel?"

"Oh! So that's you. I heard someone new was there but I haven't been by in a while." Sandy leaned closer and wrinkled her nose, as if to confide in her a secret. "It definitely needs an update."

Logan waved the book in her hand at the stacks on the coffee table. "You should come up and give it another chance."

"You know, I think I will. There's nowhere to go around here. No place for a girls' night out. Helen's is a hub, though. It's the only place we have to get together with people. I had birthday parties there when I was a kid, back when Helen served food. She threw the best kids' parties."

Logan tucked a scrap of paper in the book to mark her place and set it aside. How had Helen let the bar get from a place that held kids' parties to its dusty, cluttered state? "Really? A birthday party in there? It would need a whole lot of cleaning to hold a kid's party in there now."

"It was totally different back then." Sandy slipped into a chair across from her, crossed her legs, and folded her hands over her knee. The table shook as she tapped her foot against the leg. "It still had all that wood paneling, but there were pictures of Acadia all over the walls. The last time I was in there it was pretty dark, but when I was a kid, it was bright and cozy. I have so many memories of the place. Everybody here does. It's a shame it's not like it used to be."

"Helen said she lost a lot of business when places closed and people lost their jobs." Was that when Helen gave up?

Sandy nodded. "That was a big part of it. My dad lost his job in all that mess. The economy played a big role in it, sure. I think Helen was tired of the daily grind too. It's a lot of work, a diner. She had a few employees, but you could tell it was wearing her down."

"Tell me about it." Logan rolled her eyes. "Just being behind the bar is killing me. I feel ten years older than a did two weeks ago. This is the first soft chair I've sat in since..." Since riding the bus into town. "In a while."

"Well." Sandy slapped the arms of the chair and stood. "People will be glad to see that place get a little affection. There isn't a person in town who doesn't have some connection to it. It'll be nice to see it make a comeback."

Logan smiled. No pressure or anything. "I wish I could give the place a total makeover. Some new paint and brighten it up a bit. Everything costs money, and there's not a lot to spare. At least I can update the drinks."

"It's a step. Anyway, welcome to town. I'll have to stop by for a drink soon." With the wave of a hand, Sandy was gone. Back to her desk in the drafty vestibule.

In a world where everything seemed to cost a fortune, at least kindness and knowledge were free.

CHAPTER TEN

Logan shivered and wrapped her arms around her middle, holding in the warmth. Cold air blasted into her apartment through the open window, and her old sweater wasn't enough to defend against it. The paint fumes had already given her a headache, though. She nudged the window down a few more inches and scanned the room. It was sunny, brighter for the splash of new paint she'd applied at two in the morning, but it did nothing to make the apartment feel less like a cage. Want and grief coated the walls thicker than lead paint. At least needing a winter coat gave her somewhere to go.

She gathered the painting supplies, the hardened brushes, and paint-lined tray. She left them in the hallway, like Warren's note said, and crossed the street to the outdoor store.

Inside was colorful but silent. No music played overhead. Low racks of colorful wrinkle-free shirts and dresses on the left. Flannel shirts in dozens of plaids on the right. Shelves of comfortable denim and khaki lined the walls. Kayaks and oars dangled from the ceiling, casting shadows on the floor, and bunting made from faded bandanas was strung from one side of the room to the other. A guy waved from behind the register, and Logan nodded a brief hello.

One rack of coats filled in a back corner, coats in dark grays and earthy browns. She chose one in tan with a red plaid lining and checked the tag, not for the label but the price. She paid thirty dollars for it, more than she'd been willing to spend, and ripped the tag off at the register. She wore it up the street, threw the label in the trash can on the corner, and stepped into the hardware store for supplies to clean the office.

Logan had never been near a hardware store. It smelled of paint thinner mingled with sawdust. Rows of items she didn't recognize for purposes she couldn't conceive laid out before her. From somewhere in the back of the store, a radio station fought through the static. A man's deep voice gave rapid fire disclaimers to an ad about used cars.

She passed a giant cardboard box full of rakes with their tines entangled, racks of plastic pouches with little round screens, white plastic tubes that came in different angles and lengths, and a hundred different shapes of light bulbs—all designed to maintain and repair stuff she couldn't afford to buy, let alone break.

She crept down an aisle of cleaning supplies lined with colorful bottles and aerosol cans that solved problems she never knew she could have. On her phone, she looked up how to remove cigarette smell from a small room. There were plenty of rags and bottles of degreaser in the back room of the bar, so she spent the twenty dollars on yellow rubber gloves, dust masks, and a bag of activated charcoal to soak up the smell. She tucked the change in her front pocket, thanked the woman who rang her up, and walked to the bar.

The coat was worth every penny. What it lacked in fashion, it more than made up for in warmth. The walk seemed shorter when she wasn't cold and miserable. She unlocked the bar and left her coat in the back room, on a stack of boxes by the walk-in cooler, and gripped the key to the office door. It was cool between her fingers. What if she didn't live up to the responsibility? What if she lost it?

She unlocked the door to the office and pushed it open with her hip. It was worse than she remembered inside. Filth clung to the desk and the shelves and hung thick in the air.

She pulled on gloves and a dust mask, sprayed cleaner on a rag, and started to clean. Yellow film coated every slick surface. On the shelves, on books and ledgers, dust clung to the cigarette smoke like moss. Decades of disease-inducing indulgence went onto paper towels and into a trash can. She set aside the metal fan for a later scrubbing and pulled books from the shelves. She found a pocket bartenders guide and a set of cocktail flashcards with names of familiar drinks on one side and the recipe on the other. Two unfamiliar drinks caught her eye: a presbyterian and a horse's neck. Worth holding onto for later, she tossed them into an empty milk crate. She would take any help she could get. Something in there had to make this job easier, and something had to please Arvil.

Scraps of paper and receipts littered the desk. She raked them in an old cigar box. In the center lay the ledger, open to a half-filled page. It was the old-fashioned style she'd seen in museums. In it, Helen kept a running tally of money in and money out, staying in the black, but flirting with the red. There was so much waste. They only needed half the fruit each night that Helen prepared. The price per jar she paid for cherries in bulk was nearly twice what they charged for little jars at the market. Helen was being milked, and she wasn't doing anything about it. And then there was the marketing. The signage was old and outdated. Even their beers were stale. According to the distributor's price list tucked in a desk drawer, she could get a lot of craft beers for the same prices. Whether the crowd would drink them was another question.

Logan dropped the ledger into the milk crate to take home and study. She pulled open the drawer, and pens crashed against the drawer front. One by one, she tested them with scribbles on the corner of the blotter, a calendar page from August of 1997, until she found one that would write. On a scrap of old paper, she made notes. They needed to reduce their waste and streamline their ordering. Go through the bar book and list cocktails in increasing complexity. Offering a cocktail of the day would reduce the amount of prep, reduce waste, and save the bar resources. It would also help her learn by repetition.

The gradual chipping away at the loss would bring a general uptick in profit. She jotted a few numbers on the blotter. The money she could save on garnish alone could pay the electric bill. The idea gave her goosebumps. No wonder her father was so addicted to money.

Looking at the prices the distributor charged for liquor and mixers, and considering what the patrons ordered, they could even rebrand as a whiskey and beer bar with a cocktail menu and a daily special. Without doing the math, it looked far more profitable that what Helen was doing. But proposing that to Helen, pointing out the flaws and making bold claims about improvements, was another thing. She hadn't even worked out what to say when her finger hit the call button, and the phone started ringing at Helen's house.

There was a click and rustling, then Logan jumped in. "I have a proposal. Oh, it's Logan at the bar." She tapped the pen against the desk. "Did I wake you?"

"No, it's almost eleven. I'm up with the sun these days."

The idea was stupid, sophomoric. Logan had no bar experience, no real life experience. She had no right to tell Helen how to run her business. "It's the bar. I thought maybe we could offer a daily drink special? Something simple to make prep and ordering more efficient. And what if we had a cocktail menu? It might get people to order from there instead of buying cheap beer all the time. Lots of bars do that. I don't mean to step on any toes. It was just an idea."

"I can't see any harm in steering people toward a daily special. As long as it doesn't take anything fancy that costs too much."

"I was looking at that, too. I think I see a way for you to save some money on garnish. Is that okay with you? If I shop around?"

"If you have it in you, go right ahead." Helen's voice was weary. "I know I pay too much for some things, but it's easier for me than spending hours trying to save pennies."

Pennies? Logan circled the bottom number on the blotter with a green pen. It added up to thousands a year. "I have time to shop around for some better prices. Just in case." Logan couldn't bear to mention how much she wasted. "I'll make a list of drinks, too. A month of them. I'll show it to you, if you want."

"I'm sure it's fine. As long as its ingredients we already have, the worst we could do is use them up and make some money."

Money was just the start of it. She could make the bar a nicer place to visit and a better place to work. She could increase profit, better tips.

Helen cleared her throat. "You're doing a great job, you know. Denise… She runs the office down at the Methodist church there at the end of Main? She said your long island iced tea was perfect, and that you're a natural."

But she wasn't. Customers still waited too long for their drinks. They were angry and impatient. She'd made a mess of the coolers. She'd lied and hidden the truth from Helen and didn't deserve the kindness. The least she could do was be grateful for the chance and make it up to her.

"Thanks, Helen. I enjoy working here."

"Why is that? Why do you enjoy it?"

She drew little daisies on the blotter, like she did in the margins of her notebooks in college. The bar wasn't the most comfortable place she could have landed. It certainly wasn't what she'd imagined for herself when she graduated from Yale. God knows she'd had cushier options, even if they did wound her pride. She could have probably begged Elizabeth and slept on her sofa. She could have leaned on family connections, applied for jobs at art galleries, or started a business as a party planner and clawed her way through the fallout. She could have stood defiant against trolls who said they wanted her dead. But she'd rushed to the smallest place she could find on her phone and set up shop in a small-town bar full of angry people and decades-old cigarette dust while she waited for life to fix itself. The bar felt like redemption. Like cleaning out her own life, clearing away her own cobwebs.

"I guess I enjoy having something to be responsible for. I like taking care of the place. At first I thought it would be a great way to stay busy and not be lonely in a new town. But the bar and I are taking care of each other right now."

Helen fell silent. Had she said the wrong thing? Had she forgotten her place? Forgotten that she had no right to speak so casually with someone above her station? She'd seen her father crush men for saying less and destroy women who let their humanity slip out and their vulnerability to show.

"Sometimes you get what you need when you need it most," Helen said. "I needed you, dear. I'm glad you're finding what you need here."

Logan said goodbye, ended the call, and pushed away from the desk.

Surrounded by piles of garbage and dirty rags, old business records, and clutter, a little of the fear slipped away. The throbbing ache of her loss subsided a little. She left her gloves and dust mask on the desk and went to the bar to start coffee. Riley would bring the mail soon. And she had to prep for the day.

She daydreamed about new dishes. Nice ones with a silver band around the edge. About a pretty winter coat and a pair of snow boots. She inherited a lot from her father, some of it gone, some still plagued her. But he also taught her something about profit and loss and the value of things.

* * *

Halfway through the night and the bar was full. Logan took advantage of her surplus of limes to serve whiskey gingers. Voices bounced off the brick walls in a harmony only a busy bartender could love. The chatter and pace were hard to get used to, but the bigger tips were a great motivator.

Logan worked her way down the bar, mixing drinks and pouring beers. She added a whiskey ginger to the tab for a man who worked out at one of the farms. It was a new thing for him, refreshing, he said.

"What can I get for you, Denise? You're almost empty there."

"Paul says it's refreshing, so I'll try that whiskey ginger. What's in it?" Denise peered over the bar.

Logan grabbed a bottle of Jack Daniels. "It's about two ounces of whiskey, five or so of ginger ale. Top it off with a lime wedge."

"You're getting much more comfortable back there. I can tell. You move faster."

Logan passed the highball glass across the bar. Denise sipped it through the little brown stirrer.

"I owe it all to that cash register. Once I learned to use that thing, I figured there wasn't anything on earth I couldn't do."

Denise waved her in and lowered her voice. "Have you been paying attention to those boys at the end of the bar?"

"Yeah. I checked their IDs. They're twenty-one."

"You might want to warn Sandy and her two friends down there. They're a little rambunctious. It happens this time of year. Guys passing through on their way to ice fishing think they can reel in something extra, if you know what I mean."

"Lord, do I ever." New York was full of them. "Thanks for the heads up."

Sandy and two of her friends had slipped into seats next to Dan and Grey. Logan placed a pulpboard coaster before each of them and leaned across the bar. "Just a word to the wise. Those four boys at the corner will be annoying you soon."

Sandy hunched over her coaster and peeked down the bar. She wrinkled her nose at her two friends. "Ew. We'll stick over here by Dan, then. Just in case."

"So what'll ya have?" Logan lifted her chin at a couple at the end of the bar, acknowledging an upraised hand.

"Drink of the day?" Sandy sought confirmation from her friends, and the three women nodded to Logan. "Three of them. What's in it?"

"Whiskey and a lime topped with ginger ale. It's a simple one. Refreshing. Kind of a warm-weather drink, but we could all use a little pick-me-up in this cold, right?"

"Sounds perfect."

Logan filled three highball glasses. After doing it a hundred times, she didn't need to measure.

"Dan?" One of Sandy's friends leaned down the bar. It took her a few tries to get his attention. "Dan. My mom said there was an accident at Zach's farm yesterday. What happened?"

"One of the guys out there got his foot caught in somethin'. They wrapped him up good and took him out to the hospital. He got home this morning, but he won't work for a while. Shame, too, 'cause his wife lost her job, and now nobody's workin'."

"Are you talking about Glen?" Sandy adjusted her drink on the coaster.

"Glen?" Logan poured drinks for the couple at the end of the bar. "The guy who comes in here on Mondays?"

"Yeah." Dan slid an empty bottle to the edge of the bar. "He'll be alright. Just outta work for a bit."

"I'll talk to Helen. Maybe we can put a collection jar on the bar here and people can contribute to help them out."

Logan placed drinks in front of the couple, and the wife chimed in. "Glen's got a prideful streak and wouldn't take the money, but I've known Carla since we were little, and she wouldn't turn down some help."

"I'll make it happen then." Logan turned to Grey. "You good? Need another?"

"Another lager, thanks," he said. "Glen's kid went to school with us, didn't he? A few years younger?"

Sandy nodded and sipped her drink. "Ryan. He and Erica moved south and got married. They're divorced now, and she's with that guy. What's his name?"

The blond brushed curls from her eyes. "Karl with a K."

Logan moved on to other customers. She was an outsider on their stroll down memory lane. She didn't share their history, and it only reminded her that she'd been run out of her own. There was a time she would have been at the center of that kind of chatter. Drinking whiskey at the country club bar while they ran down the who's who list of divorces and high society scandals. Now she was just a name they tossed around. Did anyone ever wonder what happened to Logan Cole?

CHAPTER ELEVEN

"I have no intention of drinking a manhattan." Dan raised one eyebrow and ran a hand along his beard.

Logan extended a dark red drink in a cocktail glass. "Not even a sip? Come on. I need my Saturday afternoon crowd to tell me what they think. I'm trying to build the schedule for next week. I gotta order all my garnish by five for delivery tomorrow."

Warren slid his empty glass to the edge of the bar. "I thought it was perfect. Never had sweet vermouth before. And I'll have another."

"See, Dan." Logan rinsed the glass and dropped it in a tray. "People like the nightly specials. It introduces them to new things. The bar is busier, and we make more money. Everybody wins." More customers meant more tips, less fretting over quarters for the laundromat and pinching pennies for toothpaste. Dan would have to get used to it.

Dan nodded but stuck to his beer. "I'll tolerate the noise for Helen's bottom line, but I'm not drinking a manhattan out of a floofy glass. And I hope you being busy don't mean my six packs are late or get warm on me."

"Never. I promise."

Logan added an ounce of sweet vermouth to two ounces of rye. She twisted the yellow cap off a bottle of Angostura bitters and added two dashes to the mixing glass.

"Where'd all this fancy stuff come from, anyway?"

"The glasses and barware? Small distributor perks on the way to a better bar."

When she started ordering better quality ingredients, her distributors tried to lure more of her business with branded gifts. Someday, she hoped to increase prices enough to afford a nice sign, something to attract tourists on their way through town and people who stayed at the hotel across the street. No one wanted to go to a bar that looked more depressing on the outside than their musty, outdated motel room.

With contributions from the distributors, Logan could also afford to test recipes. She strained a golden yellow drink from a shaker into two glasses and placed one in front of the seat Grey was sliding into.

"What's this?" He arranged his coat on the back of his chair.

Logan dumped ice from the strainer into the sink. "It's called a gold rush."

"I hate drinks that don't say what they are."

"That's all of them then. This is two ounces of bourbon and three quarters of an ounce each of honey syrup and lemon juice."

"The drink of the day?"

"Nope. A future one maybe. I'd have to make the syrup at home. There's no working stove here, and mine is teeny. I made enough for a test batch, though. What do you think?"

Grey's eyebrows pinched; his eyes narrowed.

"Well?" Was it too sweet? Too tart? Lose the citrus squeeze?

"It's good. I like it. I don't know what I was expecting, but I like it."

He held the glass to the light. When he set it down, his expression had changed. His eyes locked on hers for a moment too long. "Did you make this up? This is really good."

Logan turned her back on his admiration. "I wish I could take credit for it, but it's a classic. I'm just trying to see if you all like it."

"Maybe you don't have to try so hard."

To the contrary. If he kept looking at her like that, keeping him at arms length could take a lot of work. "So what can I get for you?"

He tapped the rim of the rocks glass. "Can I finish this?"

"Sure can." She tugged the towel from her shoulder and wiped the counter clean.

Behind her, coffee sputtered into the carafe.

"Hey," Dan pointed at the coffee maker. "What happened to the big coffee machine?"

"It was too big. I had to make too much coffee at one time, and Riley's the only one who drinks it. I found this in the back."

Right on time, Riley's bag bumped into the door, and he tumbled into the bar, a bundle of mail in his gloved hand. Logan poured coffee into a paper to-go cup.

"You really should get a travel mug, Riley." She set the cup on the bar and placed a lid next to it. "I'd give you a discount."

"But they're insulated, and they don't keep my hands warm like paper cups do." He tugged the gloves from his fingers, tossed them on the bar, and grasped the cup.

"Suit yourself. Terrible for the environment, you know."

"So's all this junk mail." Riley left a pile of bills, magazines, and advertisements on the end of the bar and dug into his bag for the next batch of mail to deliver on his way out the door.

"Speaking of junk mail..." Dan slid from his seat and slapped cash onto the bar. "I gotta run home and sort mine before my dinner gets cold. Keep the change."

Warren stood and peeled his wallet from his pocket. "I got a pork butt in a crock pot, and it's calling my name." He laid cash on the bar. "Same here. Keep the change."

Logan collected the bills. "Thank you, both. Be safe."

She dumped the dredges of the carafe into the sink and turned off the machine. She rang up their tabs, stuffed her tips in a jar by the register, and grabbed the pile of mail Riley left on the bar. She stood by Grey to sort it. Just because he looked too long and smiled too much didn't mean he deserved a cold shoulder.

"What brings you in here so early anyway?" Logan sorted the mail. Bills to be paid. Junk.

"Nothing's broke. Heaters, plumbing. A whole town and nobody in it's complaining."

"I'm complaining about this cooler. You want to give me a quote on what's wrong with it?"

"That thing ain't worth fixing. You need to replace it."

"How much?"

"Installed? I can get a used one and put it in here for about two thousand."

"Is that two thousand dollars or pennies?" That kind of money was a pipe dream. Two thousand dollars meant nothing once. It used to be so easy to solve problems with cash. Now, every time she gained an inch, she fell back a mile. She swatted at him with a postcard from a car dealership.

"What's this bar competition about?" Grey reached across the bar and took a giant postcard from the pile.

"Junk. We get those all the time. Helen ended up on some mailing list or maybe it's through a distributor. I don't know. They have these events all over the place."

"You should go for it." He flipped it over. "Says here it's in New York. That's not far."

"Yes, it is. It's eight hours away. And it's a solid no." Logan took the postcard back and added it to the junk mail pile. She sorted more bills from the fluff.

"Come on! You've been making some killer drinks."

And going back to New York could be a killer experience. She ripped the junk mail in half and tossed it in the recycling can beneath the bar. "Like what? What drink was that great?"

"That maple syrup thing."

"It was a maple old-fashioned. Everybody makes those. They aren't special."

"I dumped maple syrup in some whiskey, and it was not special, I can tell ya that. Tell me the recipe."

Logan stacked the bills and tapped them on the bar, giving Grey a coy smile. No way was she giving up her recipes, even to a customer she didn't think she'd lose. "Not a chance. If you can't figure it out for yourself, you'll just have to buy them from me."

She took the bills to the office, and Grey called after her. "I can always look it up you know."

"I know. But you won't. Because you'd miss this place."

"That's true. But you could still go to this competition." Grey rescued the competition flyer from the recycling pile and waved it in the air. "One grand prize of ten thousand dollars."

"Ten thousand dollars doesn't go very far," Logan called out to him from the office. She knew for a fact.

"It'd get you a new cooler, though."

It could also bring her ridicule. Going back to New York would be the opposite of laying low. She'd be threatened, spit on, screamed at. The reputation she was building in Ramsbolt for working hard would be destroyed, and if they ran her out of town, she'd have nowhere else to turn. "Plus, all those fancy ingredients. I'm not good on the fly like that."

"You just lack confidence." The glimmer returned to Grey's eyes adding fuel to Logan's fire.

She threw the rag from her shoulder onto the bar. "Dammit, Grey. Can't you just listen to me? I don't want to do it, okay?" He had no right to give her a label or judge her or tell her what she was or wasn't.

"Whoa. I touched some kinda nerve, huh?"

"I am not weak."

"I know you're not. Not the way you handle Arvil. Bern ain't the easiest person to deal with either."

"Isn't. Bern *isn't* the easiest person to deal with."

"Look who's all prissy now for being a barmaid." Grey put his hands on his hips and tilted his head in a mocking gesture.

Logan snagged Dan and Warren's glasses from the bar and slammed them into the tray. "I am not a barmaid, I'm—" Logan caught herself and bit her tongue. She'd let down her guard and let him get too friendly, and almost let slip that she didn't belong there at all. She almost forgot, with all the playful banter, that she wasn't with someone she'd known forever. And now that she had to dial it back, he was wounding her ego.

"That's right. You're a goddamn professional. Not that there's anything wrong with being a barmaid. I don't even know what that means. Do they wear those push-up bra things and white poofy blouses? I don't even know." Grey finished his drink and set the glass on the bar. "Can I have an old-fashioned this time?"

"Maple?"

"Surprise me."

Logan poured two ounces of bourbon into a shaker. She added half an ounce of elderflower liqueur, an ounce and a quarter of grapefruit juice, and two dashes of grapefruit bitters from her growing shelf of ingredients. She shook it with ice, more vigorous than she needed to. Ice slammed inside the metal shaker.

Grey picked at the sleeve of his sweatshirt. "Sorry I made you mad."

Logan strained the drink into a glass with ice and slid it across the bar to him without a word. Anything she would say would end in regret.

He took a sip and lifted it to the light. "This is really good. I'm not just saying that."

"Thanks." Logan wiped a drop of grapefruit juice off her counter. She wished she could believe him, that she was good enough to be behind a bar at all.

"I pissed you off. I can tell. I just open my mouth and shit comes out sometimes."

"You didn't make me mad." She turned her back on him and put the bitters back on the shelf. There was nothing to talk about.

"Defensive, then," he yelled after her.

"I'm not defensive, Grey. When you grow up the way I did, you don't get defensive." With her back turned, he couldn't see her nostrils flare or her sarcastic smile. "You get even."

"Where'd you grow up, anyway. Not around here."

Logan refused to be cornered, coerced into making up stories. To lose control of her emotions out of anger or fear or familiarity. Something about his kindness, the way he talked to her, made it too easy for her to be herself. The risk of saying too much to him terrified her, but he didn't deserve to be snapped at or lied to.

"Nope, I didn't grow up around here. And don't forget what I said about getting even."

Grey laughed. "Did you put something in my drink?"

"I would never. I'm a professional, remember?"

She rinsed a dirty mixing glass and dunked it in sanitizer. Why couldn't her father have put her in the witness protection program as the daughter to some other billionaire? She was far too weak, unskilled, prideful, and short-fused to get by in the real world. Someone in that house should have taught her some skills. Her mother taught her how to get along in a narrow world of social engagements, her father taught her how to fight, but no one, except Marta taught her anything about the real world.

Logan carried the mail to the office, sat at the desk, and ripped open the envelopes, filing bills into their folders. Electricity. Water. Like her father's business manager did. She tried to picture her father at the bar, among those people, but in every place she tried to picture him—at the bar, in the newsstand, in the park—he was just a void. Her father and the people of Ramsbolt trafficked in different conversations and haggled with different emotional currency. Her father's brand of pride would leave him bankrupt in a place like this. So would Logan's if she didn't learn to let it go.

She stepped through the office door, back to the bar, and a paper airplane whizzed past her and into the office.

"Oops! Sorry." Grey shrugged an apology.

Logan looked over her shoulder at the airplane. It sat on the floor of the office in a crumpled crash. Money peered out from a fold. "What was that?"

"You have to look at that flyer again if you want your tip."

CHAPTER TWELVE

A late November snow fell on crunchy piles of leaves and made mounds in yards like igloos. It piled on sidewalks and stuck to windows, heavy and wet. The world slept under a gray, dark Saturday sky, but Logan needed an early start to finish the December drink specials and to place the weekly order before customers arrived for the day. She tucked her feet into two pairs of socks and the most affordable snow boots sold at the outdoor store and trudged across the street to the newsstand.

Flickering battery-powered candles glowed in every window along the street, like slides from her freshman year American Art History course at Yale. Norman Rockwell. Currier and Ives. It wasn't the America Logan knew, but it was one she wanted. And she didn't fit in the picture. She was an outsider with no friends behind those windows, no family to call on at those doors. Just one father in federal prison who didn't want to see her and a mother who had fled to France.

The window at the newsstand was decorated for the holidays with greenery and classic toys. An old teddy bear, the kind with black button eyes and no fancy bow, sat patiently in the back of a sleigh, surrounded by boxes and little tin toys. Logan had always wanted a teddy bear like that. She'd always wanted a Christmas like that, but hers had been more for show than sentiment. Ten foot trees and pristine decorations. Like something from a hotel lobby.

She stomped snow from her boots, trudged to the back wall of the newsstand, took a new composition notebook from the stack, and paid Warren in cash.

"Three cents change." He placed pennies in the palm of her hand.

"Thanks. The window looks nice." Logan zipped the change in the coin pouch of her wallet.

"Same thing every year. It's getting stale. You want a bag?"

"No, thanks." She tucked the notebook into her duffle bag with her work shoes. "It's not stale. Not to me. It looks traditional. Not like that manufactured vintage Christmas stuff."

When she turned to leave, the newspaper rack caught her eye, a picture of her father above the fold as he stepped from a car. The picture had been taken in the early days of visiting courtrooms. She remembered that day, having breakfast in bed and playing *Tomb Raider* before she showered and got ready for court. A busy task to pass the time before shuffling off to fulfill the obligation of being seen. At the time, court was just another thing to get through, another chapter. But the new headline that shouted up from the rack at Warren's newsstand proclaimed new charges for witness tampering and declared him destitute, unable to pay restitution on some state conviction. She couldn't afford to peel away the layers of what it meant for her father, his sentence, her future. She tore her eyes from the newspaper and fixed a gentle smile, forcing the corners of her eyes to lift, armor to keep any trace of emotion from her face.

"Thanks. And don't change that window." She managed her words through a dry throat. "It's comforting that some things never change.

Especially at Christmas." She fumbled out the door. Over and over, as her feet hit the pavement, a mantra ran through her mind. *Hold it together. Get to work. Read the paper. Hold it together.*

She crossed the circle and paused for solace at the foot of the sailor, but he was too busy weathering storms of his own. She trudged up the street, past the steep-roof houses. Cars warmed in driveways, puffing exhaust to heat their hides. She returned a wave from a tightly-bound neighbor who scraped ice from a Jeep and crested the gentle hill, careful not to lose her footing.

At the bar's doorstep, she rescued the newspaper from a dirty pile of snow and with all intents forgotten, she settled at the desk, slipped the paper from the wet plastic sleeve, and followed the story to where it continued on page A-2. Maybe her mother was an alarmist by nature, but that hadn't made her wrong. She should have listened, prepared herself for the news, for the ringing in her ears with the adrenaline rush when her life landed in another headline.

The article quoted a public defender, a faceless name she'd never met. A man in the shadows who spoke to her father through glass. It was more contact than she had with her father. She pushed the paper aside. She couldn't let this cloud her progress and make her weak. It could ruin her, slow her down, and cost her tips.

She would not let his sentence be hers.

She pulled the composition notebook from her bag and listed recipes for December, warming drinks to get through the winter months. The maple old-fashioned had been popular. She scheduled it for a day Grey would be around. And Christmas Eve called for a simple whiskey and cranberry.

She wiped a drop of water from the notebook, then a second. A cool, thick drop of water landed in her hair. She pushed away from the desk and looked up at the leaking ceiling. Like her father's bad decisions, her poor packing, her lack of planning, and everything else, the world was raining down on her. Another drop fell a few feet to her left, landing on the thin, worn carpet.

"That spot's cleaner now." That's what Marta would have said, anyway.

She dumped pens from a chipped coffee cup, dropped it on the floor under the drip, and grabbed buckets and bar towels from the back room. She pulled the desk back a few feet so the drip wouldn't land on her work space, and settled in again. A drop landed on the newspaper, blurring out her father's name.

"And that's what insurance is for."

She would have to call Helen. She rounded the desk, grabbed her cell phone from her coat pocket, and unlocked the screen. Above the phone icon was one she used to touch all the time, before everything collapsed. She'd deleted her tweets and deactivated her account when the threats poured in. She'd been an active user once, with tens of thousands of followers, though she'd only followed a few accounts. Mostly people she spoke with in person, like Elizabeth and Jill, some friends from school. A few guys she dated and people she saw at parties. A handful of accounts that posted pics of cute cats.

Until the rumors, the lies, and the disparaging innuendo had lined up next to Elizabeth's manx cat and vacations in the sand, the icon had been hard to resist.

She started a new account under a random string of numbers and looked in on old friends, scrolling back through the weeks and months since the news broke. The kindest tweets were distancing. A guy she dated for two years claimed to have known her once but not well. Some were ruthless. Elizabeth's cousin spread a rumor that Logan, heiress to the Cole fortune, ran off to an island harbor of offshore banking and lived off the sinew of her father's victims. She searched for hashtags like #ColeCorruption, read news stories, and skimmed comments. *Lock them all up. Drag them through Times Square.* Then Avery, the son of a partner at a law firm they'd hired years before to help with a real estate project, declared her father a cheat, her mother vapid, and her a whore. He claimed experience with her he didn't have. Probably pissed that she'd turned him down when he pawed her in the back of a limo after a Tony Awards party. The world had rejected her, but it still wanted a bite.

She crafted a threaded reply, reminding him that bitterness was a weak response to rejection, that he'd inherited his father's spite after they were sued for misrepresentation for failing to live up to their contract. It felt good to defend herself, but she couldn't post it. Someone would find her, unmask her. People would show up at her narrow doorstep, angry at the wealth. Fueled by the demise, they'd seek social justice for her father's crimes. The risk of being doxxed was real enough without putting up a neon sign. It would undo all her hard work at trying to live a decent life in Ramsbolt. God knew no one who sat at the bar would have sympathy for a Cole. She would be back on another Greyhound bus without her security deposit, all the poorer for her efforts.

The gulf she'd created between her old life in New York and her quiet life in Maine was wide. It might be lonely, but it was safe. She could never go back there, not for anything. Not even for a cocktail competition. And it helped a little to know that world wouldn't take her in if she begged. She wasn't the same person anymore. At least she'd made the right choice by leaving instead of begging for scraps of dignity and patching together an existence.

Logan clicked through the settings, deleted the new account, and said a silent goodbye to that life and those people. She didn't belong in New York, and maybe Ramsbolt wasn't home, but she didn't need validation from either of them. From anyone. Someday, her father would get out of jail, put it all back together, and they'd be sorry. In the meantime, she had to tend to the whiskey.

She closed the notebook and set it on the shelf, away from the risk of water. She took the newspaper out to the bar and left it for Arvil to fuss over. Wiping the chalkboard by the register clean, she changed the drink of the day to a Whiskey Sour. It was high time she perfected her father's least favorite drink.

CHAPTER THIRTEEN

One by one, Logan cracked eggs and separated yolks, funneling egg whites into a squeeze bottle and yolks into a container for Marissa, who owned the bakery downtown. Every evening she stopped by to pick them up and paid for them with bagels and muffins that Logan blamed for the extra five pounds on her waist. It saved her a fortune on breakfast, though.

"Logan. It's been nothing but whiskey sours for days." Grey leaned across the bar and peered into the stainless steel bowl. He fell back into his seat. "Don't your arms get tired, shaking those things?"

"Not really. It's good exercise." Logan broke the last egg and separated its white from its yolk.

"Do you ever not mix one all the way, and it comes out runny?"

"That hasn't happened to me in a while." Logan put the cap on the squeeze bottle and tucked it in the fridge beneath the bar. "The trick is to dry shake it to mix everything first. Then shake it with ice to chill it."

"Can we have something else soon? I mean, is there a sale on eggs or something? Bern even made a sign for the lobby. Tell me you've seen the sign."

"I see it when I lock the door every night. I kinda like it."

In the hall entry, past the piles of coats beneath broken coat hooks, Bern had taped a sign to the cigarette machine. Each evening, he changed the number of days by applying a new Post-it. The signed declared it to be Day 13 of Whiskey Sours. Logan considered it a goal and vowed not to change the drink until the stack of Post-its fell to the floor.

She exchanged nods with a woman at the other end of the bar, a silent acknowledgment of another round, and placed a glass beneath a tap. "You know you can order anything you want. You don't have to have the drink of the day."

"I plan to." Grey lowered his voice and leaned across the bar. There it was again. Another of those looks. She shied away. Even if she was interested, he didn't deserve the consequences of getting close to Logan Cole. "What's with all the whiskey sours anyway?"

She slapped the bar and leaned in. "Remember when I said I like revenge? This is it." She pushed away and turned off a tap, letting the foam settle in a glass of beer. "And no, the revenge isn't for you."

"What did the rest of the drinks do to you? Or is it us? You hate us? You do, don't you?" He folded his arms in mock disgust.

Logan rolled her eyes. "Is there a drink you want, or are you just here to harass me about the ones you don't?"

"I want a Sazerac. And one of those bull drinks. And something else that isn't a whiskey sour."

"Okay, but you can't have three because the law says two, and it's not a bull drink it's a Boulevardier."

"You break the law for Dan and give him a six pack every night."

Logan placed her hands on her hips. "Dan's Dan. What can I get you?"

"The Boulevard. I liked it."

"Boulevardier. It has three and a half ounces of alcohol in it. You sure you can handle that?"

Grey cocked an eyebrow in feigned disgust. "Make it a double, and I'll give you a nice tip."

"Don't tempt me."

Tips were a sensitive topic. She needed them, she counted and recorded them with a level of detail that would make her dad's accountants proud, but she hated her reliance on them, and she'd never accept them out of pity. She would earn it, not beg for it. She held her tongue, but shot him an icy look to silence him. Besides, she needed to draw a line between a friendly work environment and sentiment. She turned to his drink.

She dropped ice into a mixing glass and added an ounce and a half of rye and an ounce of sweet vermouth, but there was no Campari on the shelf.

"Dammit. I must have run out and forgot to replace it."

Logan left her bar spoon in the mixing glass and slipped into the back stockroom. Her least favorite space, it was the last frontier on her cleaning crusade. The shelves were overstocked with expired cans of fruit, old kitchen supplies from the bar's days as a diner, and stacks of dusty table cloths. There was so much junk that the slivers of light that made it through the grimy window never reached the floor.

The light switch sparked when she flipped it. The bulbs barely had time to illuminate before she grabbed a bottle off a shelf and turned them off again.

At the bar, Logan twisted the cap off the Campari. She added an ounce to the mixing glass, stirred it until it was chilled, and strained it into a glass. From a jar she kept in the little fridge beneath the bar, she added a Luxardo cherry.

"Ooh, the good cherries." Grey reached out a hand for the jar, and she swatted him away.

"These are for special occasions."

He accepted the drink and set it on a bar napkin, another perk she'd been able to afford. "What did I do to deserve this?"

"I'm doing my part to keep the heating guy alive during our two hundredth consecutive day of snow." She wanted him at a distance, but she still liked his company.

"Much appreciated. I've been meaning to tell you—"

Logan put up a hand. "Hold that thought." She leaned in. "My arch nemesis is here."

Arvil walked the length of the bar like an officer inspecting his troops, eyeing up glasses and bottles of beer. Unless an out-of-town customer who didn't know better took a liking to the corner stool, it was empty in Arvil's absence. Just as he expected it to be. He shuffled to the furthest seat from the door and shifted his weight until he was settled. He twisted in his seat and tugged his arms from his coat.

Logan placed a bar napkin in front of him, a welcome mat that kept his attention on the drink to come instead of whatever was missing.

"What'll it be tonight, Arvil?"

"Thirteen. Thirteen days of whiskey sours. This whole thing is stupid. Egg whites in the winter. Nobody wants egg whites in the dead of winter." He wrestled with his coat and fumbled it onto the back of the stool.

"You desperately wanted one a month ago when I didn't have any egg whites. Remember? And people eat those little meringue cookies in the winter."

"What's that? I don't know what that is." He narrowed his eyes at her.

"Not your usual playful self today, huh? You know what meringues are. Those little poofs? Taste like peppermint or vanilla or whatever and... Never mind. Order anything you want. I'm not forcing you to drink egg whites."

His lip curled in disgust. "Stupid frothy thing. Walk outside and your stomach turns to ice cream."

"Sounds delicious to me. You want to sit there and complain, or you want to order something to drink? You've been here before. You know this is a bar, right?"

The trick to navigating Arvil's mood was to offer a snappy comeback. If his cheeks burned red, she'd be in trouble. But his eyes widened and lit up, and she knew it would be a calm night.

"Beer. Michelob. Bottle."

She pulled one from the tall refrigerator, popped the top off, and placed it on his napkin. "I'll start you a tab."

Funny thing about Arvil, the less she tried to make him happy, the easier he was to get along with.

As another day of relentless snow drew to a close, Arvil led the charge. One by one her customers paid their tabs and made their way into the frozen air. The few stragglers closed their tabs, so Logan seized the opportunity to close early. She wiped down the bar, restocked the coolers for the next day, and prepped fruit. Anything to get a head start. She crouched on the floor behind the bar, moving aside jars of cherries and syrups in the small fridge to make room for containers of fruit.

"Logan!" Panic elevated Grey's voice an octave. "Get the cash from the drawer and run. Come on."

Were they being robbed? "What are you talking about?" She stood, and the acrid, bitter, sour waft smoke from a fire hit her. It consumed wood paneling in the back room and licked around the doorway, teasing at the bar. Did they have a fire extinguisher? There had to be one in the back. Her coat was back there. Her bag with her snow boots. They were expensive. Irreplaceable. She'd saved for so long, and without them, she'd freeze. The smoke alarm went off, the shrill screech assaulting her ears.

She lunged for the back room, toward the thick smoke that streamed through the door and Grey grabbed her arm. "Where are you going? We've gotta run!"

"I need my coat." She screamed over the alarm. People rushed past them, through the door and into the lobby. Cold air pushed in, throwing smoke across the room. It stung her eyes, and she covered them with her forearm. "The safe! My boots!"

"There's no time. We have to run." Grey grabbed the donation jar for Glen with one hand and Logan's wrist with the other. Flames licked around the stockroom door, they rushed out into the ankle-deep snow and across the street, where they stood with bar patrons and a few close neighbors in the motel parking lot.

She pulled her phone from her pocket and dialed 911, but someone had already reported the fire. She was losing everything. Her coat and boots. Her job. The source of her self-worth. She took in a deep breath of cold air tinged with the sweet smell of smoke, but it did nothing to calm her or sooth the desperation. It only made her feel worse for Helen and Ramsbolt. Flames began to eat through the roof. At least she'd be warm soon.

"It was that wiring," she said, mostly to herself. "That ancient wiring in the back."

Grey stood behind her. "The light back there always sparked when you flipped the switch."

"I know. Helen never fixed it. I have to call her."

"I can do it—"

"No, it should be me."

Logan dug her phone from her pocket and pulled up Helen's number. "It's Logan. I have bad news."

"I already know." Helen's voice cracked, broken by the sharp edges of grief.

"How did you know?"

"The Garlands next door have a police scanner. She rushed over in her nightgown. They said everyone got out. Are you okay?"

Logan glanced behind her at Grey and counted the faces. The two women who'd been sitting closest to the door were there. The couple from out of town were huddled by their hotel door. Arvil leaned on a plastic chair, his face lit by the glow of the fire. He'd barely had time to make it out of the parking lot when it started. Now here he stood, his expressionless face tinted orange by the fire. Not even destruction could please the man. "Yeah. Everyone's out. We're across the street, in the motel parking lot. Grey grabbed Glen's donation jar, but everything else..." Her mind was too busy, too scattered to count the toll. Like fireflies, the thoughts arrived and were gone, ungraspable. Her notebook. There were things at her apartment. The ledgers. A bar book. The rest of it gone.

"Should I come?"

"No. Definitely no." Helen didn't need to suffer the cold, and her spirit didn't need to endure the vision of it. "The firemen are here and—"

"It's all gone, isn't it?"

"Yeah. I'm sorry. There wasn't any time. It just came out of the back room and... Do you have insurance?" Would it cover lost wages? Logan couldn't bear to ask.

"It's not the best policy, but I'll call them in the morning." Helen sniffed through the phone. "You should go home and get out of the cold. Get a good night's sleep."

People came from town, lured by the flashing lights and sirens. They walked up the street in clumps and gathered to watch it burn, a landmark consumed by an insatiable inferno. The melting sign. The charred bricks. "Yeah. You're right. I will in a bit. Talk to you tomorrow."

Logan ended the call and tucked her phone back in her pocket. She wasn't even cold. The warmth of the fire reached across the road.

"I lost my coat in there." Logan spoke to no one, but Grey was still listening.

He stepped forward and stood at her side. "You can get another one."

"I sacrificed a lot to get that coat. I've never been this poor in my life. I don't know how I'll replace it. I hated that thing. It was ugly, but at least it was warm. Snow boots don't come cheap, either." It was a stupid thing to focus on, the loss of her coat and boots, while watching her work burn to the ground. She was lucky and grateful to be safe. But complaining about her coat kept her mind off the loss and uncertainty, and it kept the tears from streaming down her cheeks. Another job might not be so easy to find, let alone another boss like Helen. Customers like Grey. People who didn't want to eat her alive. She'd only just begun to put a life together behind that bar.

The fire raged across the street, loud and bright behind the flashing lights and idling engines of the fire trucks. Water rushed from hoses, but it wasn't enough to save the place. It was more than enough, however, to fill Logan with gratitude for the people who fought to save her home. For making her realize she'd even felt that way at all.

"Insurance. They'll wanna know what was lost. Make sure Helen tells them about your stuff." Grey bumped her shoulder with his. It was a friendly gesture, meant to console her, and the only human contact she'd had since she hugged her mother and moved to Ramsbolt. Part of her wanted to crumple into him, to fall into a hug with anyone, any random stranger.

The flames did their best to battle the night sky, but they were no match for the dark. The firefighters doused the fire in what felt like no time at all. But when Logan checked her phone, three hours had passed by unnoticed. Unfelt. Nothing could penetrate the numbness. Around her, the people from town bounced on their heels, hands in their pockets. They sat in plastic Adirondack chairs scavenged from the hotel, blowing into their hands for warmth. Some dabbed at tears with sleeves and tissues. Others stared in disbelief. Murmurs and soft chatter washed right over her. They'd all lost a thing they loved, but Logan had lost the only thing she had. She was back where she started, with nothing to lose, a defiant girl with no skills and no promise.

Her old world had been full of easy fixes. Pick up a phone and call a lawyer, call a bank, make a request or a polite demand. Now, every solution seemed as distant as the stars, and the only thing on Logan's side was the luck that went up in flames.

She shivered as the fire died out and the cold set in. Next to her, Grey cleared his throat. His words were soft, almost a whisper.

"That thing I was gonna tell you," he said. "I signed you up for that bar competition. I feel kinda bad about it now."

CHAPTER FOURTEEN

Logan shed her clothes the second she walked in the door. She sealed them in a trash bag and left them in the laundry basket to keep the smell of the smoke from saturating her apartment. She washed the stench from her hair and tried to sleep, but the uncertainties of the future rang in her ears like her worst post-concert tinnitus. When the first trucks of the morning bumped through the circle, carrying goods from the farms to towns in the south, Logan slipped out of bed, through thick, freezing predawn air, and back to what was left of the bar. The air was heavy with the threat of snow and the smell of embers. Chairs still scattered in the hotel parking lot. She dragged one to the sidewalk where she sat, like the first arrival for a morose parade, ignoring the cold seeping through her jeans and the thermal tights she wore beneath them, waiting for the seat to warm. The site smoldered through the break of day. Cinders of the life she was trying to build.

Helen's Pinto station wagon chugged into the parking lot, puffing exhaust on a drive too short to warm the car. Logan stood, and the plastic chair scraped against the cracked pavement. She climbed into the passenger seat, pulling the heavy door closed behind her with a thud.

Lukewarm air shot through the vents, not warm enough to bring her any comfort. She shoved her hands between her knees and hunched, holding in what warmth she had and making her own comfort.

"What happens next?" To the bar, to her apartment, to her tiny dwindling savings, to the meager life she'd been building for herself in a town only beginning to accept her.

The car wobbled with Helen's exhale, like enough weight lifted off the earth to shake the parking lot. "The insurance value, the maximum amount they'll give me to rebuild, is less than what it would cost to put something new here."

"It can't be a total loss. It can't. What insurance company would even bother to sign a policy like that?"

"The kind that wants to keep me as a customer when I try to save some money on the high cost of insurance."

"But—"

"I was behind on lot rent, anyway."

"No." Logan started to warm. She shoved her feet deeper into the foot well, closer to the heat. "Lean on the insurance company. Send an angry letter. We'll find a lawyer and get them to send something aggressive. It'll buy us time to talk to the landowner. Maybe we can find another site."

"Logan. Please." Helen rested the tips of her fingers on the steering wheel. "Stop. I owe too much money. And there are no other sites."

"Downtown?"

"It would cost too much to tear up the floors for the plumbing and upgrade the electrical for new coolers." Helen's hands gripped the steering wheel. "Even if I could afford them."

"Every contract has a loophole, though. The world is designed so people can get away with stuff. We can look it over. Hire someone to go through it with a fine-tooth comb," she said. Helen shook her head, dismissing the idea, and fury flamed within Logan. "Why not? Why not try?"

"Arvil will never bend. That's not who he is."

"Arvil?"

"He's owned that land forever. He's as grumpy a bastard as he makes himself out to be. Sure, you can stand up to him, and he'll shut up for a while, but when it comes to money, he doesn't care who you are. Five thousand dollars is too much to make up. Even if I could afford to pay him what I owe, and even if he would let me rebuild there, insurance is only going to cover the replacement value, not what it costs to make a new place. What was there wasn't worth much."

Logan squeezed her hands into fists and turned her face away from Helen. Water still trickled down the street and flowed down the road she'd taken into town. It ran all the way to New York for all she knew. Her nails dug into her palms with a satisfying sharpness. Arvil. It figured he'd play a role in her misery.

She swallowed hard to keep from screaming, first about Arvil and then at Helen for being so irresponsible with her money and not protecting her assets. How could she be so thoughtless?

The inside of Helen's car smelled like fast food and old cigarettes, and Logan took in shallow breaths of it. She couldn't live like that, on displacement and food that didn't fill her. "I'm telling you, there's always a way."

The car wobbled and creaked again when Helen shifted to face her. There was no pain in her face, no strain or sadness. Helen seemed emptied. "How do you know so much anyway?"

Logan didn't answer. What was she supposed to say? That her father had been shuffling money around in real estate for her whole life, and not a day went by that she didn't hear some complex problem tidied up in transactions before dinner was done? The better question was: Why didn't Helen know enough? Why didn't Helen take better care of the bar? If she had, Logan wouldn't be staring at a pile of rubble that was every bit as dismal as her future. But the answer was in the debris. All around her. In the state of the office, in the dust-covered bar, in the ripped and tattered interior of her forty-year-old car. Helen was depressed.

Logan offered up a lie. "I know a lot, because I used to watch a lot of television." She couldn't think of a single television show about commercial real estate. Doctors. Lawyers. No real estate. Maybe if she'd watched more reality shows. She hoped Helen wouldn't give it much thought. "What about a loan to get up to speed and cover the difference to build a new place?"

"I'm too old and tired to take on a loan like that."

Helen rounded herself into the seat of her car, sinking as if trying to be absorbed, to disappear and become a part of it. Though equal in age to Logan's mother, the woman couldn't be more opposite. Petra Cole moved through the world thin enough not to disturb the air but with gust enough to move a mountain. Helen consumed what she could and let the rest destroy her. Lorne Cole would have eaten Helen alive, just because he could. He would have razed that bar and turned the land into a tourist trap. The stabbing pain in Logan's chest was borne of more empathy than her father'd ever shown. She wanted to lift the woman up, repay her for all the kindness. Give back to her the bar she loved. And she couldn't help thinking that she had no choice but to help the woman rise or risk sinking with her.

"Did you have business interruption insurance?" She dreaded asking, fearing the answer would be no. Without it, she wouldn't have even her meager eight dollars an hour to hold her over.

Helen shook her head in the slightest of movement. "I really don't know. I don't even know what that is."

"It covers paychecks. That kind of thing." Logan rubbed a hand over her forehead. Her skin tightened and dried from the car's overactive heater. She pushed the vent down, away from her face.

"I'll have to call them back and ask them. They didn't mention it, so probably not."

"Will you call me and let me know? I know it's a lot to ask, and I don't want to put more burden on you, but I lost my coat and my snow boots in there, and if there's a chance that insurance covers it and at least my pay…well, you know."

Helen's nod, a sympathetic shake of the head, seemed to take all the energy she could muster. Logan grabbed the door handle.

"I wasn't always this way," Helen said. Logan released the cold handle. "I was prideful in my youth. I took big risks. You only have so much energy, you know? So much time to devote to things. Like that fire over there, once you use up all your resources, you're burned out. Nothing left."

"We can fix this. It's not all lost."

"I took too many risks, is what I'm saying. I'm older now, and I don't care so much for pride. I'm trying to say that this bar won't survive. We have to face that."

"You mean it won't survive because it seems hard, not that it has to die because it's out of options. I wish I could convince you that you love this bar enough to make it work, but only you can do that. All I can do is tell you that you don't have to do it alone."

Logan pulled the door handle and stepped out into the cold. She wrapped her arms around her middle to hold in the warmth into her fluffiest hoodie, saturated in the musty, stale smell of that old Pinto. It clunked and creaked as Helen left the parking lot, and Logan watched it go.

She crossed the black stream of water and stopped on the sidewalk before the yellow caution tape. The concrete walkway was streaked with black. Pools of muddy water formed in the cracks. All that remained of the bar were its brick walls, pierced by gaping rectangles where doors and stockroom windows once fit. Wisps of smoke curled from the charred remnants. Within, little was recognizable. Piles of melted and shattered glass marked where the bottles fell when the counter burned. She could make out heaps of scorched metal, the remains of coolers and equipment, and the frame of the metal desk. They'd been saving money, safely in the black for weeks, and there had still been places to save. Their rented dumpster smoldered behind the remains of the bar, too big for their needs. The window in the back room that had been drafty and inefficient, adding to the cost of heating and cooling the place.

It had been her home, and all of it was gone.

There had been a fire, once, at an apartment building her father owned. The property manager had taken care of it all. A few phone calls and a meeting or two. Logan couldn't recall the details, how long it took or if anyone suffered, but it had been rebuilt. She'd worn a smart suit and attended a ribbon cutting. They raised the rent after that. It was new, after all.

Logan took for granted that damage could be fixed. Someone came, patched the holes, mended the wounds, and handed off the keys. That was their job. But there were no helpers here. No safety net. Sometimes when things were lost, they were lost forever. At least Helen seemed to think so, and maybe she was right. But Logan wasn't accepting defeat that easily. She couldn't afford to. And she wasn't convinced that there would never been a ribbon cutting at Helen's Tavern.

Maybe there were no lawyers on retainer to write angry letters, no property managers with loud voices to pressure contractors into timely and quality work. But there had to be a way to rig this system in Helen's favor without pulling any of her father's dirty old tricks.

Skirting debris that littered the sidewalk, Logan rounded the corner and made her way back to town. The few people who stirred gave her a wide berth. She walked in silence past the houses, across the circle, and beneath the sunlit face of the stoic sailor, wishing for one ounce of his mettle. The biting wind stole her breath, so she kept her head down and stayed close to the buildings that lined the street. She stopped at her door and dug her keys from her back pocket. They chilled her already frozen fingers. She didn't want to face that lonely box of an apartment, but it was better than standing on the freezing street, wondering how long it would be before she couldn't pay the rent. Where would she go when her little savings ran out? Not France. She knew that much.

"If I were a bear, I'd have bit ya."

Logan turned at the familiar voice. Grey sat on a park bench in front of the post office, his arm slung over the back and a shopping bag at his side.

He stood and lifted the bag. "I got ya a present."

"What is it?" Logan knew better than to accept gifts. They created debt. Even gift bags at awards parties begged for her to be seen with

JENNIFER M. LANE

them. Nothing in life was free. "How did you find me?"

"Riley mentioned you lived up there." He extended the brown paper bag by its wired twine handle. She recognized the generic, unmarked bag from the outdoor store.

"Did you get me a coat?" The cold keys numbed her fingers. She shoved them in the lock and let them swing. There was no way she was inviting Grey inside her apartment.

"I got you boots, too. They knew what you bought, so I got you replacements."

"How? They're not open yet." Across the street, the lights were off in the store. They opened before nine on weekends and only if the opening employees showed up on time. It wasn't even eight.

"I called in a favor." He extended the bag again. "Take it. It's cold. You can't live in Maine in the dead of winter and not have a coat."

"It's not the dead of winter yet. It's barely December." Logan offered him no expression, no hint of gratitude or longing. She wanted to grab the bag, clutch it to her chest, find warmth and comfort in the ease of it. She wanted to hug it like the most precious gift she'd ever received, but nothing had been as sweet, yet terrifying, as this. Grey offered her a simple solution, and his gift made one thing easy, but she had no intention of being fragile or owing anything to anyone. She shook her head. "I can't accept that."

He lowered the bag to the bench. "Last night you said—"

"What? I said what? That I'm poor? That I worked hard to afford a coat and a pair of snow boots the first time. Insurance might cover it." Sharp wind forced its way down the street, picking up what little debris lay at the edges and rustling the bag in the municipal trash can. Logan turned her face from the cold. "I'd hate to accept this and then have it all work out." The words left a hollow space in her chest. She doubted it would work out that easily. Helen hadn't seemed confident that insurance would cover much.

"If insurance pays you for it, you can pay me back. If it doesn't, consider it a welcome wagon from the town."

She tore her eyes away from Grey, away from the gift and whatever the gesture meant to him. Her keys rattled in the lock. Across the street, Warren opened the newsstand, and the ring of the bell attached to the door bounced between the buildings.

"Logan, take it. No one has to know. It can be our secret."

"Why would you give me this?"

"The whole thing cost me a hundred and thirty dollars. Have you ever hired a plumber? Do you know what we charge?" He said *a hundred and thirty dollars* the way she used to say *we can take my plane to lunch.*

She hadn't ever hired a plumber. She'd never even met a plumber before Grey. She rolled her eyes at her own naivety. "I guess you're going to tell me you can afford it."

He pulled the coat out of the bag and held it by the shoulders, giving it a shake. "And you're going to have to accept that you can't. At least not right now."

The warmth she'd absorbed from Helen's Pinto had dissipated long before she reached the sailor statue. Unable to tame her shivers, she turned and slipped her arms into the coat, then faced him.

"Thank you. It's a very nice gesture. I *will* pay you back."

"Don't mention it. I don't know where you come from, but around here, this is what friends do." Grey handed her the bag, and it sagged with the weight of the snow boots. He turned and walked up the street, toward the market. "I got a freezer to fix. Take it easy."

"Hey, can I ask you something?"

Grey turned, hands in his pockets. He gave her a look that could melt all the snow in Maine. "Anything."

"Do you know where Arvil lives?"

CHAPTER FIFTEEN

Logan trailed her parents into the ballroom at the Plaza Hotel. The last thing she wanted to do on a Saturday night was spend it with the same people she saw at school. And graduation just a few weeks away made her more restless than ever to shed the Caroline Herrera and get back into yoga pants.

"Congratulations on your upcoming graduation, Logan. I'm sure you have your list of colleges ready." The headmaster took the napkin from his lap and began to stand and shake her father's hand. "We're immensely proud of your daughter, Mr. Cole." Her father returned the man to his seat with a firm hand on the shoulder.

"No, no. Don't stand." Her father towered over the man. "Wonderful event, Hedges. Good to see you out. Yes, we're proud of her, too. Top of her class, we presume. Graduating with honors?"

The headmaster smoothed his napkin on his lap and offered no response.

Logan tightened her grip on her diamond Mouawad clutch, a gift for her eighteenth birthday, and smiled politely, knowing her father's demand would be met, whether she'd earned it or not.

She stood taller than usual, a corset forcing her back into submission beneath her Dior gown. Many her age lost parents and loved ones on 9/11, and the annual fundraisers to support first responders topped the list of social engagements. The diamonds, fashion, and need to be seen reflected the disparity between the human toll of terror and the walls their society built to rebuff it. These people wanted to be seen. Their heart wasn't in it for the giving.

She returned an uncomfortable glance from the headmaster with a lift of her chin and half a smile. Her school work was mediocre, but their donations were substantial enough to warrant a lift in her grades, enough to put her in the sights of an Ivy League school. It would all work out, as it had for everyone else in her circle. In the end, she would sit at a desk at her father's office and run a nonprofit foundation to manage his tax write-offs and do some good in the world. She'd swap online gaming for shopping and martini lunches and find good uses for her parents' money.

"It's a talented group, that class." The headmaster's hands were wrapped in his napkin. "We should get together, Lorne. Over coffee or a round of golf."

The headmaster struggled beneath the weight of her father's hand again on his shoulder. Her father reached down to shake on it, and relief came off of the headmaster like heat from tarmac on a summer day. "Will do, Hedges. Golf. I'll be in touch."

Grateful for the short formalities, Logan slipped from her father's side. She scanned the room. It was empty of substance, but thick with the hot air of donors and schmoozers. With no allies to gather, she aimed for the bar. Knowing the bartender wouldn't question her age, she laid her clutch on the counter and asked for a glass of pinot noir. "Please," she added. Politeness smoothed the path to getting what she wanted. Though she occasionally found herself on a tabloid cover and tagged in viral Instagram posts, she was a practical girl who had bigger things to worry about than British literature and dissecting frogs. Her biggest concern that night was getting a good enough buzz to make the corset worth it.

She released the clasp on her clutch and placed a ten-dollar bill in the tip jar.

"A little young for the bar, no?" The headmaster stepped up beside her.

"Not by this standard." She offered a toast to his empty glass and reached into her clutch for another bill. "Allow me."

"You mustn't." He raised a hand in protest.

"My pleasure. It's a kindness, not a bribe. But since we're here, I was wondering if I could bother you for letters of recommendation."

"A 2.0 grade point average won't get you into Yale, Ms. Cole. It won't even get you into Princeton. I don't want to get your hopes up on that account. But I would be honored to write you a letter boasting your kindness to your fellow students, the prudence you learned over the years, and the goodness of your heart."

"That's all I can expect for now, I suppose." Logan closed the clasp of her clutch and took in the deepest breath of air the dress would allow. She didn't expect him to say much here, at the bar. After a day with her father, though, his tune would change. "I'll always have the fondest memories of Grafton. No matter where the road leads."

The road would lead through Yale, like it had for her father, her grandfather, and her mother. It was a token education. An item on a checklist. Then she'd sit at a big, heavy desk made of some rare wood, where she'd make the best of it by helping the poor. Somewhere out there, someone had to need something.

Hedges's hands shook. He folded the corner of his thin blue cocktail napkin over the base of his wine glass. Weakness. He always folded and saw to it that she got decent enough grades; he did every year. This year would be no exception.

"I'm equipped to teach students," he said, "About subjects and career paths. Unlike Ms. Graves, I'm a poor guidance counselor. And I've never known the kind of life you and your father have." He met her eye. It was a struggle, and she relished it, though she would never admit it. Her moral compass knew which way to point, even if she fed on his submission. "You are a very smart girl, Logan. You always have been. You just never applied yourself in class, probably because you didn't need to. But you will be successful in whatever you do, not just because you have learned to make the most of the privileges you've been given in life, but because of who you are. You are a good person with many talents, and though you may not believe me, there's strength in your heart as well. The sad truth, however, is that not all strings can be pulled. I've seen even fourth generation students turned away from Ivy League schools. It's a competitive place. I'm not predicting, I really don't know what the future will hold, but I want to prepare you for the possibility that it may not come to pass. Either way, you will succeed."

The wine turned to vinegar in her mouth. How dare he? His tune would change, and she would savor it. "Come by my office on Monday, Logan. I'd be happy to write you a letter." He fidgeted, creasing the corners of his bar napkin again. It was clear to Logan he had more to say. So did she. But silence was the better part of valor, as her father would say. She didn't need to narrow her eyes or raise an eyebrow to express her displeasure, to threaten the strength of the dollar she placed in his pocket. He knew as well as she did that if Cole money walked, it would take untold other dollars with it.

CHAPTER SIXTEEN

Logan stood on the fractured sidewalk and took in the details of Arvil's single-story house. It hid behind overgrown shrubs and crooked shutters. The impression she got from his attitude, his ratty coat and worn shirts—that he was self-absorbed and cared about nothing and no one—was confirmed by the view of his life from the street. She knew his type of greed. An unabashed self-centeredness that hoarded money, blind to the world. People like Arvil were hard to reason with because you couldn't lean on their sense of propriety.

He hadn't salted or scraped the sidewalk that led to his small porch. The constant freeze and thaw had broken it into chunks of concrete. She took care around the ice, crunching through the thin layer that coated the snow, and made the only set of fresh footprints to his front door. When she knocked, a series of grumbles erupted, growing louder with his approach. A curtain moved away from the sidelight window, and the door flew open against a chain.

"What are you here for? How did you find my house?"

"Property records." She wouldn't have sacrificed Grey even if he hadn't given her a coat. "Can I come in? I'd like to talk to you. I have a few questions about the bar."

"No. Nothing about that bar or my life is your business."

"I'm not here to make problems. I'm here to find solutions. At the very least, you can argue with me, and it'll add excitement to your day."

Arvil fell silent but his eyes were fire. He wasn't grumbling, but he wasn't walking away from the door either. After a pause long enough to make her think his *no* was firm, the door closed, and the chain scratched against the lock. He pulled the door open and walked back to his chair.

"Don't get snow on my carpet," he barked. He settled into the divot of a tan chenille recliner, and it creaked a weary welcome. A remote rested on the arm of the chair, and he reached for it, a clear message that she shouldn't stay long.

There were no pictures on the walls or in frames on tables, no family or houseplants. No cat curled up on a windowsill, warmed by the sun. Newspapers and magazines flowed from a wooden rack by his chair, and on a metal stand by his chair lay the remnants of an empty frozen dinner, half of it neglected. The walls were dark red, and the curtains near black, blocking out the view, the sun. The air was stale, with a hint of old cigars masked by cheap potpourri. Even Arvil couldn't stand his own stench. Beyond the living room, an almond-colored fridge peeked through a narrow doorway from an earth-toned kitchen. No magnets staked their claim, no pictures offered a hint of a life lived within—or outside of—those walls. The only thing his home reflected was a desire not to be one.

Logan kicked off her boots, but there was nowhere else to sit, so she stepped off the rubber floor mat and onto his decades-old brown shag carpet. It crunched beneath her feet.

"I came to ask if you would consider...if you've given any thought to building a new bar."

He wiggled his toes in his white tube socks. "Now why would I do that? I don't want to own a bar."

"For one, you could charge a lot more for rent if you were leasing out a building instead of just a plot of land."

He tapped the remote on the arm of his recliner. "That bar wasn't profitable enough to make it worth rebuilding before you started working there. It certainly isn't any better now. It wouldn't make enough to repay a construction loan. Helen should have had better insurance if she intended to survive a mess of her own creation."

"Are you going to stand in her way if she decides to rebuild?" Logan tucked her hands in the pockets of her coat, knowing a relaxed demeanor would make her look more self-assured, even if she didn't feel that way.

"That's between me and Helen. You really should mind your own business. It's probably not even legal for you to be here discussing Helen's financial situation. If it is legal, it shouldn't be."

If Arvil was going to pivot at every question, she was going to have to increase the pressure. "I know she was behind on lot rent. She told me that. She thinks you'll stand in her way of rebuilding the bar, and I want to see to it that you don't do that."

"She'd be dumb to try to rebuild that heap. If I do stand in her way, I'll be doing her a favor. How, exactly, are you going to see to it that I do anything, anyway? What could *you* possibly do to persuade me to do your bidding?" He smirked and wiggled his toes.

Appealing to his sense of duty wouldn't work. If he was begging for a threat, she would have to deliver, and without any resources, she stood a better chance of plying him with honey than vinegar. Perhaps there was humanity left in him. "She's depressed. She needs help. You should be trying to help her. Not force her to sink. Love thy neighbor, right? This town is small, and people remember kindness, you know. They repay it. But they also remember cold-hearted cruelty, and social justice can be savage." She knew better than most.

"Cruelty? This has nothing to do with unicorns and fairy tales. This is business. Helen's best bet is to accept whatever insurance will pay her, pay off her debt to me, and get on with her life. If she doesn't, I'll have to sue her for the back rent. I'm not a charity."

"That doesn't make any sense. If she's pays you what she owes, why wouldn't you let her build another bar?" There had to be a bigger reason. Something deeper than greed.

"It's called Breach of Contract, honey."

"Condescension from a man with an empire so small he can't replace the carpet in his living room." Running out of options, her hands shoved in her pockets, she balled them into fists and dug her nails into her palms. "What will you do with the land, then? It won't make you any money just sitting there. You have to at least make enough money on it to pay the taxes, and having the bar there was more profitable than that."

"It wasn't worth it to me. It's none of your business, but I'm going to build an office building on it." His face brightened with a self-satisfied grin.

Logan's laugh was spontaneous. "Who is going to work there? Offices need businesses. And workers. This town isn't a place to find office workers. These are hard-working people who spend time outside at farms, getting dirty, and they want a place to go after work that soothes all of that and makes them feel like a community. You've lived here your whole life; you should know them better than I do. Where are you going to find a business to move into an office building in Ramsbolt? There aren't any administrative assistants or paper pushers around here."

He pounded his remote on the arm of his chair so hard the batteries rattled. "The answer is no."

Logan returned his ire with an empty, fixed look, a trait she learned from her father. When confronted with a blank slate in opposition, people would draw their own conclusions. They'd craft their own consequences in the silence and seal their own fate. She wiggled her feet into her stiff boots and tucked the laces inside, preparing for a hasty exit, but she wouldn't leave without a fight. She couldn't let him take away the only thing she cared about. Making people happy, giving them drinks, banter with Grey. All of those things mattered, and she was not walking away without exhausting her options. Coles didn't give up that easily.

"You know, if you take that bar away from this town, you're destroying a big piece of it. You'll have that on your head forever. No one will forgive you. It's one thing to be a curmudgeon and let people make excuses for you and live their lives in spite of you, but it's another thing to go out of your way to destroy them."

His fingers drummed the buttons of his remote, and Logan picked up on the faintest hint of progress. It wasn't enough headway to launch a resolution, but she had to wring every last bit of potential from her visit. A fat cat in his recliner, taking everything he could from people, no matter how small. Forcing his way through the world like a battering ram when a gentle knock would do. He crushed people, not because he needed to and not because it achieved an aim, but because he fed on the misery and despair of others. He was just like her father.

"Why are you like this? Greedy and angry all the time? Why can't you be happy with what the world gave you, with how much you have, instead of pushing for more and more?"

His face grew red with rage. "You have no business to walk into this town and tell me or anybody else what to do. That bar has always been a failure, and you made it worse when you came here with your incompetence. Not only are you incapable of pouring liquid into cups, you bring no skills or benefits to this town whatsoever. You're a leech. How dare you come into my house and ask me for anything at all."

Logan's nostrils flared. On the verge of saying something she'd regret, she turned, pulled the door closed behind her, and made a second set of prints in the snow on her way back to the broken sidewalk and her tiny apartment.

Why did he hate her so much, anyway? And why did she care? It wasn't just about helping Helen and saving the bar. It was deeper than that. Every criticism and barked order dug a little deeper, took away a little more of her self-respect, chipped away at her self-worth. Her father had talked the same way to the help, about his drinks, how his office was cleaned. It was his way of helping them be better and reach their full potential. Is this how Marta had felt? Criticized, unjustly judged, and forced to grovel for approval with the aim of avoiding the blame by eventually getting it right?

If Arvil was the path of least resistance to getting the bar back on its feet, she was in for a fight. A fight to keep a job she wasn't even all that good at and didn't even want until it was the only thing she had. To win it, she would have to get support from people she'd worked so hard to drive away.

CHAPTER SEVENTEEN

Logan's apartment was smaller than a two-car garage and boiling hot, even on the coldest days of winter. With four radiators stuck open, heat flooded into the room, but she couldn't afford to complain. Heat and hot water were free, anyway. She pushed the bed in front of the open window and sat with her back to the street below. Cold air washed past her for three days while she lived on cereal and sandwiches. She ate soup from china that had once been fine but in the half century since, had faded and scratched. The radiator pinged and clunked, the erratic heartbeat of a depressed and lonely monster. She sat, the sun rising and setting around her, like she lived in a haunted version of her grandmother's china closet.

Piles of clutter amassed around her. The uncertainty of poverty had driven her to save what she could reuse, meaningless trash she once would have tossed. Paper bags from the market, plastic takeout containers from the deli. She'd get up, eventually, and store them in the cabinets. Tuck them away out of sight. But for now they were a source of comfort. They tied her to a time when she could buy what she wanted. Now she fought against the fear of going without.

Logan's restless mind jumped from thought to thought, from impossible method to improbable outcome. Her physical self caught up with her mind, and unable to face those four walls any longer, she climbed into the shower, into something presentable, and into the winter coat she swore was not a gift but a loan. She needed a job, a place to go, a goal to reach for. If she had to start over, she wanted to work in solitude, far from people and their exhausting egos, from the materialism that drove so much destructive greed. Those work-from-home-stuffing-envelopes schemes started to look attractive. But no one in town was hiring, and her phone offered no results from online job listings.

She found two quarters in her purse and ventured to a red metal newspaper box a few doors down where she exchanged her quarters for a daily paper. She hadn't picked one up on purpose in years, avoiding the headlines when they'd become inevitable. Slanderous stories planted in anger and fragments of the truth that tore her family apart. She rolled it tight and squeezed it, bracing against the unexpected blow, but by the time she reached her front door, she could no longer bear to sit alone surrounded by the scavenged remnants of the life she was trying to build, closed in with the fodder of who she used to be and the scraps of the person she couldn't become. Plopping down on the bench outside the post office, she pulled the newspaper apart, grateful that the lead story was about planned improvements at a county park instead of the further dismantling of her former life and the persecution of her father, no matter how much he deserved it.

The help wanted ads weren't what she pictured. They were nothing like the movies with dozens of options to circle. Local farms sought spring help for planting and clearing. Her back wasn't strong enough for that kind of work, and she couldn't operate heavy machinery. She couldn't operate *any* machinery. She needed a job in a small place where she could blend in, where she could get by without a glowing resume. At least she could use Helen as a reference if she needed one.

"Anything good happen yesterday?" The bell above the post office door rang out, and Riley stepped onto the sidewalk next to her.

She held up the paper. "Want ads."

"Giving up, huh? That's not a good sign."

If Riley was in the dark on the future of the bar, then nobody else knew either. She shrugged, gave him a sad smile, and rested her hands on the paper so it wouldn't rustle in the breeze. "It doesn't look like Helen will be able to rebuild. So it's time for me to look for something else. You're not hiring someone to put rubber bands on the mail, are you?"

"Afraid not." Riley dug his hat from his bag and pulled it down over his ears. "Wait. You mean no more bar?"

"Yup. No more bar."

"Man." His eyes clouded and scanned the row of shops across the street as if saying a silent goodbye to it all. "The whole town will be destroyed. Wait until everybody finds out about *that*. Bern will totally freak out."

Wind pushed down the street. The newspaper crinkled, reminding Logan how little she had to lose. She tightened her grip on it. Beside her, Riley blocked the glare of a rising sun. Tall and lanky, he cast a shadow on the sidewalk that reached to the next door. Without the bar, he would be the only daily link connecting the people of Ramsbolt. The only thing connecting one weary soul to another six days a week. She could hear the conversations, Bern throwing a temper tantrum. Dan stroking his beard and offering polite consolation. Sandy waxing poetic about a place from her youth, lost forever. Riley would be the only common thread now.

He shifted his weight, his foot scraping the pavement. "I wish there were something I could do. Everyone's gonna be devastated."

There was plenty he could do. He could be the fertilizer on the discord she had sown. He could do the one thing Logan couldn't: bring the town together against Arvil.

"You mean, everyone but Arvil will be devastated. He doesn't care. Did you know he wants to put an office building there? Give me a break."

"First, how can he even do that? And second, who's gonna work there. Three, even if we did get an office of some kind, our post office can't handle that kind of mail. It's just me and Marshall in there, and we're stretched as thin as we can get." He ran a hand over his forehead, as if wiping away the idea.

Logan saw enough of Riley to suspect that wasn't true, but if he was going to take up the cause, the whole town would know by dinner. "Well, don't tell anyone I said anything, but Helen owed some lot rent, and Arvil intends to evict her from the land and not let her rebuild at all. He said he plans to build an office there, and the bar brought no value to the town."

Those might not have been his exact words, but they were close enough.

"No value?" Riley hoisted his bag higher on his shoulder, his eyes narrowed. "Maybe it wasn't packed every night, but it was the only place to go around here unless you drive way out of town."

Her conscience told her to stop, not to reveal Helen's secrets. But watching Helen slip further into hopelessness while Arvil destroyed the one place where the town came together just for the sake of lining his own pockets was more than Logan could bear. It would break her heart to pick up and move to another town, to beg Warren to let her break the lease and grovel to get her security deposit back, and no one else seemed to be looking out for Helen. No else even knew what was at stake.

She'd seen it a million times, a community destroyed by a developer. Her father would find a way to raise the rents, to push people out onto the streets. She'd been eleven years old when her father bought a mid-rise in the city and closed it down to make improvements. He sold it to some foreign man for much more than he'd paid and then bought himself a yacht and her a horse. The lawsuits were inevitable, he'd said. Peasants upset about losing their rent-controlled apartments, too stupid to see that it was all for the better, for the neighborhood to improve. But her father's idea of better had been shortsighted. He'd been unwilling, unable to see past his own bank account. Logan hadn't cared then, taking for granted that her father did what was right and enjoying all the perks. But destroying a community for pleasure and gain, changing people's lives for the worse, hadn't been right when she was eleven, and it wasn't the right thing to do now. With all of her foresight but none of their power, she had to do something about it.

Arvil couldn't do any worse to her. She couldn't be any more wounded than she already was. She had nothing left to lose, and Arvil knew it. Knowing anger made people unstable and forced them to make hard decisions, she knew pushing Arvil's buttons would make him lash out to bring an end to the irritation. If she could knock him far enough off balance, he would flail. Crush himself under the weight of his own anger. She wouldn't have to do a thing. Turning the tables felt a bit like absolution, and Riley was a heck of an ally.

"Arvil said the bar was a waste. I'm sorry."

His eyes sought something in the distance, somewhere along the rooftops. Logan's request to keep the news to himself was already forgotten.

"Wait until people find out about this. There'll be a riot. Would *you* want to tell Dan and Bern they can't go to the bar anymore? It's been less than a week, and they're probably imploding from the lack of stale air and sticky floors."

Logan folded the paper on her lap. "They'll come up with somewhere else to go. People are resilient. It's just a shame because it really was the hub of the community. It's where everybody talked to each other, you know? Now this place won't be any different than a big city. All those people wandering around, and they don't even know each other."

Riley's grip tightened on the strap to his bag, and his jaw clenched. Whether she'd done the right thing or not, only time would tell. But seeing Riley take on the fight was a small achievement in weeks of failure.

He said his goodbye and left. From the corner of her eye, she watched him enter the bakery and heard him issue his morning greeting to Marissa. It took a few minutes for him to emerge, much longer than necessary for dropping off a bundle of mail. Her work had been done. People would stop Arvil in the street, tell him how much they would miss the bar. Bern might even yell. Arvil would be forced to see the truth.

Logan climbed the stairs to her apartment and sat on the bed by the open window. At best, the message would grow legs and spread, and like all good gossip, it would evolve. If it got to Helen, she would suspect Arvil. Under pressure from the town, he would cave and forgive Helen. They'd come to an arrangement about payments or a personal loan. At worst, Logan would have to leave town and rely on some other group of strangers to take pity on a young woman and her suitcase. But there was too much hope in her plan to entertain that possibility.

She opened her notebook and the bar ledger on her little kitchen table and calculated the money she'd saved through frugal spending and cautious pouring. She'd come so far, and there'd been miles still to go. The dumpster, new windows. A cooler and a better sign out front.

"Not bad for an art history major," she said out loud to herself. The radiator pipes banged a retort.

She swore, if they ever got the place up and running again, she'd beg for a laptop and some accounting software.

Desperate for lunch and high on opportunity, she decided to splurge on the makings of a salad. She grabbed her coat and bounded down the stairs and onto the street where she found Riley returning from his early rounds, delivering mail on the east side of town.

"Back for lunch?" She tugged her key from the lock and shoved it in her pocket.

"Yup. Finished with one corner already. Ran into Arvil." Riley balled his empty mailbag in his hands.

She shoved her fists deep in her pockets, and prayed that Riley wouldn't make her drag it out of him. "What did he have to say?"

"Not much. Got all red in the face and closed the door on me. I wouldn't have to knock if he'd fix his mailbox. It's a law. Most people don't know that. Of course most people actually want to have a mailbox." Riley turned to the post office door. "He did say one other thing. Something about it being a matter of economics. That the town has to shake off some fleas. And something about how in nature forest fires happen on purpose, to clear the land so the woods can thrive. He rambles. Anyway, he was never meant for a small town like this. You gotta be nice to people here. Nobody will want to work on that land now, just to spite him."

CHAPTER EIGHTEEN

Logan stepped onto the street, into the swirl of a dusting snow. With a ten-dollar budget, she had to find a gift for her mother. Candles on timers came on in the windows, illuminating nothing for no one. What was it about Christmas that made everyone nostalgic? Was it the habit of putting out the same decorations year after year, dragging up warm memories in a season of gloom? Logan wanted that familiar tug of holiday sentiment, the nostalgia and warmth. But she'd been left behind. Those were things for other people, for people who still had pieces of their past. Logan didn't even have the reindeer ornament she cut from construction paper in kindergarten.

Around her, Ramsbolt moved at its own pace. Light and relaxed without obligation. As if Christmas were a well-rehearsed show. Logan was an outsider with no role to play, waiting in the audience for the show to start.

She crossed the street and cut through the turning circle. A young couple sat on a park bench, their backs to the sailor, cradling warm drinks in their mittens. Their laughter bounced off the statue and lassoed Logan, tightening the coil in her chest. She passed empty storefronts and stepped into the toy shop, where overhead, a low voice crooned a classic holiday tune Logan couldn't place.

Shipping to France would cost a bundle. She skimmed the shelves for something small and light. On a shelf in the back corner, past rows of puzzles, shelves of children's books, and bins of stuffed toys, she found a row of snow globes. She shook one and snow fell on one of Maine's indomitable red lighthouses. She took it to the counter where the owner sat on a wooden stool, eating a chocolate bar. She accepted the little paper bag from the man behind the counter and shoved her four dollars in change in her purse.

"Thanks, Nate."

"Sure thing. So it's true then?" he asked. "No more bar, huh?"

"Looks that way. How'd you hear?"

He hunched and lowered his head, sharing a secret in an empty room. "Arvil."

"Arvil was in here?" One eyebrow raised, Logan didn't bother to hide her surprise. "In a toy store?"

"Ran into him this morning in the market. He was buying canned soup. Lazy, if you ask me. Nothing beats making your own soup."

"What did he say about the bar?" Logan fought the bag into her coat pocket, feigning disinterest in the topic Nate raised but wouldn't address.

"Said you'd been up to his house, asking about his business, trying to get him to build a bar. That's a nice thing to do for Helen. Took guts."

She waved a dismissive hand. "Not really. I haven't been here long, but I picked up on Arvil pretty fast. He wants people to jump and run. He was probably surprised it took me that long to get there."

Nate let out a small laugh. "That sounds right." He ran his hands over a stack of flat paper bags, the kind he used for penny candy, smoothing down the dog-eared corners. "And you know that bag boy?"

"Sean? The tall one with the glasses?"

"Yeah. Well, Arvil gets up to the register to pay for all them cans, and Sean tells him it's a shame he won't let the bar open again 'cause he's just about twenty-one and never got a chance to go. We all know that's not the truth 'cause Helen would serve him, but that's not the point. Anyway, Arvil got all red in the face and slammed cans on the counter and said what he did with his property was nobody's business. Never seen him so mad. Said the whole town's been at him about it, and it's his to do with what he wants, and he don't think we need a bar. Not that bar, anyway."

She'd knocked Arvil off-kilter, made him wobble on his axis. Lashing out more than usual and being defensive, Arvil could break if she could crack his shell. "Slammed his cans on the counter, huh? Sounds like he was pretty pissed."

"Yeah! He said the whole town's been at him." The electric chime rang through the store, throwing Burl Ives's "Jingle Bells" off key. Nate nodded at a woman in a tea-length dress who strode in, purse hooked over her arm. "Keep at him, will ya? We might break him after all."

It wasn't a confrontation she looked forward to. She was off-kilter herself, suffocating under the weight of a Christmas she would celebrate alone. The fifty-dollar Amazon gift card she received from her mother wouldn't go far, and she didn't know how to cook Christmas dinner for one, even if she could afford to. She wasn't hungry for Christmas dinner anyway. "We'll see. I don't know what I can do about it, but if I get a chance, I'll certainly try. You're not hiring in the meantime, are you?" She'd inquired once, but it didn't hurt to try.

"Afraid not. I'm not doing that well either. Not terrible, but not good enough to add more to the payroll." He wore the same look as everyone else when she asked, a mix of apology and imposition. "The summer months, tourists stop here on their way in and out. We're busy this time of year. But it's fits and starts, you know?"

"I totally get it." She waved a hand. "Forget I asked. Happy holidays."

"Same to you. Take it easy."

Logan closed the door behind her. It was barely four thirty, and the sky was dark. Flurries dusted the lamppost at the corner. It should have been romantic, festive. She should feel good about making progress with Arvil. It's what she'd wanted, to put him on edge so she could strike a killing blow. But she had no idea what that blow would be, how to get him to break. And she was far from home. Far from the ornaments and decorations and the magic of her own traditions.

She passed empty storefronts and paused at the circle for a passing car. The risk of disturbing the giggling couple was worth the reward to pause at the sailor's feet. Snow frosted his cap, his hands at the helm. He looked to a distant horizon only he could see with a ferocious tenacity. A plaque she hadn't noticed before was affixed to the statue's base, brushed with snow. *In memory of Degory Howland. In homage to those who never saw the sea.* She had no idea who Degory Howland was or what the inscription meant, but it stirred a hope in her that even on land far from shore, distant beacons still called to her. If she looked hard enough, even on the darkest night, the horizon was still there. Somewhere, if she never got through to Arvil, there was a place where she belonged. Where she could find friends, a job, and comfort.

She turned from the sailor, heading for the warmth of her apartment, and slipped into the path of Arvil, his head down, a bundle of envelopes clenched in one hand.

"Good. You can save me some trouble instead of making it for once." He thrust the mail at her, pushing it toward her chest.

She stepped back in alarm. "What am I supposed to do with this?"

"Take it to the post office. It belongs to Helen. I keep getting the bar's mail, and I don't want it."

"Isn't that mail fraud? I can't take that. You have to put return to sender on it or something. And don't ask me to run your errands for you. I'm not your assistant. I'm incompetent, remember? How can I possibly be trusted to return some mail?"

"You listen here. How dare you smear me all over this town. This is my town." His face grew red, and the sailor threw his words back at him in a metallic echo.

"No, you listen to me." Her voice was calm and steady, belying the surge of vengeful hubris that took hold of her. She welcomed it. In another world, he wouldn't dream of talking to her with a raised voice. He would pay her deference. "This is not *your* town. You own two little slices of it that you don't care for, and you treat people poorly. If they dislike you, it's a consequence of the person you are. It has nothing to do with me."

"Don't care for...Helen didn't *take care of* that bar, and it burned to the ground, so I have no income, and I have to wait for someone to show up from her sham insurance agency to get that soot off my property. You're lucky I'm not suing both of you to pay for the cleanup and cover the damages. You're just a useless..." His nostrils flared and eyes darted from side to side. He blew a fuse. Fury took hold of him, and Logan knew silence would make him bend. It was checkmate in a game of chess she wasn't prepared to play. She didn't have her father's foresight or power to back up her threats. All she had was desire. Desire to help Helen, help herself, and help the town.

In the quietest whisper she could utter and hold steady in the chill of a December night, she did what her father would do and talked to him like a child. "I feel sorry for you. Your life didn't turn out the way you thought it would at all, did it? The world didn't meet your expectations so instead of learning how to get along, you turned those expectations into demands. And when you still didn't get your way, you decided to take it out on everyone around you."

He stared back, unblinking.

Logan didn't relent. "I hope you find what you're looking for one day, because it doesn't look like all that anger is working for you, and God knows it's nobody's fault but your own."

He pulled a large envelope from the stack and waved it in her face. "You're not good enough anyway. Go. Make a fool of yourself. Then leave this town and be foolish somewhere else."

He dropped the envelope at her feet and stormed off to the post office. She let him have the last word, but her own words stayed with her, playing again and again in her mind. It was nobody's fault but her own that she didn't have a job. That she couldn't fix the bar. That she hadn't closed this chapter of her life already and started a new one. It was her own fault that she had no plan for the future that didn't involve taking down someone else. And she had no one to blame but herself for thinking that her father's worst traits were her best assets. She would have to do something different before she became angry and bitter and took it out on the world like Arvil. Like her father. Lorne Cole tore his family apart with his unbridled ambition. Logan might have inherited his appetite, but it didn't have to consume her.

She was sick of clinging to a life raft, being pulled on by the tide. She plucked the envelope from the ground and dusted off the snow, then headed for home, cold paper chilling her ungloved hand. She looked for traffic, though none came, and crossed the street. At the corner, she paused to dump the registration packet into the town recycling can and take in the smell of snow. Change was in the air.

CHAPTER NINETEEN

The thud from the envelope falling into the empty recycling can echoed like an exclamation point on the end of Logan's career as a bartender and followed her up the street.

"Whoa, whoa, whoa." Grey's voice bounced off the brick buildings, and his feet pounded the pavement as he gained on her.

Logan spun on her heel, her hands in her pockets, to face him. Of course, he would show up when she needed solitude the most. She fought back tears that made blurry stars of the streetlights. She mustered an excuse to flee. "I'm not in a very good mood right now."

"I was coming out of the hardware store, and I saw you and Arvil fighting over there. Actually, I *heard* you fighting, because Arvil's so loud he could wake the dead. I saw you throw something away in a huff."

"So?"

"I dug it out." He held it out to her. "Here. Take it. Don't throw away the registration packet. You need this. There's no reason you can't still go."

"Why are you digging in the trash?" Logan waved a hand and turned away. "I'm not going to stand out here and argue with you about garbage."

He grabbed her wrist and stopped her. "Come on. Talk to me. What's going on?"

"You don't know? Everybody knows."

"I don't talk to people. I crawl around under their sinks. What don't I know?"

"Arvil is going to block Helen from rebuilding the bar. That's what we were arguing about. So, no. I can't go to this bar competition because I don't have a bar to represent. I can't afford any liquor to practice with. I can't afford to get there or find a place to stay. Because—"

"Wait. Breathe." Grey took a step back, and Logan saw the opportunity to escape. She turned her back to him and strode toward her apartment, but he darted around her, walking backward in front of her.

"You're gonna trip on something and fall over walking backward like that."

"Then stop walking."

"No. You stop. I'm serious, Grey. I really don't want to talk about this. I just want to go home."

Grey planted his feet before her and came to a halt. Too exhausted to pick a fight and smart enough not to argue with one of the few people she could trust, she faced him. He could say his piece.

"Arvil's just a grumpy old crab. Helen will rebuild it. It'll be back. A place like that can be built in a month."

"Then why hasn't the site been cleared? It's been three weeks. I'm telling you it won't be rebuilt. Helen can't do it, doesn't want to fight for it, and Arvil wouldn't let her if she could because she's behind on lot rent. That's it. It's over."

"What are you going to do? Did you get another job?"

Logan blinked up at the cast iron lamppost, willing her eyes to reabsorb the tears that threatened to fall. She would not cry about a stupid bar and certainly not in front of Grey. "No. I pinned my hopes on fixing this mess. I ran my mouth to Riley, and let him spread it all over town because I'm foolish and selfish. Now Arvil's totally pissed, and I blew it for Helen. Even if he would have been flexible, he definitely won't be now out of spite. I haven't even talked to Helen. She probably hates me."

"Helen doesn't hate you. You can't give up that easy. There's got to be a place to get a job around here. Did you look online?"

"Yes. Useless. There's nothing around here. I checked the paper, too, and every store downtown and everywhere I can walk to. The only jobs are at the farms, and I don't know anything about working on a farm. And I don't have a car. I don't even know how to drive."

"You don't know how to drive?" Grey lowered his chin and gave Logan a comical sneer. It was an obvious attempt to lighten the mood, but she wasn't taking the bait.

"Look, smart-ass. I grew up in the city. You know that."

"Sorry. You can't give up, though. There has to be an answer. Start your own business. Everyone here needs something. Find something people can't live without and sell it to them. Or do it for them. The right thing is out there. It seems dark right now, but there's something out there for everybody. There has to be."

"Exactly. It just won't be here. Or at that bartending competition. So thank you, but no thank you."

Logan pulled her keys from her pocket and gripped them in her fist. They dug into her fingers and into her palms with a good kind of pain.

The kind that brought feeling back from the cold. She stepped around Grey and walked toward her apartment, flurries scattering at her feet, and he fell into step beside her.

She sighed, her breath making icy clouds in the cold. Why wouldn't he just leave her alone? "I don't want to talk about this anymore. I just need to take a break and look for something somewhere else. I can't keep waiting for something to happen. I have to make something happen on my own."

"Wait. You said you want the bar back, and Arvil won't let her rebuild because she's behind on lot rent. How far behind is she?"

"A few thousand."

"What if you won this competition, and you gave Arvil the money?" Grey waved the registration packet. Logan gave it a playful swat. "I read the flyer. It didn't say anything about needing to be employed to enter."

"Nice try. But like I said, I can't afford to go, so it doesn't even matter."

Logan stopped in a shadowed patch between two lamps, where the pools of light wouldn't meet. Half of her wanted Grey to call her out on the lie, and the other half wanted to run and hide so he would leave her alone. Here was this person, trying to help, and she couldn't even let him in. The familiar taste of anger rose with a vengeance. Her father had destroyed her life, forced her into exile, and now she couldn't even accept some kindness when she needed it the most.

Grey tugged on the sleeve of her coat and gestured behind them. "Come back here with me. Please. I wanna show you something outside of town. The snow's not that bad. It's just flurries. And I'm a really good driver. I promise. If that's what you're worried about."

"Where?" she asked.

"It's a surprise. Just get in the truck. If you want to give up and leave town, that's fine. Just do it for the right reasons." He turned to leave.

Her heart wanted to follow, but her feet were planted. "I can't."

"You're a terrible listener, you know that? The universe is screaming at you, and you've got your fingers in your ears. Come on."

She followed, a reluctant slog to Grey's truck. She didn't want to leave town on any terms but her own. A heartfelt journey to discover some part of herself she'd denied wasn't one of those terms, but she humored him. The smallest act of atonement she could give herself for her father's dereliction. Grey was the closest thing to a friend she had, and she deserved one. He opened the truck door for her, and she climbed in.

The truck's yellow headlights shot up the road, and Logan took a tally. She hadn't been in a vehicle since she rode a Greyhound bus into town many weeks before. Thumbing through memories like snapshots, she tried to find a truck in her past. Town cars, taxis, limousines. Her father once had a Lamborghini Countach he kept at their house in Dubai, sold to the highest bidder when the investigation first started, and he pulled his assets out of the country. She couldn't think of a single time she'd been in a pickup truck. It felt like the school busses she'd ridden in on field trips as a child. It leapt into and out of potholes and sounded like a steam engine a hundred years its senior. It tossed her from side to side, and it smelled like diesel fuel and something else, too. Something rancid.

Not wanting to seem prudish, Logan sat in silence as the truck bounced past wisps of grain that blurred along the shoulder.

Grey cleared his throat. "So, I dropped that donation jar off at Glen's house."

"Yeah? How's he doing?"

"Gonna be fine. He was huffy about it, but his wife said it was real nice of you to do that. It'll help pay some of his medical bills. She'd like to thank you in person some time."

Logan didn't know what to say. Everyone had troubles. In another life she would have paid the bill for them. Too bad the goodwill had done nothing for her karma. But she couldn't mourn the loss out loud.

She grasped the only thing in reach to change the topic. "I like your truck."

"It's horrible. It breaks down all the time, and I hit a skunk yesterday."

"Is that what that smell is? I didn't want to ask."

"I wouldn't ordinarily ask a nice girl to come out with me in a smell like this, but I forgot about the skunk."

"This isn't a date," Logan said.

"I know. Not a date. You just happen to be a nice girl, and you're in my stinky truck, that's all."

"I'm just clarifying." She made sure her voice sounded as firm on the topic as she felt.

"Okay. It's not a date, but it's still okay with me if you're not so adamant about it. Kinda kills a guy's ego, if you know what I mean."

"I don't want you to get the wrong idea." Logan could picture herself spending time with Grey. She could use a friend sometimes. But that was it. Just a friend. And she couldn't imagine a world where this truck was a part of her life.

"No wrong ideas had. I promise."

"I thought skunks hibernated in the winter." Contrary to popular thought, rats and humans weren't the only mammals that roamed the streets of New York. She'd seen enough skunks lurking in parks and near doorways, searching for food, to know their numbers diminished in the colder months.

"They don't." Grey adjusted his hands on the wheel. "They get real slow, and they sleep off and on, but they do come out sometimes. That one picked the wrong time."

"Maybe you had the wrong time."

"By the smell of my truck, seems you're right."

Grey slowed the truck and put on his turn signal for no one. A road appeared from the darkness, and he turned left.

"Where are we going, again?" It came out hesitant and high pitched.

"You really hate surprises, don't you? You're like a skittish stray cat. Every time somebody tries to talk to you, you run under the porch."

The world passed by the window as they picked up speed again, but all Logan could see of it were flashes of fence posts and the blur of grasses by the roadside. She had no retort, no snappy comeback or reply. He wasn't wrong; she was skittish.

"I guess. That's just the way I am." She hadn't always been that way.

"I'm taking you someplace I like to go. You'll like it. I promise. Change of topic? What kind of cars did you have growing up?"

The Countach was unmentionable. "City people don't own cars. We walk and take taxis."

"They're so expensive, though."

"But we don't need them much. Everything's closer. We don't have to take a car to the grocery store. You guys have to drive everywhere." Not that she'd ever walked to a grocery store, but it wasn't a total lie.

"Wasn't that restricting? A little less free? Didn't you wake up on your sixteenth birthday and smell freedom? I did."

"Riding around in skunk fumes is your idea of freedom?" Freedom meant something different to Logan. Back then it meant a calendar free of obligations, no charity functions, no dinners for the useless committees her parents belonged to, and not having to put on tights and a girly dress and wear a happy face for the people her father was tearing apart in the courts. Now, it meant being able to go to the market and buy food without doing math on the way to the register. "We just wanted a different kind of freedom, I guess. Different rite of passage."

Lights appeared as they crested a hill, and Grey pulled into a parking lot, kicking up gravel and crunching on patches of slushy snow. Strings of lights circled a barren porch. He brought her to a bar.

"I don't know how to say this without sounding rude, but dining out isn't in my budget and I—"

"I didn't bring you here to spend money." He silenced the truck and pulled the key from the ignition. "And I know it's not a date. I'm being friendly. We do that around here. You can buy me a drink sometime or make me stew. I love stew. This place has amazing stew."

Grey stepped out of the truck. The door closed behind him with a solid finality. Logan pulled the metal lever, but the door wouldn't open. A hollow *thunk* echoed in the cavity of the door. Grey stood on the restaurant's porch, looking at her and speaking words she couldn't hear. She could barely see him through the dirty windshield.

He returned to the truck and unlocked the door from the outside. "My truck is making me inhospitable. I forgot the lock is all messed up." He offered her a hand, and she declined, scrambling to the ground and landing close to an icy puddle. The door closed behind her, and she walked beside him into the restaurant.

Inside, it was every bit the log cabin the exterior predicted. A large, open room with a bar in one corner and stone fireplaces at either end.

There was no hostess, but a note taped to the half wall inside the door told them to seat themselves. Grey extended an arm, and Logan took the cue to choose.

She circled the room, sticking to the edges. Most were occupied, either by families who pinned their unruly kids by the wall, or groups of friends with beer bottles scattered like pieces in a drunken game of checkers. She slid into a booth by a window nailed shut.

They were barely seated when a waiter dropped menus on the table and declared he'd be back for their drink order.

"Talk about a fire hazard." Logan handed a menu to Grey and kept one for herself. She examined the front cover, a grainy, black-and-white photo of the log cabin restaurant from a century before and text in too many fonts. "We used to stop at places like this on the way home from ski trips."

"Never been," Grey turned the laminated menu pages, settling on a list of burgers.

"Me either. I like my feet on the ground. But I'm really good at wearing ski outfits and drinking hot chocolate by a fireplace." The last time she'd been, they'd still owned a lodge in a bundle of luxury hotels. She'd taken a dozen friends for New Year's, where they stayed for three extra days, trapped by a blizzard. It devolved into arguments and accusations, and they'd run out of hot chocolate. Looking back, Logan wondered how she'd ever been comfortable in that skin.

But she wasn't comfortable in this new skin, either. She'd never been without money of her own, hesitant to order a twenty-dollar entree in case it might cost too much. And she'd never been so reluctant to talk, to give so much of herself away.

"What are you gonna order?" she asked, hoping for a hint at the budget.

He dropped the menu. "Do you like nachos? With pork?"

"The more guac, the better."

"I thought I wanted stew, but I'm in the mood for something salty. Want to split a massive thing of nachos?"

"That's a great idea. I miss nachos. It's one of those foods you don't think about. It's not like you can order them for delivery or walk down the street and take them home."

"Can't order anything for delivery in Ramsbolt. Maybe that's your next venture. Pick up and drop off food for people who don't want to leave the house. You could call it Nacho Takeout. Get it?"

Logan grinned and dropped menu. "I get it. But wouldn't that be hard to do without a car?"

"There's that." Grey set his menu to the side and folded his hands, his eyes fixed on hers. "Other than nachos, what else do you miss?"

The list was long. And it wasn't just places and things. At the top of the list was the feeling you get from walking through a place you've known forever. Every crack in the sidewalk and which red lights were new and remembering a long line of retailers that occupied a place on the corner. She couldn't get that feeling anywhere but home, and she'd tried really hard not to wallow in it. "I've tried not to go down that rabbit hole."

"I mean food."

"Oh." Logan unfurled her silverware from her napkin. It wasn't the type of napkin that belonged on a lap so she creased it and let it lie where her plate would be. Fork on the left, knife and spoon on the right. "I miss holiday markets. I miss walking around and eating anything I want because there are no calories at Christmas. Drinking cups of coffee with obscene amounts of whipped cream drizzled in sauces that have no business being in coffee. I miss that stuff a lot."

"We don't have those. What's it like, a craft fair?"

"Bigger. And they're outside. They bring out these little sheds, and vendors fill them with holiday stuff. Toys and clothes and hats. The kind of stuff you'd give as a gift. They fill up with people."

"Sounds claustrophobic. We do that in the basement of the church, but it's mostly crocheted toilet paper covers and googly eyed things made out of pom-poms."

"Different stuff, same theory. But this is outside, and everyone's in a good mood. It's just a nice place to go."

The waiter returned with glasses of water, friendly but aloof. Grey ordered nachos.

"You want to pick the drinks? That's your forte."

"I'm not a tequila person. I mean, with nachos you want a margarita, right?"

"Not necessarily." Grey shrugged. "Get whatever. I'll drink it."

"A Rob Roy with bourbon and a godfather?" Logan returned the menus to their place against the wall, propped up by ketchup, mustard, and a ceramic dish of sweeteners. The waiter nodded receipt of the order without eye contact. "Oh, can they hold back a little on the amaretto in the Godfather? Not quite fifty-fifty? Thanks."

The waiter nodded and sauntered off. Logan searched the room for clues, for hints at conversations to fill the void. It felt like a horrible date, reaching into the clutter of her mind hoping to find something interesting to talk about that didn't give away too much or too little of herself. "This place is neat. Has it always been a diner? I mean, is it really old and repurposed or built to look that way?"

"You know, I don't know. It's been like this since I was a kid. The menu's changed a few times, though. Used to be a steak place."

"I can totally picture that. If I looked hard enough, I could probably find the nail holes from where they put the horseshoes."

"There were plenty of those. There was a statue of a horse outside. I was little, but I'm pretty sure it was a life-size thing. Somebody ran into it in the parking lot. Drove right into it. That was a big deal around here."

"I can imagine." She didn't mean it to sound facetious, as if her city upbringing gave her cause to look down on the quiet. "I don't mean that in a condescending way. I mean when landmarks get destroyed, everybody suffers. Whether you're in a city or a small town. But I guess sometimes they have to go, to make room for new things. Like nachos."

"We would have fought to save that horse, though. Just like people would fight to save the bar."

Logan rubbed her eyes with her heels of her hands. It felt good to scrub at her skin, dry and tight from heaters and air saturated with road salt. She got his point, that the town was willing to do what it needed to save the bar. What he couldn't see was that she'd blown it for everyone. She didn't have the words to say how sorry she was. When she pulled her hands away from her eyes, the waiter had dropped drinks on the table, and left as quickly as he'd come. A welcome distraction, but it only delayed the well-deserved blame Grey would lay at her feet. She didn't need to hear it.

Grey pointed to the drinks. "Which is which?"

"The red one is yours. That's the Rob Roy." Logan pushed the glass forward. Liquid the color of a manhattan rippled in the glass, and Grey pushed it back.

"You taste it first."

"Why?"

"I want you to tell me what's wrong with it."

Logan raised an eyebrow. "Like testing your drink for poison?"

"More like bad bartending than poisoning, but yeah. I want your take on it."

The rocks glass was room temperature. She sipped, letting the liquid touch her lips then holding it on her tongue. She drew air over it and swallowed. "Seems fine." She slid it across the table to him.

"Would you have done it different?"

"Of course. I'd have stirred it with ice a little longer. Used a little less sweet vermouth. It should be an ounce and a half of scotch and just under an ounce of vermouth. This is almost one-to-one. I wouldn't garnish it with a cherry either. I'd use a lemon peel, but there's probably no real rule about it."

"What about yours?"

Logan sipped water to clear her palate and took a sip of her godfather. Ordinarily, it would be half bourbon, half amaretto, but she'd requested a drop less amaretto to let the bourbon shine. A wheaty, spicy kick competed with the amaretto. "I think they used rye instead of bourbon. Not sure. It's still good, though."

"And if you were making one?"

"I would have used a milder bourbon. Something that goes well with amaretto and doesn't fight with it in the glass, you know? And stir both of these longer so they're chilled. These are almost room temperature. Garnish matters, I guess. I never really thought about it, because I was always trying to save money, and most of the people at Helen's don't care." She stopped herself. Thinking of the bar in present tense wouldn't help her move past it. "Didn't care, rather."

"They care about what matters, Logan. Cherries and lemon peels don't matter. But the bar matters. Not a place like this with booths you sit in that keep you separate from each other. An open place where we talk and hang out. A place to relax and be yourself in Ramsbolt and not half an hour through the fields. It was right there at the top of town, where it belonged."

A large plate of nachos landed between them. The waiter warned them it was hot and left them with a stack of napkins and two small plates.

"Is that why we came here? So I could pick apart the drinks?"

"We came here so you could see that Arvil's wrong. You do know your shit. And if he's wrong about you, he can be wrong about that bar."

CHAPTER TWENTY

"Arvil doesn't want a bar on that site, period." Logan licked salty nacho dust and oily melted cheese from her fingers. A treat like this would have been sinful in most of the circles she once moved in, not just for the contents but the method of eating it. And she wouldn't dream of licking her fingers at any other table. "He wants an office building. Not a bar."

Grey took a sip of his Rob Roy. "If you show up on his doorstep with the money and all of the legal boxes are checked, he can't force Helen out."

Logan shrugged. "He can do whatever he wants, within reason, because she's already breached the contract. At least that's the way he tells it, and it's what Helen seems to think. She doesn't even seem interested in rebuilding it. It's just a waste of effort."

"But if you show up with the money, do you honestly think Helen would say no? Not everybody is opposed to accepting help when things get hard. Can I tell you a story?"

Logan delayed biting into a nacho chip loaded with pork and guac. "Sure."

"I know this girl who lost her coat in a fire, and I thought she was gonna knee me in the balls for buying her a new one. That's the kind of reaction you get out of people who've never had to accept help from anybody. If I went back and asked that girl, I bet she'd say that's true, that she's not used to taking help from people. But Helen might be. That girl with no coat offered help to Helen once, and Helen jumped on it. Maybe she would again."

"Yeah, yeah. Snark aside, I get it. Maybe Helen's in so deep, she'll accept any help she can get, and if something came along that made it all easier, she wouldn't turn it down. Again."

"I'm telling you there's a reason you showed up at this town. You might think you needed Helen, but maybe she needed you, too. Maybe we all need each other." Grey pulled on a nacho, and the pyramid settled. A dollop of sour cream shifted, and he rescued it with a chip, smearing it across the pile.

"I'm not some magical being sent here to save you guys from a future without a bar. That's insane. I came here because I—"

Grey looked up from his little plate of chips and pork and gooey guac. "Because why?"

Logan rolled her eyes. "Because I have my own stuff to sort out. All I wanted was a job, and it didn't pan out, so now I have to find something else. It's no big deal."

"It is a big deal." Grey waved a chip. "You aren't like us. You react different than we do to things. You don't know how to be poor."

"What do you mean, *I don't know how to be poor?*" Poor wasn't something she aimed to master. It was something she aimed to be rid of. Like not knowing how to have polio.

"You can't make do and mend the way people here do. You don't know how to cook, you couldn't make a basic cocktail, but you knew Helen was wasting money and how to fix it. Not the way someone who's poor knows how to cut corners, but like someone who knows their way around a business."

She was not letting Grey drag anything out of her. He could make all the assumptions he wanted. "I watch a lot of television."

"No, you went toe-to-toe with Arvil, and I saw you earlier. Back at the park. You looked at him like you were gonna make him your bitch. You're not here 'cause you're running from a man. You're here because you're running from something else. I just haven't figured out what it is yet."

He leaned across the table, an eyebrow raised in expectant wonder. She'd seen the look before. Helen had wanted assurance that trouble wouldn't follow her. Logan was more than happy to give her that, but Grey wanted an inside scoop. He wanted more from her than she was willing to give. Not because he wanted the secret of her past, but because he wanted a miracle. A savior for the bar. She didn't have the power to make a grilled cheese sandwich. How was she supposed to save the tavern?

If she could throw money at a problem, she would. Like when Jill got caught shoplifting for the fun of it and did her community service at a pet shelter. She'd signed up to volunteer at weekend fundraising events, but Logan was more interested in going to Europe, so she wrote a check for fifteen thousand dollars and bought Jill out of her trouble. There was no check this time, and it wasn't about being selfish. Logan's heart hurt, watching the town yearn so much for something that would have been so attainable just a few months before.

The light above the table picked up early strands of white in Grey's hair. Just a strand or two. And bits of gold reflected in his eyes when he looked up from his drink. His intentions were just as good as hers, to save the bar, to save her by offering an ear. But Logan didn't need saving, no matter how much she hungered to unburden herself of heavy secrets and feel the weightlessness of telling Grey who she used to be, what she'd lost, her father's crimes. The slow creep of realizing your own father valued money and lies more than the safety of his family. Telling the truth couldn't save her from the pain. Her father's reputation would follow her to the ends of the earth, and she would forever wonder if women were holding doors for her only to spit in her face. If men in newsstands would turn on her and hold her accountable for transgressions she never committed. In Ramsbolt, things were calm, but if Grey gave her away, she would be right back where she started. No safe place to go, the world nipping at her heels. The consequence of telling the truth would be losing everything all over again.

But it still hurt to lie.

Grey took another sip and set his drink on the table, making yet another wet ring. "You're not going to tell me, are you? What you're running from?"

Logan pushed pork around on her small plate, and kept her eyes pinned on it. "Nope. I'm sorry. I can't. I just can't."

"Who was he?"

"It's not like that."

"Are you in the witness protection program?"

As many times as she wished for it, she couldn't resist the laugh. "No. Wouldn't that be fun, though? I'm pretty sure they set you up with sheets and towels and real dishes when that happens. I don't think they drop you off in the middle of nowhere."

Grey lowered his head and scanned the room, a sly smile crossing his face. "Are you, like, James Bond? Are you CIA? Did you kill someone?"

"I was in a taxi that ran over a squirrel once. They're really crazy in Manhattan. And I was in Central Park when someone had a heart attack. He was running and just fell over and was gone. Like that." She snapped her fingers. "Wasn't my fault, though."

"Did you steal things from Wall Street? Like a big stocks heist?"

"I don't think they keep them in a safe or anything. If I did, would I be sleeping on unicorn sheets?"

"Your sheets have unicorns on them?"

Logan nodded and killed the last of her drink. "Unicorns were a lot cheaper than solid colored sheets. Don't know why. I really regret I didn't bring any with me."

"So you fled in the middle of the night. Dropped your suitcase out a window, jumped to the ground, and ran for it?"

"Not that dramatic. I had a ride."

"But why? There's no way you were running to something that you could only find in Ramsbolt. What were you running from?"

Across the room, a baby cried. Adults fell silent, turning their heads to stare. "I just like to keep to myself, that's all. I'm a private person. It's just the way I am."

The waiter dropped the bill on the table, a black plastic folder with a slip of paper poking out. Grey nodded. She was grateful that he scooped it up so it didn't sit there like a billboard reminding her of poverty.

He pulled cash from his wallet, paid their bill, and shuffled in his seat, stuffing his wallet back into his pocket. "You're entitled to that. That's okay. I wish you'd trust me, though. You have this vibe about you, like you're a fish out of water. I'm sitting here with a hose and a kiddie pool, and you'd rather flail. It makes no sense. You could enter that competition, buy into the idea of saving this bar. You could use some of the money to help grease Arvil's wheels and solve your own problem. But you won't, and I don't get why."

Grey shook his head and dark curls brushed his eyebrows. It hurt to disappoint him. She didn't want to risk exposure by entering a competition, but she didn't want him to give up on her either. The pleather bench cushion crinkled as he slid to the end and stood. Logan followed him into the parking lot, across the crunchy gravel and into the truck where he closed the door behind her with a soft thud.

He steered toward town, back the way they had come, and Logan set her sights on the quiet peace of her apartment, on curling up beneath the window in a puddle of blankets and letting the radiator pings sing her to sleep. The sky had cleared and out there in the fields, away from the lights of Ramsbolt's tiny downtown, Logan could see for lightyears.

She ducked her head to peer at more of the sky through the window. "I've never seen so many stars."

Grey slowed the truck, and it shuddered, kicking up gravel and salt that clinked against metal. He turned right, down a path cut into a field.

Logan held onto the door to steady herself as they turned the corner. This was not the path they'd taken out of town. Sensing she was further from her apartment and her warm bed, and closer to another ploy by Grey to get her to talk, she squeezed the edge of the seat.

"Where are we going now?"

They crested a small hill, and Grey cut the engine. "I thought you might like to see the stars. Come on."

She rolled down the window, the glass squeaking as it dropped, and reached outside for the handle. Her feet landed on flattened grasses, crunchy, hardened by the cold, and Grey motioned her to the rear of the truck. She followed his lead, climbing into the back in a graceless fumble. Sitting on the wheel well, she tilted her head back to look up at the sky.

"Some people live in New York City their whole lives." Logan gripped the side of the truck so she wouldn't fall backward. "They're born, and they die there and never step foot outside to see this many stars."

"Wanna tell me more about New York?" Grey's boots made a hollow sound in the bed of the truck when he shifted his weight.

She could only deny so much about her life. She had to accept that he knew some facts. The alternative would create a web of assumptions and lies. But that didn't mean she was obliged to tell an elaborate truth. She nodded, but he missed the gesture, his face turned toward the heavens.

"All these stars. They sure do make you feel small," she said.

"Billions of years old. When life gets weird, and I think that my drama is such a big deal, I come out here and look up. These stars have seen it all. My crap looks pathetic next to everything they've seen."

"I can't imagine you with drama. You're so laid back."

"Oh, I've known my share. My mother spent years trying to hide bruises from this town, applying makeup so thick she'd look ridiculous, so she'd send me to the store instead with change in my pocket. No one questioned a seven-year-old boy in the market, buying stuff for dinner, but they did wonder why my mom stopped making plans and going to church. They'd ask me all the time, and I had to learn to lie to my neighbors to keep the truth to myself."

"Jesus." Logan's father hadn't been that brutal, but he'd left plenty of scars. And learning to hide them, to cover them up, and craft lies to cover the wounds was an emotional requirement. The only way to hold onto normalcy. "There's some comfort in the lie, sometimes. Like, if you said the truth out loud it would make it real. It would become such a big part of you that you'd never be able to get past it."

"Those lies stack up, too. Even the ones you don't say out loud. I was thirteen years old when my father beat her to within an inch of her life. I got between them and took the keys to his truck. First time I ever drove a car was to take her out of town to my aunt's. We told everybody they were gettin' a divorce because that was a cheaper sin than saying he beat her. I'd like to think nobody here knows the real story, but now I'm older, I suspect there were plenty of rumors and somehow, one of 'em probably landed on the truth."

"You never told anybody?"

"Just you. Family knows. But we never told anybody in town. I just let 'em think what they wanted."

"What happened to your mom?"

"She's fine. When my aunt got a real divorce, the two of them went all *Thelma and Louise* and moved to San Diego. I talk to her all the time, but I don't see her as much as I'd like. It's a shame she had to leave here, though. Real justice would have been running him out of town instead. But she couldn't afford to stand on her own, so there was no use pursuing that kind of justice."

"I don't know what to say." The truck bed creaked when she shifted her weight, like an anguished cry from a burdened soul. "Does your dad still live here?"

"He had a heart attack and died in the shower four years ago, and I've never seen a town put on a bigger display of diplomatic mourning. Nobody here misses that man. Everybody stood around a hole in the ground and nobody said a word. That's around the time I figured people arrived at something that resembles the truth. Even though I didn't have to tell 'em. But sometimes I wish I had. It coulda gone a lot different, letting people think what they wanted."

Grey kicked at a length of pipe, and it rattled in the bed of the truck. He seemed lighter somehow, and Logan envied his release. But the lines etched in his brow said telling the story was still painful.

"You don't need to tell me this." Logan tried to let him off the hook.

"I know I don't need to. I want to."

"So we can swap truths? You told me yours, now I tell you mine?"

Grey shook his head. "That's up to you. All I know is, people put the pieces together all by themselves, and they make a story about who you are and what you deserve. This town coulda figured my mom cheated on my dad and treated him like a victim, but they didn't, and that was luck. The risk of not being who you really are is that people will decide for themselves what you deserve. When people know who you are and who you want to be, they go out of their way to help you get there."

Logan turned away from the stars. Mud from the parking lot had dried on her sneakers. Sneakers she couldn't afford to replace and had no idea how to clean. It wasn't that easy to let it all spill out, not like it was for Grey. No matter how nice it might be for someone out there to know the real her, she'd kept the secret for so long. Keeping it had kept her safe.

"That may be true here, that people help each other," she said. "But not where I come from. In my world, you don't show your hand. You protect the cards until it's time to play them, and then, when you have a full house, you throw them on the table and take what you earned. Life is about playing defense. Not about teamwork."

"See what I'm saying? You coming from money. People are gonna put the pieces together, Logan Cole. It's not that hard to do."

The cold air stung her cheeks. He knew. He knew her last name. Where she was from. Not just New York but the money. He'd already figured it out, but how long ago? How long had he been keeping her secret? It was too late to deny it.

Logan rubbed one shoe against the other, knocking off bits of mud. "How do you know my last name?"

"Warren told me."

"How long ago was that?"

"Coupla days, I guess."

Then why didn't he say? All this time, this drive to a restaurant and nachos and drinks, and he knew all along. Was it a joke or a notch in his wallet, buying dinner for a former billionaire's daughter?

Logan locked her fingers together and squeezed until her knuckles hurt. Nothing on Grey's face said he was proud or happy to have unraveled her mystery. And if he'd known for days, he hadn't told anyone. She had to give him the benefit of the doubt, but he still held all the cards.

She released her shaking hands, unwound her fingers, and gripped the cold edge of the truck bed. She cleared her throat to steady her voice. "If I told you the truth about who I am, and if you told anyone, I could lose everything. I don't have a lot to lose. That just makes it way too risky."

"Your name? That guy on the news? People are gonna figure it out either way. I bet there's a lot going on with you that you haven't been able to talk about, and an ally would be a good thing to have." Grey held out a fist and stuck out his pinky finger. "And don't worry about Warren. He sells the news, but he never reads it. Does a pinky swear help?"

Logan smiled, but didn't accept. "I wish it did."

She wished her father hadn't put her in this position, that he'd put his family first. That her mother wasn't living off shady money in sunny France. That consumption hadn't been so all consuming and something had been left for her to hold onto. But all of that was the darkness between the stars, unreachable and unattainable. She couldn't fix or change any of it, but she could take charge of her own situation, and she could always change her mind.

Logan folded her hands in her lap. "Okay. I know you already figured it out. That my family is a little famous. Lorne Cole is my father. Do you know who he is?"

"I've heard his name in the news. I know he's a superrich guy who went to jail."

She couldn't say it. She couldn't put the words together. Not because the truth was hard to say but because the sound of her own voice staking claim to it made the shame harder to swallow.

Grey's eyes were fixed on an invisible, darkened horizon. "I know the government took all the money and that there was some kind of appeal that's not going so well."

"I wouldn't really know. I don't know any more than what's been in the papers or on the news, because he told me not to contact him, and the more time goes by, the happier I am with that arrangement."

"You were, like, one of the richest people in the world." Grey's eyebrows lifted, his eyes widened and fixed on Logan's.

It was almost a relief, basking in the rays of his fascination. It was better than facing his judgment. Nevertheless, the familiar ache of suffocating scrutiny crept over her.

"Don't look at me like that."

"Like what?"

"That look. Like if you were on the other side of the counter at the market, you'd try to gift wrap my groceries. I'm not an object. I'm a person." She knew from experience the only way to retain her humanity was to make sure he couldn't forget it. Waiters in restaurants could think what they like, but Grey's opinion of her mattered.

"Sorry. I've just never met anybody who had that kind of money before. It's like you had this whole life I can't even fathom."

"We had a lot of money, and it's true, I never gave a thought to how I spent it, but I'm probably not what you think. I wasn't into partying, and I wasn't a reckless diva. I wasn't mean to people who had less than me. I was no better than anybody else when I had a big checking account, and I'm no less now for having lost it."

"Okay. No awe. Just curiosity. So what was it like, having all that money?"

"To be able to do anything any time I wanted? It was normal. We had our own plane. I could go anywhere as long as I had my passport with me. I could get any table in any five-star restaurant by walking in the door. I could throw money at problems to solve them, and I can't anymore. I didn't ask for that life; I was born into it. I didn't have anything to do with my father's business. I'm not guilty of anything. I just want to make a life somewhere and start over without all the painful parts, but everything is so damn hard. I didn't know where to buy sheets. How to do laundry. I never even owned a real winter coat."

"What happened to all of your stuff? They just took your clothes and everything?"

"Not all of it. Just the high value stuff. But there was no use keeping it anyway. I wasn't going to need it, because I couldn't live in that world anymore."

"What about sisters or brothers?"

Logan shook her head. "Only child. My mom moved to France."

"That's awful. To have no one you can turn to, no place you can go where people get you."

"Tell me about it." Logan smoothed a loose thread in the sleeve of her hoodie against the seam. She couldn't afford for her warmest clothing to unravel. "No one knows more than me. The worst part was the threats. That's why you can't tell anyone. People sent me pictures they doctored of me in...really bad situations. They spit on me in the street when I was walking into the courthouse. I felt really unsafe then. I never knew when someone was going to lash out at me, and I don't want to go back to feeling that way."

"They'll forget. That's the way this stuff is. They'll move on to something else. I mean, no one bothers you in Ramsbolt, right?"

"No, they don't. I hope you're right, and they do move on. But I *need* privacy."

"So that's why you run off when people ask you questions. You're afraid they'll figure out who you are and some mob will show up."

"And that's why I can't do that competition. I can't be seen in New York." The truck wobbled when Logan shifted her weight and shook her head, an adamant exclamation point on her rejection. "And don't hate me. You're the only person who knows. I'm not trying to be sappy about it, but I could use a friend. Someone who knows the truth. I never liked being the kind of person I had to be to get along in that world. Household help and assistants and strange friends who aren't friends and *real* friendships that don't last because the money gets awkward or they can't go where you go. Maybe I can't hide from the threats and the anger forever, but I want to be the kind of person who belongs in a place like this. Okay?"

"I get it. I wouldn't want you to face that. Ramsbolt does take care of its own, though. What is it about Ramsbolt, anyway? Why here?"

"I wanted somewhere small. I took a bus north and got off in the smallest place I could find. Part of it was economic, I guess. I wanted my money to stretch as far as it could and bigger towns are more expensive. And I wanted to make my own way in the world. I guess I thought I'd be anonymous here, you know? That people in small towns have their own lives to live. You're not in each other's face all the time, so there's less gossip. Naive, I guess. But I love it here. I don't wanna have to leave."

CHAPTER TWENTY-ONE

The calendar app on her phone declared it the twenty-second of December. Three days before Christmas, and she was supposed to be at a children's hospital like she was every year, serving dinner to families stuck there for treatments. Her mother started the tradition as a tax deduction that came with a side order of good public relations. Her father tolerated the ritual, but Logan cherished it. She didn't want kids, but their unforced joy had a way of keeping the magic alive. Without it on her calendar, the season was a little emptier. A little colder. In Ramsbolt, she stood in line at the market, trying to convince herself it was just another day.

Christmas carols took their last dig at her while she paid for hot chocolate mix and a small box of animal crackers, the kind that looked like a train car with a little white fabric handle. She scrambled out the door and clomped back to her apartment to celebrate the season with the only childhood memories she could afford to relive.

She flopped on the foot of her bed, pried open the box of cookies, and ate them one by one while water heated on the stove. Even the animal crackers were different. There'd been no giraffes or hyenas when she

199

was a kid. Nothing was sacred anymore.

It was hard to think about Christmas without remembering Marta, the two of them sitting in forts made of sheets and pillows, watching Rudolph and Santa in classic stop motion animation films on VHS tapes, eating plates of sugar cookies and drinking hot chocolate from a thermos.

There were no traces of Marta on the internet. She'd looked a million times. After Marta was fired for not cleaning her father's office, a task that wasn't even in her job description, she disappeared from the house, and Logan never saw her again. Their driver once said Marta was in Philadelphia, but whether that was true or a rumor, Logan never learned. It seemed more reasonable to think she returned to her home in the Dominican Republic where Logan pictured her with a family of her own and a billion people to clean her house and wash her dozens of windows. The woman deserved it.

Logan did a quick Google search on her phone. Still no Marta on the internet.

She had hot chocolate, though, with its freeze-dried marshmallows. Not half as rich and creamy as Marta's but warm in a Cookie Monster thermos she got for a dollar from the antique store. And she found Helen's address without any trouble. With nowhere else to go and no festive obligation to tie her down, Logan walked four blocks to Helen's, Cookie Monster warming her hands.

It took some time for Helen to make it to the door, but she flung it open and gestured for Logan to enter, a warm welcome that made a bit of the dreary weather fall away. "It's wicked cold out there. Why are you walking all the way out here?"

Logan stepped into the cluttered but cozy living room. Every surface held a plant, but the same yellow film from decades of smoking that plagued the bar also covered every surface of Helen's home. The curtains were streaked with tawny drips of smoke pollution.

Logan followed Helen's outstretched hand to a tattered loveseat covered in pillows and hovered by it. Not wanting to seem ungrateful for the hospitality, she risked the soiling and took a seat, pleased she was wearing the same jeans as the day before. Mileage was everything when the laundromat ate your quarters.

"What brings you by?" Helen clasped her hands on her lap, lit by the kaleidoscope colors of the television on mute.

"I was lonely. This time of year always makes me want hot chocolate, and it's not nearly as yummy when you're by yourself. Want some?" Logan held out the thermos, and Helen smiled. "I'll get the mugs if you point me in the right direction."

"Above the little coffee maker." Helen pulled the lever on the side of her recliner, and the footrest shot into the air.

Logan strode to the kitchen. If not for the decor, Helen's house would mirror Arvil's, as if the town had sprung from the ground in a building boom with one genetic blueprint. She chose two mugs, one with a kitten and one that declared its contents to be wine. Steam rose from the thermos when she opened the cap, still hot despite the walk, and she filled the two cups.

Helen patted the drum table between them when Logan returned from the kitchen. "Place them here. Tell me what you're doing now. Did you find a job?"

"I haven't. I'm holding out hope. I know you said not to, and it seems a little stupid, but I really believe there's a chance."

Helen shook her head, a gentle dismissal. "I wish you wouldn't."

"There's a lot of farmland out there, right along the major roads that take you out of Maine. If we set up a partnership with a local farm, we could open up a bar, a brewery or a distillery even, and attach it to a restaurant. People would go a long way for something like that."

"It's a lot of liability."

"That's what insurance is for." Logan caught Helen's side-eye. "Good insurance. I looked into it, and it's not that hard. It could be really profitable with a few small investors to help with up-front expenses like equipment and construction."

"Logan. I don't want to break your spirit. That does sound like a very good business idea, and maybe you could pursue it, but I can't help. My debts were big before the fire, and they're not getting any smaller. Bills still arrive, and I still have to pay them. And taxes. The tax man cometh whether the profit caught on fire or not."

"What if the answer were easy? What if someone came along and did the hard work?"

"I don't have it in me anymore. You're a really smart young lady..." Helen tugged at the hem of her shawl, pulling on a loose thread. "I shouldn't say that. You're a smart woman. In just a few months, you transformed that bar. Everybody knows it. I was terrible. Mostly because I hide from anything that seems hard. I wasn't always like this."

"You said that before. But what changed? You're too young to retire, and I'm not saying that because I'm being selfish. I'm saying that because women ten years older than you are still obsessing about their companies and don't want to quit. You're entitled, if that's what you want, but look around you. You quit smoking ten years ago, and this place still looks like you smoke a carton a day. No offense, it's lovely. But ten years and you never got up and cleaned? You retired from *you*."

Slumped in her chair and picking at the loose threads of her shawl,

Helen seemed little more than parts of the person she once was. She certainly wasn't the same woman who'd run a much-loved diner.

"Helen. Come on. I like you too much, and I owe you too much, not to try to help you up. We need to pick each other up, here. I just can't accept that this is all there is to it. That this is how it all ends."

"I have to cancel the lease at the end of February. That's when it would have been renewed. There's no way Arvil will let me renew it. He's already told me that." Helen set her mug on a coaster and reached for a tissue. She moved slow like honey, as if movement were draining. Logan had accepted Helen's molasses movements as bad knees and the stress of a larger frame, but as Helen's tears fell, she couldn't dismiss the impact of her mental state on the picture as a whole. Helen dabbed at tears below her eyelashes.

"Keeping myself afloat doesn't mean what it used to. It used to mean putting food on the table and paying the mortgage, but the house is paid off, and I stopped caring if I drown or not. It's a big commitment, jumping into something else when I don't even know if I can get out of bed every morning."

"I am not going to let you drown in this. Every time I tell you there's hope, you give me a reason there isn't. What if I told you, for sure, that there is hope out there? That it's real, and I'm going to find it. What if you didn't have to do the hard work to find the door, and the door just opened for you, would you walk through it?"

Helen's fingers ran along the stitching on the arm of her recliner.

"It's not just about me," said Logan. "Or you. The town really misses the bar."

"I know they do. I was at the newsstand, and Warren said how much he missed it. I saw Riley on the way to my car. He said nobody got together anymore. Without the bar, there's no place for people to talk about things. I destroyed it, because I didn't care enough."

"That's not true." Logan cursed Arvil for planting that seed, for making her believe she wasn't good enough. "You did the best you could. It doesn't matter. Looking back isn't going to help you move forward. There are two of us here, and we can do even more now. This town needs a place to be a community. They're all out there waiting. What if you got the money to pay off Arvil? We could fight him for the right to build there again. He'll cave; I know he will. We just have to give him the money."

"And where are we going to get that kind of money?"

Good question. She'd wasted so much of it on selfish endeavor. Now that she wanted to do something real with it, it was so far out of reach.

Would her father's old friends do her a favor and give her a loan to secure her future far from town? Many of them had escaped consequences when her father agreed to plead guilty. One of them must feel some sense of obligation. It was a scant sum to them and absolution of guilt on their part, if she found the right people and the right questions to ask.

And there was her uncle, eager to help her mother and generous with the space on his farm. Logan would never accept her mother's money, but for the right cause, she could be inclined to take a loan from a man who made his way in legitimate business. But Helen lacked the confidence to extend promises to investors, even if Logan could ensure it would be profitable.

That left the competition. She could sacrifice, take a trip to New York. She could end up on the cover of a tabloid. The consequences could be dire if she were splashed all over the newsstand and lined up on the magazine rack at the market. Losing the bar and not being able to pay for her apartment would suck even more. Being rejected by the town, by the people she'd grown to care for, would be worse, a second exile from a second home. It would be more heartbreak than she could bear. But what if no one noticed her in New York? If she blended into the scenery and returned to Ramsbolt unscathed? What if Grey was right, and nobody cared about her father's crimes, his reputation? With too much life of its own to live, Ramsbolt might let her live hers in peace. Best case scenario, they saw in her what she saw in them. Someone who worked hard to get by, helping others along the way. Someone worthy of redemption.

"Helen, I think I know what to do. This is going to sound strange, but do you have Grey's phone number?"

"I do. Everyone in this town does. He did some plumbing here at the house when the pipe in the kitchen froze a few years ago. He's been doing small things at the bar... did work for the bar for years."

Helen lowered the footrest and pushed herself up from the recliner. It rocked when she stood.

"Can I ask you one other thing? You can say no, but maybe another set of eyes on the lease will help? Would it be okay if I looked?"

"It couldn't hurt, I guess." Helen used the edge of the chair for support. "It's in the filing cabinet back here."

Logan carried their empty mugs to the kitchen and left them by the sink. Except for a few dishes, the room was clean and cozy. A spider plant hung from a hook in the ceiling by the back door, its wafty tendrils dripping toward the floor. The fridge was covered in pictures, like the bar had been. Happy moments with contented patrons. Logan recognized some. Others, she assumed, were long gone.

Helen's feet shuffled across the linoleum. "Some of these pictures are very old."

"I can tell. This one may be older than me."

"I suspect it might be. Midseventies, I guess. We couldn't fit half as many cars in that parking lot, they were all so big. Terrible things. Smelled awful back then." She extended a scrap of paper and a few stapled pieces of legal document. "Grey's cell phone number for you. And this is the lease. I need this back, though."

"I'll take good care of it. Promise. And thanks." Logan tucked Grey's number into her back pocket. "There are no guarantees in life, right? I don't know what the outcome will be, but I'm not giving up, and you can't either. You sit tight while I go out there and try."

"What does Grey have to do with this?"

Logan waved a hand. "I left something in his truck."

"You and Grey?" Helen tilted her chin, a curious smile spreading across her face.

"No, not like that. He's been very nice since the fire."

Helen patted Logan's arm and used it as leverage as she turned back to the living room. "This town is full of supportive people."

"I promise not to wear out my welcome. And I swear that I will pay back every ounce of kindness. Just hang tight, okay?"

Logan shrugged into her coat and stepped outside into the coldest air she'd ever felt, freezing her cheeks and numbing her nose. A cold front pushed in behind already freezing air, and her gratitude for the coat warmed her even more. She pulled her phone from her pocket, made a new contact for Grey and sent him a quick text message.

It's Logan. I left something in your truck. Can I catch up with you today?

His response came before she'd plucked her gloves from her coat pocket.

Reg packet, right? Lunch? Meet at the market at noon?

CHAPTER TWENTY-TWO

Logan waited for Grey inside the market, out of the wind and chill. Customers came and went. With each ringing of the bell, heat from the store escaped onto the street, and gusts of icy air pushed in to fill the void. She declined an offer of help from a girl stocking the shelves, and instead browsed the dairy products. The cases were far from the door and icy blasts of December air. She craved a big breakfast. Eggs and milk. Bacon and yogurt.

"Breakfast for lunch?" Grey's voice preceded his footsteps.

That would mean cooking. Inviting Grey into her apartment. Letting someone see how small she lived, how raw. He already knew the worst of her secrets, so letting him in on the small ones couldn't hurt. "If you don't mind my cooking. My place is tiny, but I can make pancakes." The trick was to keep the heat low. She'd eaten a lot of burned pancakes to learn that valuable lesson.

Grey opened a door to the dairy refrigerator and grabbed eggs. "I won't turn down an offer like that on a cold day like this."

Logan snagged the bacon. She let him pay, a gesture that still hurt when he offered it and added to the debt she owed him and the town. She climbed the stairs to her apartment, Grey in her wake. She couldn't recall if she'd made her bed, if her clothes were neatly folded and placed in the dresser, if the bathroom was tidy.

"I hope it's clean. You'll forgive me if it's not, right?"

"It can't be worse than my place." Grey stopped on the stairs behind her while she unlocked the door. "I'm a plumber, so I've seen a lot of mess. Makes you numb to it."

She appreciated that he would forgive her mess, even if she was horrified at the thought of what he lived in. "This is it." She pushed the door open. "One room. And a bathroom."

Logan saw her apartment for the first time through someone else's eyes, and it wasn't as bad as her wounded ego made her believe. Her tiny table and two mismatched chairs looked rustic and loved against the buttercream yellow walls, though the table was still covered in Helen's old ledgers. The counters were clean, but for the ancient French press she found at the antique shop when she added to her collection of plates, cups, and bowls. Her unicorn sheets were hidden beneath a blue comforter. It wasn't much, but it wasn't an embarrassment.

"So this is it, huh? The famous apartment for wayward souls?" Grey set the eggs and bacon on the counter.

Logan hung her coat over the back of a chair. "This is it. It's a pretty exclusive address, I hear."

"Indeed. Penthouse, even." Grey shrugged out of his jacket and handed it over. It smelled like cologne applied not too long ago. "How do you like living here?"

"Not bad." She draped his coat over the back of the other chair. "That's not true. I hated it. I still do. It's small and suffocating. It can be lonely up here, and it gets really quiet at night. I'm used to knowing there are things to do if you leave home and go out into the world. New York never sleeps."

"What's all this stuff?" Grey ran a hand over the cover of a black leather-bound book of Helen's records.

"That is every bill Helen ever paid and every day's income." Logan lifted the books and placed them on the floor. "I was going through all of this, looking for ways to cut corners. I found a lot, but then the bar burned down. I have to get these back to her eventually. Coffee?"

"Sure. Paper bookkeeping. That's crazy."

"Not how my father did business, that's for sure. Just another bit of culture shock." Logan put grounds in her French press and heated water on the stove.

"Must be strange moving from a place like New York to this. I've never been to New York, but just from TV, it seems chaotic and loud and dangerous to me. Too much going on."

"You get used to the sensory overload, I guess. Here, I'm alone with my thoughts. There's a lot to think about, and sometimes I could use a distraction."

"What kind of stuff did you do in New York?"

"Shopping. Hanging out. I didn't live in the city, but my dad had an office there that was a lot like a condo. We stayed there sometimes. We lived in a house on the Hudson. It was quiet at night. I had a big yard with lots of trees, and I played a lot of video games."

She pulled two small skillets, both older than her, from a lower cabinet and placed them on the stove. She made pancakes in one while Grey tended eggs in the other. Bacon sizzled on a baking sheet in her tiny oven, and for the first time, Logan's apartment smelled like a home. They talked about growing up, being connected to the soil of their home and struggling to find a sense of belonging anywhere else. The more they discovered what set them apart, the more they found New York had in common with Ramsbolt.

"I know I'm the one who pushed you to enter this competition, and now I feel like I have to play devil's advocate. You were afraid of unmasking yourself and asking for trouble. Have you thought this through all the way?" Grey scooped scrambled eggs from the pan onto two plates.

"I've thought about it a lot. Mostly at two in the morning. There are too many unknowns. I read the news, but I don't do social media anymore, so I wouldn't know what people are saying. It's hard to see the forest for the trees when people are sending you hateful messages, you know, to tell what's a real threat and what's just someone spouting off? But I have to keep living. I can't be afraid forever." Logan added hot water to the French press and stirred it. "I still wonder sometimes if the town would turn against me if they found out, but I don't think so. I'd have to move if this fails anyway, to find a job, but that just means I have to work harder to win."

Though she couldn't admit it, the hurt she feared the most wasn't from strangers but people she used to know. Those empty relationships with people like Elizabeth played no role in her life anymore, but her pride would still take a beating, knowing they laughed at her and mocked her for the fall.

Grey took two cups from the shelf. "What about the terms and conditions."

"What do you mean, terms and conditions?"

"Of the contest. If you win, and that's your goal, there are promotional materials, pictures, social media, magazines. They put your picture and the winning recipe in emails and stuff like that."

Of course there'd be pictures and press releases. She hadn't thought that far, past the consequences of cashing a check. It stung, but it didn't change anything. Just another consequence, falling dominoes she couldn't control.

"The packet's out in my truck. I read it last night. I wanted all the ammunition I could get to convince you to do it."

"And now you're trying to change my mind?"

"No, not like that. I'm trying to make sure you know what you're getting into. When all this started, I thought you were being shy. I didn't know there were actual consequences. Now I'm just making sure that all the bases are covered."

Logan took utensils from the drawer. She could take care of herself just fine. "You don't have to worry about me."

"It's kinda hard not to." Grey's voice was barely audible over the sound of the creaking floor as Logan carried everything to the table. She lay utensils in their proper position by their plates. Old habits die hard. "There is another way, you know. In case you want to make sure you've exhausted all your options."

"If it involves not competing against people with more experience than me in a competition I'm bound to lose, I'm all ears."

Grey skimmed coffee grounds from the French press and lowered the plunger. He poured coffee into their cups and sank into the wooden chair. Leaning across the table, his eyes twinkling, he said, "You *could* be your father's daughter."

"What's that supposed to mean?" Logan speared eggs with her fork, and they crumbled.

"Set Arvil straight. Rage at him. I bet your father was a scary man when he wanted to be. Pull out all the stops, and do what he would have done."

"I tried that. Well, not to my father's exact playbook, but I tried to pressure him. It didn't work. You saw us in the park."

"What would your dad have done? Screamed?"

"Hardly." Her father plotted the demise of his enemies in silence, from behind a solid walnut door. And when he had a plan, he pounced like a panther. Silent and unseen. "If this were his problem, he would have bought the bar and the land and thrown so many lawyers at Arvil that he would suffocate under the angry letters. There would be unreasonable deadlines for producing documents and statements filed to keep him on edge. The paperwork would have been endless. And just when Arvil started to slip, some public accusation, even a total lie in some tabloid, would set his family against him. Arvil would beg for mercy." She speared a sliver of pancake with her fork and wagged it in Grey's direction. "You see, everyone has a breaking point."

"That seems harsh." Maple syrup dripped from the triangle of pancake at the end of Grey's fork.

"It was. But it didn't seem that way at the time. That's just what my father did, and it felt like part of doing business, like a defense mechanism you build up in a game of business warfare. But now it all seems different. Dirty."

"And you don't want to be like that."

"Of course not." Logan smoothed the paper towel on her lap. "He would have ruined Arvil. He's just a lonely man trying to make money off some land he owns in a small town."

"He's not that lonely. He's got kids."

"Here?"

"No. They live in Florida or something, with kids and lives of their own."

"That makes it even worse. He has enablers."

"I'd be an enabler, too, if I stood to inherit a sprawling estate like Arvil's. That tiny, haunted-looking house and a plot of burned land? It's a pot of gold at the end of a rainbow." Sarcasm dripped from Grey's voice. He finished the last of his eggs. "And he's not that nice of a guy. He's had his neighbors' cars towed, he screams at kids for trick or treating. He deserves whatever he gets."

"Well, I've got enough trouble. I need to find a legitimate way to handle this that doesn't involve dirty tricks." Or trying to stab scrambled eggs with a fork.

"I just don't get how he can deny you the right to rebuild the place. It's probably in the contract somewhere that if something happens, Helen can rebuild."

"Tried that, too. Helen wouldn't budge. She's depressed. She's given up. But when I asked her if she'd embrace a solution if one were put in front of her, she seemed hopeful. She didn't promise me anything, but I said I would try."

"So you're in it to win it then."

"I guess so."

Grey set his plate by the sink. "I'll run down and get that packet, and help you clean up."

There was more at stake than a few thousand dollars on her way to clearing Helen's debt and bringing her back to the living. Giving the town its bar back meant sticking it to Arvil, knocking him down a peg and seeing a small-town version of her father lose a battle in the war of right and wrong.

The only time she saw her father suffer was when he couldn't beat the system, when no lawyer or public perception campaign would bring his enemy to his knees. Logan would have to use the system to cripple Arvil, and when she was done, she would make her own life, instead of living in the shadow of Lorne Cole.

Grey's footsteps on the stairs preceded him, and he dropped the letter-sized envelope on the counter before rolling up his sleeves. "Want me to wash?"

She tossed him a towel. "Wanna dry?"

"Sure."

Water dripped from a clean plate into the sink. When the stream turned to dribbles, she handed it off. "There's gonna be some stiff competition. I may not win this thing. Compared to the experience these other people have, this whole thing seems stupid, but I have to try."

"Maybe you can get Arvil to agree to some terms before you take the risk. Get some kind of agreement out of him that you can throw in his face if he still puts up a fight."

"Good idea." Logan handed him another plate. "This is probably the only time in my life that I've had to compete for something, instead of getting it by default because I knew the right people or had the right last name. It's horrifying."

CHAPTER TWENTY-THREE

Logan waved goodbye to Grey and stepped into the street, away from the afternoon thaw that dripped from awnings. She crossed the road and spent three dollars on a Christmas card with a wreath on the front, borrowed a pen at the register to sign it, and kept to the street, hopping over puddles, on her way to Arvil's house.

The sour timbre of vinegar between her and Arvil hadn't served either of them well. Honey wasn't easy to pull out of thin air, but she painted her face with a generic business smile to cover her reservations, wearing the mask of a woman out to woo her enemy. It was the same smile her mother wore when she complimented the undeserving that had made Logan's skin crawl. It felt skeevy to wear it, but it was for a good cause.

On his porch, black water splashed from the gutter onto her coat. The house didn't offer her a warm welcome, and she didn't expect one from Arvil either, if he even bothered to open the door. She brushed the sludge from her sleeve and knocked. Through the closed door she could hear the faint hum of a machine. A vacuum cleaner.

Arvil flung the door open and faced her with the look of a man who tasted bile. "What the hell do you want?"

She extended the card. "Merry Christmas."

The unexpected gesture carried enough power to force him upright and put a suspicious glint in his eye. "What do I want with this?"

"Jesus, Arvil. It's a Christmas card. You came to the bar every day, and I want to spread a little holiday joy. See?" She shook the card at him. "It's joyous. Just a card."

"I don't need a card from you."

Logan cocked her head to the side and let half her face smile. "You don't need anything from anybody, but a festive holiday greeting won't hurt you, will it?"

He ripped the card from her hand. "You don't need to come in, do you?"

"I suppose not." She shoved her hands in her pockets and shrugged. "I just wanted to say Merry Christmas. And I'm sorry."

Arvil leaned his weight on the door knob and amusement crossed his face. "You're sorry, huh? You tell the whole town you're sorry?"

"I will. But I wanted to say thank you, too. Because you pushed me to learn more and work harder, and because of that, I'm going to a bartending competition next month. I wouldn't have learned all I did and come so far without the little shove, so thanks."

"Letting all the heat out." Arvil stepped out onto the porch, clusters of ice crunching beneath his moccasin slippers. He pulled the door shut and folded his arms. "Let me tell you something. You are grasping at straws, child. You aren't confident enough to be a good bartender, and you aren't competent enough to win a competition. Those two are inseparable. You can't become competent if you're not confident. But people like you need competence in order to gain confidence. That's how I know you're going nowhere."

Arvil was an immovable mountain. All she could do was smile at him and take a small pleasure in seeing him unnerved. "Thank you for the advice. Can I ask you something, though? I sometimes wonder if you wanted me to fail. Because if Helen kept losing money, you'd have justification for not letting her renew her lease."

"That's quite an accusation."

"No, not accusing you of anything. Just curious. It seems like you were really angry at even the smallest things. And louder than you needed to be to make your point. Almost like you were trying to get other people to be angry right along with you. I didn't want to think that about you, that you were trying to sabotage Helen at all. So I thought I'd ask why? Why all the histrionics? There must have been a reason."

The glint snuffed out of Arvil's eyes. "So what if I want more money out of my investment? That bar's been sinking for longer than you'll live here. I'm not a charity. I told you before, there's no obligation in our contract to let her accrue a lot of debt. You can call it greed if you want, but it's not against the law to run a profitable business."

Logan folded her arms and looked down at his slippers. They were getting wet, probably soaking water into his socks. If she didn't strike soon, he would turn from her, go back inside where he would shake his head and toss the card in the trash. Maybe like her father, he would put it on a mantel where it would sit as a reminder of the prey he hadn't yet eaten, a stash saved for the lean winter months. But she wasn't done. She wasn't prey.

She was the only one in this town who could break Arvil down, because she was the only one who spoke his language, who knew how to use business to manipulate people, and the stakes were high. Winning the competition would mean nothing without his assurance that they could rebuild the bar. And to get it, she would have to force Arvil to make the next move. To turn the tables and make him need that bar on his land. She couldn't just lay it on him. He had to beg. And that's how she would know he heard her loud and clear.

Logan lifted her eyes from Arvil's slippers. "Like you said, your karma's your business. Your shoes are getting wet, though, so I'll let you go." She turned to leave, knowing he would stop her, that he would need the last word.

"I don't care what you think. You know that, right? You're just a wayward traveler who couldn't hack it anywhere else. You brought no value to this town, and now you'll just have to pack up and go annoy someone else. I don't know why you keep picking at this."

Her back to Arvil, she let herself smile, chewing on a chapped lower lip to hide her pleasure, then spun on her heel to face him. If only he knew. "I keep picking because you have no legal basis to keep Helen from rebuilding. If she comes up with the money and clears the debt before the end of her lease, you have no reason to expel her from the land. You've been letting her think all this time that she's in more debt than she is, because you think she'll just walk away."

"What are you talking about? She's a disorganized woman who can't run a business."

"No. She's not. She's depressed, and she needs a little hope, but she's not disorganized." Logan reached inside her coat and pulled out the lease. "She keeps pretty good records, actually. Every bill she ever paid written out in ledgers like it's the turn of the century. Anyway, she's been signing extensions of this original lease she signed with you back on..." Logan flipped to the back page. "February third of 1981. That was a long time ago. So, sure, you both might forget the details."

Arvil rolled his eyes. "Here we go. Little girl thinks she knows how to read a lease."

"Oh, it's not hard to read a lease. And I also know how to find every record of her paying rent in the bar's books. But here's the important bit. Paragraph three." Logan flipped back to the first page and read aloud. "If fees or late changes are accrued to the Lessee's account, payments made to the account, rent or otherwise, are to be first applied to any accrued fees and second to any utilities, prior to being applied to rent payments. Do you know what this means?"

Arvil's face scrunched into lines of anger. "Of course I know what that means."

"You've been telling Helen something different. You let her believe that past due interest was accruing on bills she hadn't paid years ago. That's not true. If you back out the interest you're not entitled to charge by the terms of this original contract, she's not five thousand in the hole. She's sixteen hundred in the hole. And I have the receipts to prove it."

His every breath seemed labored, like an effort driven by his rage.

Logan plowed on. Victory really did taste sweet. "Basically, because nothing in the contract explicitly says so, if she gets current on the last few months' rent, you'll have to let her rebuild. You can't stand in her way."

"I can do what I want."

"No, you can't."

"That's my land."

"But you signed a contract. And I can guarantee you that you'll make more money if you renew it than if you don't. Because there isn't a judge in this country that would side with you if you try to crush that woman to satisfy your own gluttony, and you'd be on the hook for all the legal fees when you lost."

Logan stopped before she said too much, before she gave away how she knew about real estate. Arvil's nostrils flared in a last gasp of defiance, but his shoulders fell, and Logan recognized the slow death of hubris. She'd seen it from her father as they put handcuffs on him and led him from the courthouse.

"Arvil, this doesn't have to be so hard. Everybody's afraid of the future. We're all trying to build safety nets so we can take care of ourselves. Some of us just forget that we can do that without depriving someone else of the same right. You don't have to be so lonely."

He lifted his head and spit his words. "What do you know about being lonely? I'm not lonely. Opposite. I'd appreciate it if you got off my property."

"I know what lonely looks like. It looks like that." Logan waved the rolled-up lease toward his front door, to the dark and dingy home within. "You're terrified of being alone, but greed is a habit that destroys your ability to connect with people. You just take and take."

"Don't tell me—"

"You sit in a bar next to these people every night, and you can't even see that they need each other. Or maybe you do see it, and you're jealous that they have someplace to go, and that they get something out of that place that you don't think you deserve, because you're so deep into this isolated grumpy guy thing that no one wants to be around you. If you push them all away first, they won't be able to reject you."

"How many times do I have to tell you that I don't need these people?"

"Fine. If greed is the real reason, then you'll accept Helen's money when I give it to you. You'll let her get current and let her rebuild, however long it takes." Her work was done. She'd proved her point. She turned and took a long stride over a muddy puddle in his broken sidewalk.

"Fine." His voice boomed and echoed off the brick homes. "I'll get plenty of satisfaction out of watching this whole thing crash and burn, and everyone will know I was right. They don't need that bar. They'd be better off with a place to work."

Logan didn't care what he told himself or how he justified doing the right thing. "What's in your best interest doesn't have a dollar sign in front of it, Arvil. I'm sure you're smart enough to figure that out without some kid spelling it out for you."

* * *

Logan sipped a blueberry whiskey sour, a new concoction that needed some work but brought a tough day to a sweet end. She slid her finger under the lip of the letter-sized envelope and gave herself a papercut that she stuck in her mouth. She scowled at the small streak of blood on the flap.

"Nice try," she said.

She shook the envelope and application pages tumbled onto her little kitchen table. It asked for the usual information. Contact details. Questions about the bar where she worked. Payment information for her registration fee. There were questions about the cocktails she wished to enter, the type of drink, the type of primary liquor. They wanted two drinks, a modification on a classic and another that represented how she felt about the place she called home. And they wanted an essay. They wanted her to explain why that drink represented her feelings about home.

Home.

Why did it have to be that? The one thing she didn't have.

Logan had phoned in every test she'd ever taken. She'd met the requirements for graduation not as an accomplishment, but as an obligation. She didn't need to write grand essays to earn a place at Yale or secure her seat at the head of her family's foundation. And in the face of objection, all she had to do was pull some money from a jewel-covered purse, buy the headmaster a drink, and remind him that, for the school, so much depended upon the satisfaction of its benefactors. But this time, it was personal. And knowing they didn't give points for good grammar and punctuation didn't take the edge off the fact that what she had to say really mattered.

Ice settled in her glass, and a wild blueberry bobbed to the surface. What did it mean to her, those frozen blueberries she got from Helen, the local honey, and the thyme she simmered with them to make that syrup? She'd arrived in Ramsbolt a vagabond, displaced and dispossessed by circumstance. On her walk from the bus to Helen's Tavern, she couldn't miss the blueberry bushes growing in yards and empty lots. She'd endured the bitter chill of a cloudy autumn day on her way to a better life. It may not look like much, her life or those bushes, but they thrived in Ramsbolt despite the odds. It was supposed to be a stepping stone to something else for her, a place to pass the time until fortune came around again. But while she was waiting, she'd taken root, and now she couldn't imagine calling any other place her home. Like the blueberries that bordered Ramsbolt's yards and lined its crooked sidewalks, her life there was rich in aspect and indelible in spirit.

CHAPTER TWENTY-FOUR

Logan leaned across the post office counter and peered through the doorway to the back room. All she needed was one stamp. "Hello? Riley? Anybody home?"

"That you, Logan?" Riley's voice echoed from the storage room, followed by a crash of cardboard boxes.

"Yup. I need to mail something."

Boxes shuffled. "Just one stamp? Do you have exact change?"

"No, but it's only three cents. You can keep the change." Every penny mattered, but she wasn't going to put that much importance on three of them.

"You can peel one off the display there. One of those flag stamps. Just leave the change on the counter."

"You got it." Logan left two quarters on the counter and took a stamp. She pressed it onto the envelope, running her thumbnail over every corner. If she was going to diminish her savings to enter that contest, the $250 entry fee better get there unscathed.

With only two months' rent left in her savings and a little to spare, things would be tight. But two days before Christmas was hardly the time to fret about what she didn't have.

Logan let the envelope fall into the outgoing mail slot and hoped that somewhere, someone needed part time help, and she could at least make enough money to afford a New York hotel room for the length of the competition. At the very least, maybe Grey would teach her to drive, and she could borrow his truck to sleep in. Desperate times called for desperate measures.

"Thanks, Riley! Quarters are by the register."

"You got it. Merry Christmas, if I don't see ya."

"Same to you!" Logan stepped out onto the street, and the door slammed closed behind her. She sat on the bench outside the post office, as close to holiday tradition as she could get without a feast of her own to attend. People walked in ones and twos between the market and their cars, resting paper bags on their hips while they opened car doors. A toddler crashed through a thin film of ice and splashed in a puddle while his mother loaded the car. All the things Logan missed out on as a kid came into focus. Shopping. Cooking. Decorating. She didn't even know who'd done their food shopping. The cook would bring out a turkey or goose and all of the trimmings on Christmas evening, and the help ate in their common area or with their families. All that help seemed a cheap trade for empty tradition.

She slipped her phone from her coat pocket and texted Grey.

I did it. Reg form mailed! Thanks for the encouragement.

Ellipses flashed across the screen, Grey crafting his response. She lay the phone on her lap. Pigeons roosting in lampposts flew to the ground to pick at pebbles and crumbs, a seasonal feast of their own. Her phone buzzed.

Celebrate?

She wanted to say yes to the distraction, to the friendship. But if she was going to get the bar back, she needed to study. *I should head to the library b4 they close. Need books to study.* It would keep her occupied for the next few days, at least.

More ellipses. *Practice and celebrate? I'll bring stuff.*

His persistence was charming and irresistible. *K. After 4? Going to library first.*

4 is good. We can run to market for anything I forget.

Perfect. See u then. She deliberated over a happy emoji. An exclamation point. Then left it alone and hit send.

She tucked her phone in her back pocket and aimed for the library, two blocks behind the newsstand, nestled among houses on a residential street. She would need a library card this time and was glad Sandy was at the desk, hoping the rapport they'd established would buy her some privacy. If Sandy even figured it out.

Logan closed the door behind her, the first step to pleasing the librarian.

Sandy lowered her tablet. "Hey, Logan."

"Hey, Sandy. I could really use a library card this time."

The drawer slid open, and a manila folder landed on the desk. Sandy held up a piece of paper, a form as old as the books within. "You need a pencil or a pen?"

"Nah, I'm good." Logan filled out the form. Her full name. Her social security number. Her address and phone number. For so few fields, it was a monumental admission. She handed it to Sandy with a steady hand and searched her face for any sign of recognition. None came.

If Sandy put the pieces together, she didn't let it show when she handed the card across the desk. "I'm really sorry about the bar."

Logan accepted the plastic card and tucked it in her back pocket. "Me, too."

"Riley said it's done. Over. Helen's not rebuilding it."

"Maybe not." Logan didn't stick around for the conversation. Time was short. "But I'm working on a plan."

Sandy's chair rolled into the wall behind her when she stood and followed. "Really? Tell."

"There's a bar competition, and if I win it, I might be able to pay off some debt and save the bar." Pulling books from shelves, Logan paused. "Is there a limit?"

"It's supposed to be six, but if there's a good enough reason, I can make an exception."

"Awesome." Logan handed a stack to Sandy, who fell back at the weight of them.

"You really think you can get the bar back?"

"Maybe. But I have a lot of studying to do first."

"Well, keep them coming, then."

* * *

"Why are you making a gold rush if you're not making it at the event?" Grey opened the fridge and scanned the shelves for the bottle of lemon juice. "I thought your specialty cocktails were the blueberry thing and that whiskey sour?"

"They are, but they're also going to surprise us with a classic, and I want to be prepared. It's there, behind that milk." Logan reached past him and collected the bottle. She squeezed lemon juice into a little plastic measuring cup.

"I still think you should have used fresh."

"It's just practice. Real lemons get expensive." Logan added the lemon to a shaker. "It might taste a little better, but I need to cut corners right now."

"Talk about cutting corners. I should have cut out the drinking two drinks ago. How much did you say?" He wobbled when he put the bottle back in the fridge.

"Three quarters of an ounce. You should sit."

"Nah, I'm good. I'm really not that much of a lightweight." He took a seat at the table, though, and ran a hand through his curls while Logan finished making a drink for herself.

She poured the last of the honey syrup into a container left over from wonton soup and tucked it in the fridge. Taking the seat next to him, she propped her elbows on the table and looked through the glass. "Drinks are a lot clearer when you use fresh juice, too. Still tastes great, though."

"Tell me about it." Grey tugged his baseball hat back on his head. "You make a great drink."

"Thanks." She touched his arm, a gesture of gratitude too close to affection. She recoiled from it and wrapped her hand around the drink, letting her fingers get cold. "Thanks for your advice. You know a lot more than you thought you did."

"See? And now you know enough to be able to say that." He placed a hand over hers. "I really enjoyed tonight. Obviously."

It would be a terrible idea if he stayed. As much as Logan wanted comfort, and as good as he was at offering it, she knew her need would leave him dry. She couldn't possibly give as much as she'd take. But she couldn't bear for him to leave, either. "You shouldn't drive."

His eyes held hers for an eternity. "Where will you stay?"

Ice settled in her glass, and Logan tore away, took a sip. "What do you mean?"

"In New York. For the competition. You can't afford a hotel room."

She centered her glass over a scratch in the table's surface and peered through her drink at the dividing line. "I haven't given it a lot of thought yet. I'm kinda hoping a miracle happens." She had thought about it, about calling Jill and asking for a place to crash or looking up a guy she used to date and begging for a couch to sleep on. But nothing felt right.

"I got this." Grey leaned to the side and reached for his phone on the counter. "One room with two beds."

For all the drinks, her mouth went dry. If he came along, she wouldn't celebrate success alone. But he would be there if she stumbled, and he would see her fall.

"You don't have to do this." It took far too few clicks for him to find a place to stay. "You already had it planned out, though, didn't you?"

"I hoped you'd let me go with. I bookmarked some places near that colosseum or whatever the place is where that thing is held. Figured I could at least cheer you on. I mean, I followed you this far."

That he did. When he wasn't following her, he was pushing her along. "It's just a convention center. And we got this far. Why wouldn't I let you go?" Logan gave him a playful shove.

"Someone had to do it, or this would end up a dry town." Grey adjusted his hat. "No pressure. It's not a date. It's just a thing. Okay?"

Logan couldn't find the words to suit her gratitude. She wasn't used to accepting generosity. That it wasn't a date, that he had no expectations, took the weight off.

"Consider it my investment in the bar." He leaned close and whispered. "I know you hate to accept gifts."

"I am going to repay you for all of this one day."

He waved a hand, pushing the notion aside. "So are you ready to have your name out there?"

"I think so. You think the town would treat me any different?"

"Maybe. They'll probably have some questions. Like why did you feel it was necessary to hide who you really are. And what was it like living in that big house and flying to New Zealand because you wanted a snack."

"I never did that. I did fly to London for dinner a few times and to Belgium for chocolate because theirs is the best." Logan tipped her head back and closed her eyes. "I miss Belgian chocolate."

"I don't even know the difference."

"Someday I will get you Belgian chocolate." Logan downed the last of her drink and carried their glasses to the counter. "I've been thinking about that safety thing, and I'm not afraid like I was before. Maybe it's because I feel like I belong here now. When I left New York, I was running from trolls and threats and looking for anonymity. I didn't think that Ramsbolt would be the kind of place where people take care of each other, you know. I don't think they'll turn on me the way New York did."

"I'm telling you, nobody in Ramsbolt cares about your father. Maybe it has something to do with money. I met a guy who won the lottery once. He was saying how it was nice to have all that cash, but everybody got jealous and started treating him like shit. Maybe New York was so hard on you because you had so much to start with. In Ramsbolt, nobody has anything."

"Maybe some of it was the joy of seeing the mighty fall, but a lot of people lost money when my father went to jail. And among our friends, where we were financial equals, it was really bad. We were shunned. It feels dirty to say it, *financial equals*, but it's true. You're ranked by wealth in that world, and everyone is so fake. I never really knew those people, and they sure didn't have my back." Logan dumped ice from the shaker and collected dirty dishes in the sink. "This might be the first time I really wanted to do something for the right reason. It's not about winning the competition. Even if I lose it, I know I did this for Helen and for the town. And in spite of Arvil, you know? He tried to make me believe I couldn't do this. I *am* worthy of that competition, and I'm just as capable of winning it as anyone else."

Grey reached past her for the dish detergent. He nudged her out of the way and drizzled blue soap over the mountain of glass and plastic. "I'm really proud of you, you know that? I couldn't have done what you did."

"Sure you could have."

"Are you going anywhere for Christmas?"

She took a clean dish towel from a drawer, leaned back against the counter, and folded her arms. "It's my first Christmas here. My first Christmas with no family. I figured I'd call my mom and read those books."

"We used to have these great Christmas mornings when I was a kid, as long as my dad wasn't being a dick. I'll be alone, too. Why don't we do something? I can call Helen, and the three of us can get together? No gifts, just good company."

Logan dried off the first clean glasses. "That sounds like a really nice idea."

A delicate silence fell between them, broken by water running and the clink of glasses. She stacked cups in the cabinet. Grey's curls covered his eyes. His hands washed a delicate yellow plate adorned with flowers, his sleeves of his thick black hoodie pushed up his forearms. Grey, the guy who sat across the bar washing her used dishes, teased at a domesticity

Logan had never needed.

And he was drunk. She couldn't let him drive. "If you need to stay—"

"Nah, I'm good. It's just a few blocks. Almost a straight line."

"But you shouldn't. What if—" She didn't want him to stay. It would be a mistake. But she didn't want him to go, either.

"I could walk, but I don't want to leave my truck out front."

"It's a safe place to park. Cars are out there all the time. Besides, what could happen in Rambsolt?"

"It's not that." Grey washed the last dish and dried his hands on a plain white towel. "I don't want to do that to you. People will talk."

"Screw 'em," she said. "Who cares what they think?"

"You might in the morning. I'm totally cool to drive."

"I really don't care, Grey. I just don't want you to get hurt or get into trouble. Or for something to happen to anyone else."

Grey stood close. Were his eyes heavy or was the way he looked down at her? He shook his head and his curls bounced. "I can walk. I'll come get my truck in the morning. You're right. I shouldn't do anything I might regret, whether it would be easy or not."

CHAPTER TWENTY-FIVE

Logan ran her hand down her hip, smoothing the fabric of her little black dress. If it weren't for the walk to and from the bar, the bagels and junk food would take their toll. But in the reflection of the cracked full-length mirror screwed to the bathroom door, the dress fit just as well as it had the last time she wore it in New York. No tights, but they'd only be torn to shreds by her cheap strappy black sandals anyway. Was it too dressy for lunch at Helen's? Did it send the wrong signal? It was Christmas, after all. Her first on her own. Better to celebrate it than to start a new tradition of wallowing in bed.

Church bells peeled through the apartment, marking the end of the eleven o'clock service. She grabbed a red ribbon from a box of chocolates sent by her mom, applied some lipstick, and packed a paper bag from the market with liquor bottles, dredges that remained from her practice drinks. At the sound of Grey's truck, stuttering exhaust and rumbling engine, she took one last sip of water to sate the butterflies in her stomach and took the stairs down to the street.

Outside, Grey took the bag, pushed it to the center of the cab, and held the door while she climbed into his pickup. His jeans were worn, but his sweater had fold lines along the sleeves. He'd gone shopping.

"I feel like I should have brought more than this." Logan fastened her seatbelt. "Rolls or something. I don't even know how to make rolls."

Grey closed the door for her and settled into the driver's seat. "When I called Helen yesterday, she wouldn't hear of it. Didn't want us to bring a thing."

"Still feels wrong. Thanks for picking me up. It would've been a hassle, walking in the cold with these bottles making all this noise. Do you know what we're having?"

"She's making a turkey. I think she's excited for company."

Logan touched the truck's window and let the cold bleed from the glass into her fingertips. Snow decorated the houses as if a generous baker had dolloped frosting with precision. Through the windows of every home, trees glowed white or red, green, yellow, and blue. Inflatable Santas and reindeer dotted yards, some bloated and joyful, others melted in colorful vinyl puddles. And inside, families made memories like the ones in old movies. She imagined fathers scrutinizing faulty instructions and assembling toys with questionable accuracy. Mothers basting Christmas dinner and complaining they had no time to change out of their pajamas.

Logan's mother was hours ahead, well past dessert and well into drinks when she'd called. Logan had thanked her for the gift card and learned the snow globe had arrived unscathed. They shared the usual promises to talk soon and get together someday, but Logan knew her mother would never return to the States, and Petra Cole accepted that her daughter had no use for France. It wasn't the end of a chapter or the start of a new life for either of them. It was simply another call between a mother whose daughter bore her no resemblance and a daughter who knew that without affection, only distance could make their phone calls stronger. There was no melancholy in it. To the contrary, Logan was happy, passing by homes full of happy families on her way to a family of her own.

Her thoughts drifted to her father, celebrating under a tree in some common room of a sterile prison. She liked to think he made friends there because the solitary alternative was too bleak to imagine. It made her think of Arvil, the distant sons he never mentioned and the lonely life he chose.

Logan pulled the bottles onto her lap and hugged them to keep them from clanging when Grey pulled into Helen's pockmarked driveway. She rolled down the window, opened the door from the outside, and stepped onto the shoveled walk. She declined the offer of help and carried the bag on her hip to Helen's door.

Plastic candles in the front window flickered to life, and Helen rustled behind the door, flinging it open and waving them in with the broadest smile Logan had seen from her. She must have been just as excited for company as Logan was to be part of it.

"You kids beat me to the door. I wanted to have the lights on before you got here. The turkey is in the oven, and I made a blueberry pie for dessert. Making a pie with frozen berries is blasphemy, I know, but the pie will be a blessing anyway."

"I won't know the difference." Logan slipped out of her coat and held out a hand for Grey's. "Want me to put these down the hall?"

"What kind of hostess would I be if I let you hang your own coat? Logan, you look so pretty." She tugged the coats from Logan's hands, and her voice faded as she shuffled down the hall. "Go on into the kitchen. It's small, but three will fit at the table just fine. Dinner's not ready yet, but I made sugar cookies. Just don't fill up before the turkey's done."

Logan smiled at Grey and elbowed his arm. She whispered, "She seems like a different person today."

A yellow candle burned on the coffee table, filling the room with the scent of cookies. The label declared it would smell like Frosted Moments. The shelves had been dusted, the books arranged, and small clusters of decorations placed around them. Plastic Santas and reindeer, yellowed and brittle with age rested between dog-eared romance novels and paperback classics. Unlit candles shaped like carolers midsong sat on an end table. A small Christmas tree, only a few feet high, sat on another, decorated with a string of popcorn and ornaments made of paper and painted plaster. Logan had done that as a girl scout. Pricking her finger with the needle as she strung together pieces of inedible, plain popped corn. If she held them too tight, they would crumble.

She leaned in for a closer look. "Did you make these ornaments?"

Helen appeared at her side and turned a mitten made from construction paper and covered in elbow macaroni so it faced outward. "When I was little, of course."

"We did this when I was a kid." Were hers shipped to France? Were they on a tree in her mother's cottage? Maybe they were on a tree in an FBI office somewhere.

"I don't think my parents kept any of mine." Grey sat in the spare recliner. "My mom had that stuff for a while, but I don't know what happened to it. We used to use cranberries, too."

"Thank God you said that." Helen jumped and moved for the kitchen. "I have cranberry sauce on the stove."

"You can *make* cranberry sauce?" Logan followed with Grey on her heels.

"Where do you think it comes from?" Helen lifted the lid of a saucepan and maroon liquid popped and splattered.

"I thought it only came from a can. In our house, it was always can shaped."

The three of them fit into the kitchen like a hand too large for its glove. The room was small but warm and inviting. The oven clicked as heating elements kicked off and on, warming pots that steamed on the stove. A crock pot took up half the counter and a tray of cookies covered the rest. Logan had seen Christmas dinners prepared in movies and on television, but household help hadn't prepared her for the chaos of steaming pots and ticking timers.

Helen waved a hand at the small table. "Go ahead and sit. Eat some cookies while you wait. If there are any left, you two will have to split them and take them home. I don't need them here. So eat up. Don't be shy. But save room for the bird."

"Do you want us to do anything?" Grey eyed the cookies as if they topped his to-do list.

"Not a thing. I haven't had anyone to cook for in so long. I don't even decorate for Christmas. I just cuddle up with a blanket and watch those corny movies. But when you called and suggested we all get together, I was so excited. It's like our own little orphan Christmas. But then I got to thinking how sad it would look without decorations, so I dug through the closets and found my old ornaments. It's been so festive here the last few days." Red sauce splattered when she lifted a lid and stirred, and the unmistakable smell of cranberry sauce, bitter and sweet, filled the air.

"It smells so good. And it looks really nice in here." Logan covered her mouth and talked through a cookie. "And these are really good.

Like... really, *really* good."

"I used to make these for customers. Sold 'em at the diner. I'm old enough to remember a time when we rationed flour to make cookies at Christmas. It would snow so hard up here we couldn't be sure to get to the store for any. So we'd plan ahead when the weather was better."

"It's funny how life changes so fast, but it seems to rewind every Christmas." Grey settled at the table, his back to the refrigerator, with a salad plate loaded with cookies. "Remember that old catalog? *The Sears Wish Book?* My mom would give me one of those every year after Thanksgiving, and I'd circle everything I wanted. Then I'd go running downstairs on Christmas morning to see what was under the tree. There'd always be one big box that they'd tuck in the back and save for last. It was an emotional roller coaster. Is it for me? Is it a new radio for Dad?"

Logan took the seat across from him, her back to the window. "I remember that catalog. Folding the pages down and making a little tree out of it after Christmas. I think I used it as a doorstop." She made it with Marta. Sitting on the floor of her playroom. She wished she'd never taken for granted that she could have anything from that catalog she wanted, but even more she wished she'd held tighter to Marta.

"I remember the food more than the presents, but I do remember some of the dolls I got when I was young. Still have a few." Helen opened the oven and removed something that looked like green bean casserole. She sprinkled something on the top and returned it to the oven. "My father killed an elk one year, and we had a huge dinner after that. Some years were thinner than others, but that's not what you remember when you grow up. You remember the whole of them and how they felt. Being with family."

"And the smells. The smell of my mother's stuffing." Grey's nose went into the air, as if he could find it there if he searched hard enough. "Onions, celery, and carrots cooking in some butter on the stove always remind me of my mother's stuffing."

"For me, it's my grandmother's bread." Helen rested her back against the counter. Beside her, a timer shaped like a tomato counted down the seconds. "It smelled like heaven. I can make it any time I want, but it never smells the same. Like the shape of the house and the way the smell moves around the rooms is different. It didn't smell the same when I made it at the diner, and it doesn't smell the same here either."

Logan picked at a pull in the tablecloth. Her family's kitchen had been a floor below, far from the rest of the house, so smells didn't travel. There were no family recipes, no traditional scents or holiday dishes that appeared on the table year after year. The only consistent thing about Christmas dinner was the table. They drank from crystal glasses and ate from fancy seasonal plates. In some ways, it was an untouchable season, a delicate dinner, when extra care should be taken not to scrape a knife on a plate. Logan's Christmas dinners had none of Helen's warmth or Grey's nostalgia. Hers had been all about the formality. There'd been no pulls in tablecloths in Logan's Christmas past.

Grey's eyebrow raised over a poised cookie, as if he expected her contribution. She had no anecdote about stuffing or elk. Anything she'd say would only widen the divide between them.

"Eggnog." Logan covered over the pull in the white cloth with her plate of cookies. "One year we had eggnog. We turned off the lights in the great room and drank it by the fire on Christmas Eve. I'm sure mine didn't have alcohol in it, but it was fun to think it did. We didn't have any food traditions, but I remember that eggnog by the fire like it was yesterday."

"We were lucky to have working electricity up here when I was little," Helen said. "It was a lot more reliable by the time you were born, Grey."

Grey nodded his agreement and swallowed a bite of a sleigh-shaped cookie. "It would go out in the summer with bad storms or when it was really icy."

"And it took days for it to come back on. We would store food outside in the winter and stay bundled up. We'd get updates on the radio."

"My dad had a little hand-crank emergency radio. I still have it on top of my fridge. Don't use it. Never will with the cell phone and all, but I keep it around just in case."

"Life was tough before indoor heating." Helen patted Grey on the shoulder and dropped a dish of sweet potatoes on a trivet. "You kids and your fancy technology made it easy on us old folks."

For the bulk of Logan's life, people had passed her on the street, wrapped up her purchases or served her at restaurants and looked at her with such envy for the things that she had. Until stepping foot in Ramsbolt, she'd never envied someone for the wealth or the things that they lacked, for the bond between them at the making do and mending. For the light they created and shared with each other in times of darkness. They had so much, radios and handmade ornaments and family recipes. Logan had nothing from her past, no puzzles or games or scrapbooks of memories. What hadn't been taken, she chose not to keep, and she had no one to blame but herself for what she didn't have. Except maybe her father.

In her hunger to fit in, to find sincerity in the holiday, she lost her appetite for turkey and stuffing. She picked at the royal icing on her candle-shaped cookie but couldn't bear to eat it.

Helen brought plates loaded with food and covered the table with casserole dishes of sides. The table gave a lurch, its uneven legs quaking against the linoleum when Helen sat. She giggled. "Everything in this house is just a little bit off, but I like it that way. Wouldn't appreciate what I have if it didn't jump out at me from time to time."

Logan couldn't deny the truth in it. It would be a waste to spend the day immersed in what she lost when so much of what she gained was right before her.

Helen folded her hands in her lap. "We should say grace. It's Christmas, after all."

"Me." Logan's napkin was neither spotless nor new, but she smoothed it over her lap with more sentiment than any of the linens her mother ever used. They could have been rented for all Logan knew. But there was nothing so special about any of them that measured up to Christmas in Helen's kitchen. "I have a lot to be thankful for."

"Wrong holiday, Lo," Grey teased.

"Shush." Logan lowered her head. "I don't know what the formula is for saying grace at Christmas, but I know it's a holiday about redemption. About wiping the slate clean not because we ask for it to be, but because something bigger than us says we're all worthy of it. I'm grateful for that, and I think the world needs more of it. Thank you for this food, this friendship, and the prosperity. Amen."

Prosperity.

Her mother always ended grace that way, thanking God for food, family, and prosperity. It rolled off the tongue like a habit. Like a mantle she was supposed to wear as an adult saying grace. But what prosperity was her mother truly grateful for? For cut crystal glasses and diamond necklaces? Logan would much rather belong. Affluence was little more than luck, and money had nothing to do with character.

She pierced a sliver of turkey and smeared it in a trail of gravy, her eyes fixed on her fork to hide the embarrassment of having said too much.

"You must miss your family, Logan. I'm sorry you couldn't be with them this year." Helen patted Logan's arm.

She did miss them, if she was honest. But she couldn't be honest with Helen. Not about that. Maybe someday she'd visit her mother in France. Or Petra Cole would get on plane and spend a weekend in Ramsbolt. Maybe her father would allow her to visit one day. They'd sit in the family greeting room, share a snack from the vending machine, start a new tradition over granola bars and potato chips. But she couldn't tell Helen and Grey any of it. There was no use bringing everyone down. It wasn't easy to move on, but she hadn't expected it to be. She choked back the past with a mouthful of sweet potato and melted marshmallows.

"It's time to make my own traditions. This is much better than spending the holiday alone. We could turn into an annual thing, maybe."

Grey swallowed his forkful of mashed potatoes. "Count me in. Our own orphan Christmas."

The nagging feeling that someone out there was alone, and didn't want to be, crept over Logan again. "I keep thinking of Arvil."

"Arvil? I wouldn't worry one second about Arvil." Helen pushed a toasted marshmallow next to some sweet potato on her fork. "He's exactly where he wants to be, shut up in that house away from the rest of the world. It's the one day of the year he keeps his grump to himself. I guess there's just too much happiness in the world, and he knows he'd never be able to win a war with it all."

"I don't want to be alone like that. I don't want to be that angry and bitter and hateful about things. It feels like it's inevitable sometimes, like the world just keeps getting more annoying until one day, you're yelling at kids to get off your lawn."

"Not everyone comes through life like that," Helen said. "I do wish I'd taken better care of my knees and my health and maybe learned a little more about how to hang onto my business, but I'm not angry or bitter."

Grey laid his fork on his plate and ripped a roll in two. He dredged it across a pat of butter on his plate. "I worry about my knees more than my sense of humor. They're my bread and butter. If my knees go, I'll be stuck under some woman's sink for the rest of my life."

Logan hadn't thought about how much she relied on her feet until then. She didn't even have health insurance.

"Oh. I almost forgot," she said. "I brought stuff to make after-dinner drinks. Who wants to toast our new Christmas alliance with a cocktail?" She needed every moment of practice she could get, and time was running out.

CHAPTER TWENTY-SIX

New York dripped its thaw down the back of Logan's neck, where it clung to her shirt in a blob of slime. She rubbed it dry, straightened her baseball cap, and crossed 28th Street beside Grey, in a crowd of thirty people who had somewhere to be, whether freeze or thaw. She had no way to predict what would happen if she were recognized. If one person stopped and pointed, yelled her name, where would she hide? How would she face that embarrassment next to Grey?

He kept pace. "Three hours, right? Before it starts?"

"Yeah. I have to check-in first, though."

Grey's eyes were fixed on his phone, on the thin purple line on his map. "What's it like to be back here?"

"Weird. Trying to keep my head down, you know? I don't think anybody will recognize me. Not this far south in the city. But I'm still edgy."

"Well, we don't have a lot of free time to wander around. That'll help." Grey's phone buzzed. "This is it."

A small sign out front declared the house to be a hotel, but without it, the building could have been any New York row home, tall and narrow with a solid wood door. Tucked between a church and a 7-Eleven. A scraggly tree grew from a void in the sidewalk, protected by a low wrought-iron fence. A bell rang out when they opened the door, and a voice called from a room somewhere, telling them he'd just be a minute. They waited in a hallway, the once-stately entrance of a New York residence, with its elaborate stairway and thick craftsman trim.

The man passed them a key and a word of warning. "The bathrooms are tucked into corners. It was built before plumbing, right?" He motioned to Grey. "So watch your head. And if you need anything, yell. There's a phone in each room that connects down here. Extra towels if you need them are in a closet on each floor. Checkout's at ten."

And he was gone.

Logan followed Grey up the stairs to a room on the third floor. The hallway smelled like cat litter and stale cigarettes. Like a loneliness and despair deeper than her own. An oddly relieving glow of daylight fought its way through a foggy window at the end of the hall.

"How did you find this place?"

"One of those apps." Grey unlocked the door and paused with his hand on the knob. Through the thin walls they could hear a couple arguing. "Looked better than one of those travel lodges. Got good enough reviews. You want to go somewhere else?"

"No way. This is great. It has character." It wasn't the room; it was the new side of New York. And she didn't want to seem ungrateful.

Grey held the door open, and she stepped into the room. Pink wallpaper, dry and cracked, faded and peeled down the wall, exposing a patchwork quilt of even older patterned wallpaper and dingy paint. Two twin beds took up most of the space, one nightstand between them. On the other side of the room, daylight streamed around the blinds that covered a single window. Logan dropped her duffle bag on the farthest bed and opened the blinds, which hung at an angle, broken. They wouldn't lock into place. She wound the cord around her fingers.

Through the cloudy panes of glass, the view of the city was unlike any she'd known. Trash cans and dumpsters, broken fences. Windows cracked and patched with cardboard. The gleaming condos and concierge services of the uptown world had shunned her. Begged for her money and attention, then shoved her aside as guilty by association. If the city below was the one she was left with, she was glad she had Ramsbolt to go home to.

"You look like you'd jump if the window weren't nailed shut." Grey plopped his overnight bag on the little stand outside the bathroom door.

"I used to belong in New York. I don't even recognize this place. I'm an outsider at this competition. I don't know why I'm doing this. It's so stupid and such a waste of money. How dumb am I to think I could win this thing? They're all from big bars and took real classes for this, and they can do all those tricks with shakers, and I just learned how to cut a damn lemon."

"Listen to me." Grey took her by the shoulders and sat her on her twin-sized bed. "None of those things mean anything. There are no categories for fancy tricks with shakers here, and you don't get points for naming the place where you learned to slice into a lemon. Nobody knows who you are or where you're from. They don't know a thing about you. They've got the same insecurities you do."

Logan shook her head and tossed her hat to the side. "Nope. That's not true."

"Think back. Remember when you had a shit ton of money? You still felt like that sometimes. Did you ever use your fancy plane to impress somebody? I bet you did. We're all like that, no matter what our circumstance is. Every person in that competition will be thinking they're the worst one in it."

"Except the girl who won last year."

"And next year, that will be you."

"Why are you so calm?" Logan flopped back on the bed, her eyes searching the ceiling.

Grey leaned back beside her. "Because I just drove for eight hours in the middle of the night." He propped up on his elbow. "Plus, I'm hungry, and I'm in New York for the first time ever. We have a little time. Wanna go explore?"

"Explore? With all those people out there with their cell phone cameras and their Instagram pages? They'll—"

"They'll take pictures of their breakfast and annoy the crap out of their high school classmates." He grabbed her by the arm and pulled her up into a seated position. "Come on. You can't hide in here. You'll turn into Arvil. Besides, we should get a move on."

"Fine, but I'm not taking this thing off." Logan grabbed her baseball hat. It was green with a fish on it, but it only cost a dollar at the outdoor store. "Come on. I'll introduce you to a real New York bagel first."

"You lead." Grey patted his back pocket for his wallet and checked his front pocket for the room key.

The convention center was five blocks away, across heavy traffic in the cold. She walked as fast as New York foot traffic would allow, Grey keeping pace, and they slipped into a deli a block from the convention center for two bagels with lox and coffee. Logan sat with her back to the door, and Grey kept up a constant stream of chatter, but Logan caught little of it, and it did nothing to settle her nerves.

They followed a stream of traffic into the center, teenagers carrying winter coats and adults in cosplay costumes. They followed the signs for the bartending competition, past a cooking demonstration and a talk from an inspirational speaker. A slip of paper taped to a door staked claim to the check-in room. The large block font screamed like a warning. An omen. Logan's skin prickled despite her coat.

"It was a last minute room change. Sorry for the confusion." A woman pushed past her and tugged open the door. Logan barely heard her through the ringing in her ears. "You're here for the bartending competition, right?"

Logan's tongue was thick, stuck to the roof of her mouth. Her throat was dry and a hard swallow didn't help. "Yeah."

"What's your name and where are you from?"

"I'm Logan. From... From Maine."

"Well, come on in and find your line here. They're sorted by last name." Logan followed the woman inside where competitors waited at tables. None of them look frightened or insecure. They were all well dressed, in vests or jackets. Logan slipped out of her coat and draped it over one arm, regretting that she hadn't done more research on what to expect or what to wear.

"Last name?" The woman focused an expectant gaze on Logan.

"Why?"

"So I can point you to the right place. *A* through *H* is over there. In the middle is *I* through *R*. The rest of the alphabet is all the way to the right there. It'll go fast if you have your ID ready."

Logan dug into her purse for her wallet and passport card, and stepped to the first table. Only one person waited in front of her, asking questions of the woman who staffed registration. A small trash can overflowed with paper coffee cups. Empty boxes surrounded the woman's chair. Logan checked the time on her phone. Registration was ending soon. She should have arrived earlier, given herself more time to settle in and prepare. Panic fizzled beneath her skin, like forgetting to do her homework and having no paper to turn in with the rest of class. Grey's hands on her shoulders grounded her, brought her back to reality, and she took in a long breath.

"Hand me your coat," he said, stepping next to her.

She held it out by the collar. "Thanks. Look at these people. They have fancy outfits. They look so professional. I look like I just stepped off a bus."

The man in front of her stepped aside, sorting papers and stuffing them into a plastic bag full of registration freebies. He left the room, went into the hallway, to a fate that Logan feared was worse than death. She was envious of him. He looked confident. Casual, at least. Not at all like the lamb being led to slaughter.

"Last name."

"What?" Panic overtook her voice, and the tired woman on the other side of the table hissed her reply.

"Last name? Registering? You're running out of time here."

"Cole." Grey filled in for Logan's missing mind.

"First name Logan?"

"Yes." Logan laid her ID on the table. With barely a glance, the woman shoved papers in a bag and pushed them into Logan's hands.

"Hurry up, so you have time to prepare. Out those doors, to the left. At the T, go left again, and it's the doors right in front of you. Big double doors. Your bar has your name on it. Find your spot. Someone will come up to you with instructions."

Logan turned for the door. From behind her, the hushed words of one woman to another were unmistakable. "Cole. That can't be her. Can it?"

Logan twisted the bag into a knot. A complimentary bar towel rolled around a shot glass and she squeezed it, hard but not enough to break. Her face went cool and clammy, the blood drained. She clutched the bag to steady her shaking hands, and on legs like jelly, she stepped into the hall. The door closed behind her. Distant voices swept past, chatter and laughter from a small crowd of people who weren't destined for a gladiator ring. Her heart gave a squeeze, and she wanted to run, to blend in with them, to slip into a crowd and glide away.

She swallowed hard, but her throat was full of cotton. "I'm making a big mistake. I don't know what I'm doing here. I don't know how to do this."

Grey wrapped a hand around her wrist. His grip was warm and anchored her to the hallway. "You know what you're doing. We practiced this."

"What if I don't remember the classic recipes? What if I just go blank? I could get eliminated before I even make it to the specialty drinks."

"So what. Then we'll explore the city for the day. You won't forget, though. You knew all of them in the car, and it was only a few hours ago. Not even."

"What if I get that far, and I can't remember how to make the blueberry syrup?"

"Logan. You know how to make it. You did it yesterday."

"One cup water, one cup blueberries, half a cup of honey, five sprigs of thyme. Boil, simmer for eleven minutes, press and strain." She pulled in air through her nose and controlled her exhale through parted lips, like her old yoga instructor would have said while she held some insane pose with her foot behind her shoulder.

"What if I forget the rules and make a fool of myself."

Grey spun her and took both her hands. "You read the rules a million times. You were so nervous your first night at Helen's, and you know way more than you did back then. You got this." They walked down the hall, and Logan turned right.

"Left." Grey grabbed her arm and steered her around. "Left."

"God, I can't even get the directions right."

They stopped outside the big double doors. "You're gonna walk right in there, just like you did the day you walked into the bar and talked yourself into a job. You are goddamn Logan Cole. You have been through more in this last year than any of those people. And you're going to stick it to Arvil and help Helen get her bar back."

He pushed the door open, and Logan let go of his hand. His reassurance was nice, but she didn't want to need it. She filled her lungs with stale convention center air and let it go, sending with it the fear. All she had to do was make some drinks. It couldn't be any worse than serving Arvil on a Tuesday night. "Thanks. I almost forgot for a minute that Coles never break a sweat."

She gave him a smile and swept the curtain aside. She wound her way around the bars, simple setups with a rail of drinks and mixers. Shelves lined the back wall, with fruit and sweeteners, bitters, saucepans, and hotplates. She found her name on a tent card and pushed it aside. A set of instructions on the table ran down the schedule.

She had less than an hour to get settled, to become familiar with the bar and available ingredients. At the ring of a buzzer, the host would announce a classic cocktail. She would be judged on speed, cleanliness, demeanor, and drink presentation. After a break for judging, a second classic drink would be announced. Specialty cocktails would come after lunch. She would present her twist on a classic and end the competition with a drink of her own creation, the blueberry sour inspired by her home.

In the cabinets below the bar she found shakers and mixing glasses, spoons and pipettes, bottles of bitters and cleaning rags.

"Are you as nervous as I am?" The guy at the bar next to her arranged his barware. He wore a crisp white shirt and a snazzy vest, part of a work outfit mandated by some snooty bar. He fidgeted, a nervous fumbling that made him easy prey. Logan would have no problem finding his weak spot, putting him on edge, setting him up for collapse, but she offered a reassuring half smile.

"Nah. No nerves here. I'm good."

It was less a lie than it would have been before she stepped up to her bar. She was at home, at ease with the bottles and tools and supplies she knew well. She tugged the hem of her cap-sleeved polo shirt down over the top of her jeans, though, conscious that she was under-dressed. The outfit she chose to blend in made her feel like she was under a spotlight. But she knew it was just her overactive imagination. Like Grey said, everyone had their own insecurities. She ducked beneath the bar to take inventory. Cleanliness had never been her strong suit, and she was determined to take out only what she needed, once she knew what the drink would be. It might cut into speed but every point would matter.

"And this is Logan Cole?" A man with a clipboard hovered over her bar.

"It is." She stood and reached out a hand that he didn't accept, so she collected a bar rag from the top of the stack and tucked it into her front pocket.

He checked her name off a list. "Lights will go down, we'll make an announcement, and the lights will come up on your station. Don't start until you hear the buzzer. You're in for the first two sessions. If you come back from lunch and your light is out, you've been eliminated." He moved on to the next bartender.

"Logan Cole, huh? Any relation?"

She could have ignored the guy next to her in his snazzy vest with his nervous fidgeting. Instead, she shook her head, and he seemed to accept the coincidence.

"Must be tough with a name like that."

He didn't know the half of it. The lights dimmed and a spotlight fell over her station. The small audience of judges, family, and friends disappeared behind the flooding lights. She blinked to let her eyes adjust. A deep southern drawl prattled through announcements, thanking sponsors and introducing contestants. Her patience wore thin. She clung to each word, waiting for the cocktail to be announced, while trying to quiet her cluttered mind. She would have to move fast, grab a shaker or mixing glass. Then the base liquor, whether it was rye or whiskey or vodka. Then the extras. Liqueurs, bitters, fruit, and garnish. The voice dropped out of the room, and music intensified. This was it. She had one shot. She couldn't dump it out and start again. She rested her fingertips on the stainless steel countertop and heard the word Boulevardier.

She knew it well, but there wasn't time to celebrate. The buzzer sounded through the room.

She dumped a scoop of ice into a mixing glass and used tongs to place a square cube in the rocks glass, which she set to the side. By count, she measured an ounce and a half of bourbon and an ounce each of Campari and sweet vermouth into her mixing glass and stirred. She strained it over the ice block into the glass, then she ran a peeler over the rind of a lemon and let two twists fall to the bar. She selected the best, dropped it into the drink, and placed the glass on the presentation circle so gently the liquid didn't slide up the walls and leave trails on its way back to the bottom.

Beside her, the man in the snazzy vest had already finished. A slab of lemon rind lay at the bottom of his glass. By comparison, what she lost in time making two twists she gained in presentation. And what she risked by not dragging all of the supplies onto her counter she gained in cleanliness. One red drip of Campari stood out on the otherwise pristine bar surface, but she knew the rule. No touching once the drink was presented. She twisted the bar rag in her hands and tried to glimpse the competition, but every drink was obscured by a competitor or barware. She shoved one end of the rag in her back pocket. At least she'd outdone Snazzy Vest Guy.

Judges scattered among the tables, tasting drinks through sips siphoned from straws. A woman approached Logan, checked items, and made notes. She commended her tidy table. "You may reset for the next round. And good job not throwing away your lemon. You get a bonus point for not being wasteful."

She lifted her chin and gave a knowing smile, but unplanned points from saving a simple lemon also meant simple mistakes might ruin her chances. She wiped her counter clean and set her dirty dishes in the tub below the bar.

"Who would have thought saving a lemon could earn you a point?" Snazzy Vest Guy wiped down his counter.

"I had no idea there were bonus points."

"Me either." He shrugged and tossed his towel in the plastic bin. "I caught your name but didn't give you mine. Harvey."

"Nice to meet you." Logan held up a hand. "I'd shake, but we'd look suspicious."

"Yeah, probably better not to. Nice to meet you too."

The lights flickered and dimmed, and the spotlights returned. "That was a fast break."

"That two-hour lunch will fly by."

Logan hoped he was right. The suspense of finding out if she made it to round two would give her a heart attack, if she managed to stay awake that long. The lack of sleep set in, an exhaustion that spread with the heat of the lights into every cell of her body. She'd napped in the truck but anticipation had kept her on edge, and now that breakfast had run its course, she was tired and hungry.

"The cocktail chosen for round two is a simple four-part drink. At the sound of the buzzer, please begin crafting the classic cocktail known as the blood and sand."

The air was tangy with vermouth and whiskey. She held in a breath of it and let it go at the sound of the buzzer. She measured equal parts, three quarter ounces of whiskey, sweet vermouth, and Heering Cherry Liqueur into a shaker. She squeezed a blood orange and double-strained an equal amount into a shaker, shaking until the metal froze in her hands. She strained the drink into a coupe glass, and her heart fell at the sight of her orange. One orange, and she'd used the whole thing, forgetting to peel it for garnish before juicing it. She salvaged what she could, garnished the drink, and placed it in the presentation circle on her bar. Despite her stupid mistake, she'd made the best of it.

The judge offered no smile. No compliment. She clicked her tongue and made notes on a clipboard. Was it the garnish? The speed? As the woman tasted the drink, Logan scanned her face for anything, the tiniest twitch of a muscle that might offer reassurance. Eyes closed, the judge held the drink in her mouth, then swallowed. The corners of her eyes relaxed, and she gave a nod, no expression, and moved on. She offered Logan no relief.

The presenter announced lunch, putting emphasis on the two-hour limit and the potential for elimination. Logan cleaned her station, wiping the counter and placing her dirty dishes into the tub. After her dismal garnish, if she didn't return, at least she could make cleanup easy for whoever would wipe her slate clean.

"What are you doing for lunch?" Harvey followed her to the double doors, toward the hallway and two hours of freedom.

"Haven't thought that far. I have a friend with me, and he's never been to New York before." Down the hall, Grey waved above the crowd. She raised a hand in return.

Harvey nodded. "Where are you from?"

"A tiny town in Maine no one's ever been to. Well, we get tourists that stop in on their way to other things. We used to anyway. The bar burned down a few months ago, and we're still getting back on our feet."

"That's a bummer."

"No kidding. What about you?"

"Miami. Hey, enjoy your lunch, okay? It's nice to work next to a friendly face. Hope to see you when we get back."

"You, too."

Grey caught up to her and put a hand on her shoulder. Logan appreciated his calming influence. "That judge seemed to like you."

"I screwed up at the end. With the garnish."

"Maybe not. You never know what other mistakes people made. One guy didn't even make the time limit."

"That's bad. Good for me, maybe."

"Exactly. Now point me to a great New York lunch that won't make me fall asleep before we get to round three."

Logan didn't expect a round three, but she didn't want to sound dismal. She led Grey back onto the streets of New York, into a maze of diners and delis and food trucks. A few stood out for their fame or infamy, but Logan's standards were low, and Grey's stomach was growling loud enough to be heard over traffic. She didn't even know the restaurant she stepped into sold tacos until they stepped up to the counter, but Grey was pleased to be anywhere at all, and Logan was so hungry she'd have eaten in a shoe store.

Grey took their tray, and she carried their drinks to a table in the back. Sauce dripped down her hand and onto her paper plate as she ate through a row of tacos, trying not to think about the competition and keeping a close eye on the clock. She wiped her chin with a napkin and a shadow fell over her food.

"You're that Cole girl, aren't you? Logan? The daughter of that man who went to jail for—"

Logan squeezed her napkin in her fist. "No, you have me mistaken for someone else." Across from her, Grey froze, his eyes wide. A woman her mother's age stood next to the table, hands on her hips and her head cocked to the side, as if she'd found the holy grail in a thrift market full of old coffee cups. She wagged a finger.

"No. I saw pictures of you in the paper, and I used to follow you online. You posted the best pics."

Logan shook her head. "No. I don't know who that is. Sorry. I'm not on social media."

"Can I take your picture?" The woman raised her phone, aiming it at Logan.

Grey put his hand up. "Please, she said no."

"It is her. I knew it."

"Don't make a scene. You've got the wrong person. We're just trying to eat." Grey's temper was palpable. Logan had been there before, someone on the street wanting to take a picture, excited by a celebrity sighting and forgetting their manners. A hand would push away a phone or shove a camera to the side and lawsuits would follow. Grey didn't deserve any of that.

Logan grabbed his wrist and leaned across the table. "Are you done eating?"

"Yeah. Let's go." He stood. "We should take these trays to the..."

"Let the camera lady clean it up if she wants dirt on somebody. Come on." Logan pulled her fish hat from her purse, wishing she'd never let her guard down. She pushed past the woman, careful not to bump her too hard but with just enough force to let her frustration out. She was hungry, tired. And her emotions crackled like a radio station out of tune.

They slipped into the mass of people slinking along the sidewalks, through the symphony of New York in the winter. Car tires thudding into potholes and splashing water onto the sidewalks. People laughing and yelling across the street. Beeping trucks in reverse, delivering packages.

Safely back at the convention hall, Grey tugged Logan toward a sign for coffee. He spent a small fortune on snacks and caffeine at a tiny snack bar, and they slouched in the back row of the darkened theater, their legs tossed over the chairs in front of them. Grey made jokes, poked fun at the competitors. Logan accepted that it was for her benefit and giggled next to him like a schoolgirl. She couldn't let the woman from the taco place get to her.

"Swedish Fish?" Grey held out a box.

"I love those. Yes, please." She took a handful and popped two in her mouth and grimaced at the blend of bitter coffee and sweet cherry candy. "They go terrible with coffee."

"This is gonna be one hell of a sugar crash."

"Thank God we're young and resilient." Logan unstuck red candy from her molar with her tongue.

"People are really upset about your dad, huh?"

"Yeah. That was mild compared to some of the stuff that happened when he was on trial. Someone spit on me once. And this woman. I'll never forget her. She smiled so nicely and held the door open for me and my mom, and when I walked past her, she whispered the most vile thing. You can't trust anyone. No matter how nice they look."

"But it's just words, right?"

"Not always. I mean, in person people are usually pretty tame. But on the internet they send you doctored pictures of gruesome things, and they hide behind avatars. It can be really scary. I used to have security, but that ended with my dad's plea deal. When they were gone, I was exposed and kind of raw. I closed all my social media accounts so I wouldn't see stuff like that anymore."

"I'd be really pissed. But I'd have no idea who to be pissed at."

"I know exactly who to be pissed at. My father didn't protect us. He put us in harm's way when he was doing shady shit. He didn't protect us during his trial, and he didn't take care of us after. I just assumed that he would always look out for me, and in the end, he just threw us away. The last time I saw him, he asked me not to visit him anymore because it was painful for him. I was so shocked by everything that I didn't even think to ask for a name change."

"I wouldn't have thought of that either." Grey shoved his thumb into the perforated corner of a box of Junior Mints. "Want some?"

"Please."

"But look how far you've come. You moved all the way out to some tiny town. You learned not to be afraid of people. You got one of the most thankless, sticky jobs on Earth, and you're taking a chance on something huge. Look down there." Grey motion toward the stage with his box of candy. "There are twelve tables. There's no way of knowing how many people tried out for this thing, but you got this far, and they didn't."

To Logan, her little table in the back row seemed a million miles away. "Yeah, but that little bar down there should have belonged to someone who worked hard and loves their career. I'm passionate about squashing Arvil and saving Helen's livelihood."

"Maybe that's what motivated you at first. You think I'm passionate about plumbing? I do it because I learned it, I'm good at it, and it pays the bills. You're no different. You're good at it, and you deserve to be here."

"I guess." She let a Junior Mint melt in her mouth.

He shook the box. "More?"

"Sure. Thanks."

He dumped a pile into her open hand. "So what are you going to do if you don't get through?"

"I don't know. I mean, I'll go back to Ramsbolt, of course. I don't want to think about losing right now. I just got used to the idea of being here." People shuffled in, coats draped over their arms. Logan sat up and brushed pretzel crumbs off her lap. "Besides, contingency plans only lower the stakes. I'm a high-pressure kind of girl."

"The lights are still out."

"I know. This waiting sucks."

"You think everybody else is backstage? Are you gonna be late sitting out here?"

Logan's breath hitched in her chest. "I can run. It's only a few feet."

The lights went down over the audience and four spotlights made pools on the stage. One of them was Logan's. Her heart nearly stopped.

"Shit. I spilled Swedish Fish."

"Who cares?" Grey stood to let her by. "Go!"

CHAPTER TWENTY-SEVEN

Logan stumbled over Grey's feet and down the aisle toward the door.

Grey caught her arm. "The bottle. You need the bitters." He fumbled with her coat in his arms, and dug out a tiny brown glass bottle. She gripped it tight and shuffled down the row of seats, tripping over the leg of the chair at the end of the row and catching herself before she fell. She shoved through the doors and into a crowd of disappointed bartenders, congratulating each other and offering condolences.

"Excuse me. Sorry. Have to get by." Logan made her way onto the stage. The presenter had started to speak, to relay the rules to the audience. The other three bartenders were already busy, sorting their equipment, so she followed their lead. Two shakers, glasses. Plenty of jiggers. In the small fridge, she found a bottle of egg whites. She memorized their placement and set the small bottle of her homemade bitters in the corner of her bar.

"For round three, we give the bartenders extra time to prepare," the announcer said in his southern drawl. "Each of our contestants has submitted two specialty drinks. In round three, they will make a variation on a classic cocktail. In the fourth and final round, the bartenders will compete with a drink of their own design, inspired by their home. Over the next half hour, they can prepare any specialty ingredients they require. Time starts at the buzzer."

The siren sounded. Logan plucked a hot plate and sauce pan from the supply shelf. She added a cup of water, half a cup of honey, a cup of blueberries, and five thyme sprigs to the pan and set it to boil. Once the honey was dissolved into the boil, she lowered the temperature and let it simmer for ten minutes or so. There was little to do but wait and stir. She tasted the syrup. There was plenty of thyme flavor to the dark purple liquid. She strained it into a bottle and set it in the fridge. She wouldn't need it until the last round.

When the buzzer sounded to start the first round, she prepared her remake of a classic cocktail. It was fitting to make an honest, earthy version of the drink her father hated most. One she would be proud of. She measured two ounces of rye, half an ounce each of lemon juice and maple syrup, half an ounce of egg white, and four dashes of her black walnut bitters into a shaker. She gave it a long, dry shake without ice to break down the proteins in the egg, to mix the ingredients and give it a frothy texture. She added ice and shook some more, and strained it into a rocks glass. With the pipette, she dropped bitters onto the foam and traced a maple leaf design into the frothy head.

She stood back and admired her work. The color was off. It was a little redder than she made it at home. The slightly darker tinge said she'd added a dash too many bitters. The flavor could be off. Would it be improper to taste it? She couldn't make another one; there wasn't time. There was nothing left to do but hope the flavor was balanced, savory but still palatable. She clasped her hands behind her back, tipped back on her heels, and lifted her chin. If they were grading on a curve, her drink had a one in four chance of coming in at the top. She eyed the competition. Being in the back row gave Logan the advantage of sight. Colorful layers filled a poco grande glass, topped with what might be a chunk of coconut. A concoction the color of thin iced tea filled another. The third she couldn't see. It was hidden behind a bartender who shifted her weight in a nervous box step.

The judges gave nothing away. They used straws to sample Logan's drink, nodded and stepped back from her bar. They talked among themselves in whispers, and she strained to hear without appearing to listen. They offered every contestant the same steel expression. Her competition was on edge. The nervous woman in the front row clenched her wrist to steady a shaking hand, and Logan saw the weakness. She was nervous enough to make a mistake.

The lights dimmed, a cue for them to clean their stations. Logan placed dirty dishes into the tub, satisfied with her work and proud of herself for overcoming her nerves. Even if the judges hated it, she was content to know her father would have loathed that maple black walnut whiskey sour. And he would despise that she called Maine her home.

The microphone crackled, and the announcer began. His voice faded, muffled by her mirth and exhaustion. Logan missed the start of the monologue, but something in his tone caught her attention, and she focused. He was reading an essay submitted by the man with the tropical drink. He longed for the hurricane-ravaged tropics of his youth, which inspired his cocktail. Had that been in the fine print, that their submissions would be out loud? She tried to remember what she had written, that she'd moved from New York. Had she said something in the essay she shouldn't?

A competitor ahead and to her left nodded at his story, inspired by Old Bay seasoning and the smells of his small hometown on the Chesapeake Bay. The wobbly woman in the front row missed the mesquite of Texas. And Logan missed nothing but the news that her essay would be read aloud to a crowd she couldn't see from the stage. Who was there? Who would know?

"Unlike our first three contestants who are tied to a place of their childhood, Logan Cole is inspired by the natural ingredients of her new home. Her blueberry thyme Amaretto sour is influenced by the blueberries that grow wild in Ramsbolt, Maine."

It was a kick to the gut, hearing her name so loud. It set her throat dry again. They had no right to take that from her, the privacy and security, to tell the world that Logan Cole now lived in Ramsbolt. She wouldn't allow her hands to shake. She wouldn't be that weak. She clasped her fingers behind her back and raised her chin with the pride she'd earned. If the audience reacted, if they made any sound at all, it was drowned out by the buzzer.

An ounce and a half each of bourbon and Amaretto and three-quarters of an ounce of lemon juice went into a shaker. She added half an ounce of egg white and a quarter ounce of her blueberry thyme and honey syrup. She gave it a dry shake, with no ice, for half a minute, taking out the anger she harbored for her father. She added ice and shook it more. Then she poured into the glass the dredges of any desire she had for her his return, the last of her will for any kind of homecoming to the life she once knew. She belonged behind the bar. In Ramsbolt. She had fought for it with everything she had.

She garnished the drink with blueberries strung on a cocktail pick and placed it in the presentation circle. She'd done all she could. No matter the outcome, she'd landed in the top four and would return home with enough cash to pay Grey back for the coat, her boots, and the hotel stay.

A bottle smashed to the ground, and Logan jumped. The fidgeting woman in the front row scrambled out of the way of the glass, and Logan lowered her chin. "There but for the grace of God go I," as Marta would have said. She didn't want to relish the moment, but it did increase her chances.

The small audience offered weak applause at the end of the round, and the judges took their tour. They poked straws into glasses, capped them with fingertips, and tested each drink, some more than once. They were stone-faced and offered no hints, but nodded to each contestant in silent assent. They made notes and conferred while the woman in the front row hunched her shoulders, her face turned to the floor. If Logan went home empty handed, at least she left without regrets.

"Would all of our contestants please come to the front here?" The announcer pointed to four white x's marked on the stage in masking tape. Logan took a place next to the woman. The smell of rum traveled up from her shoes, and she reached out for Logan's hand. Wounded pride deserved a friend, and Logan was happy to offer it. There had to be comfort left in the world.

"In third place…"

Logan's hand was in a vice. That poor girl. They put four people on stage, and only one would leave without recognition, and it was all down to the toss of the dice. The drop of a bottle. She returned the squeeze with gentle pressure.

"Doyle Collins."

Logan did the math. Could her drink be worth less than a broken bottle? She glanced to her right, at the woman's cocktail, light glimmering off the red elixir. It was perfect. Not a drop spilled, her bar immaculate. The woman was a master at her trade. Never mind she dropped a bottle; she could still win.

"In second place, Terrence Lawson."

The man stepped forward, hand extended for a shake. He smiled for a camera and accepted a small trophy shaped like a cocktail shaker.

"This is it," the woman said, squeezing Logan's hand. "You won."

"No. No way. Your drink is perfect. I made a mistake on my first one." Logan's mouth went dry. Was it possible she could win with so little experience? "I didn't see anything in the rules about breaking some glass."

She dared to think there was a chance. The judges hadn't hated either of her drinks. No one scowled at her first one, despite the extra dash of bitters. And she'd kept her cool the whole time, putting everything she had into every ounce, every dash, every shake and stir. Even Arvil would have been proud of the drink's she served. But was it enough to win?

"In first place, winner of the ten-thousand-dollar prize..."

It couldn't be. Logan had never taken a single bartending course. She'd never read a book about it from cover to cover. If it weren't for YouTube, she'd never have learned how to stir with a bar spoon in a mixing glass. She'd still be clanging it against the sides, splashing liquor and ice everywhere.

"There's no way it's me. You have so much more experience. It has to be you." Logan returned the woman's grip and scolded herself. *How could I have been so foolish to think I'd win this thing? All this wasted effort.*

"Oh, come on. It's you. You won!" The woman squeezed Logan's hand.

"Logan Cole from Helen's Tavern in Ramsbolt, Maine."

"I told you. It's you. You won." The woman released her hand and nudged her forward, but she couldn't move. Her feet were stuck to the floor, her knees locked. She'd done it. She'd saved the bar. A chill washed over her, a coldness at a win that wasn't hers. If the other woman hadn't dropped the bottle, Logan wouldn't have won.

She shook hands with the announcer and a woman in a dress who handed her a glass trophy shaped like a Boston shaker. She clutched it for all it was worth. It was worth her family's pride, and it earned her the town of Ramsbolt.

The presenter mumbled on, all of it lost on Logan. Numb, she was ushered off stage, down a hall, and into another room where a woman pointed to a mirror and asked if she wanted a hairbrush.

"Have you seen Grey? He's—"

The woman craned her neck, peering at Logan's hairline. "I don't see any."

"No, he's—"

"You're way too young for gray hair."

Behind the woman, against a far wall, two people set up a backdrop covered in sponsor logos. Logan had seen them a million times. A photographer positioned a camera on a tripod while an assistant aimed some lights.

"No. Grey's my friend. He came with me, and I don't want to leave him alone out there. Do I have a second to go grab him?"

"They'll send him back. You probably missed it, but the announcer told the plus ones where to go to catch up with you all."

"Is this just pictures?"

The woman in the dress appeared from nowhere, spinning Logan around. "Pictures first, then interviews. Hi. I'm Kath. Chief of marketing for Endeavoir Brands."

"Logan. Nice to meet you. Interviews with who?" *For how long?* Kath didn't give her time to ask.

"Some industry publications are here. Magazines and websites. The New York Times' Food and Drink section is here. People like that. There'll be some questions from us too, that we'll use throughout the year to keep publicity flowing." Kath pushed Logan in front of a wall of logos. "Put your right hand here. On the trophy. Like I'm handing it to you."

"Should I be nervous?" The question was more for herself than Kath.

"Not one bit. It's just a picture."

It wasn't the first photographer Logan had faced. She angled herself for the camera, and the smile returned, second nature. Like riding an expensive bicycle she couldn't afford to buy. A line formed of employees and the runners-up, and the photographer shuffled people into place. Logan found herself next to Harvey in his snazzy vest.

"No one deserves this more than you. What a great story, with the bar burning down and all."

"Your bar burned down?" The photographer's light caught Kath's eyes. "No one was hurt, I hope."

Logan turned for one last picture, posing with a bottle of whiskey. "No one was hurt, but the bar is struggling to reopen. It's been hard, and this award will help a lot."

If Kath was going to leverage Ramsbolt's misfortune, Logan was going to force her to share the profit. She let herself be swept into Kath's flourish, ushered to a folding table where she faced reporters in cheap padded chairs. The second and third place winners took their seats on either side, trapping her in front of a hungry crowd of information manipulators. They looked unassuming, in polos and jackets, T-shirts and jeans, but she knew better than to trust even a modest food blogger. She scanned the faces for Grey, for the comfort of a familiar face, but couldn't find him.

Kath introduced her to the press, spelled her name and stated the vitals. Just before handing the microphone to the first journalist, her voice fell somber. "Days before the competition, Logan's bar was decimated by fire, burned to the ground in a savage tragedy. This award will help restore it to its former glory. I know this will be of interest to you, Harold, so I'll let you start the questions."

A man in a cheap sports jacket stood, pulled a recorder from his pocket. He took the microphone from Kath. "I'm Harold. I cover New England for the ADZ network. You're local affiliate would be WMEZ out of Winterville, I think?"

She knew it well. Not from television but from checking the local weather on her phone. Traffic incidents and DUIs, high school sports. They were harmless enough. She cleared her throat and leaned forward, to a thin microphone clipped to the table's edge. She offered what she hoped was a disarming smile, just in case. "Yes, I'm familiar."

"Can you tell us about the status of your bar?"

"We're working with insurance to get back on our feet right now. The land owner is our biggest challenge. He wanted to put a new office building there, but the town has no other place to go for drinks, so there's a big fight about it. This bar is the heart of the town. Just don't tell that to our postman."

Thin laughter from the crowd. Playing to their sympathies would gain her favor.

"Can he do that, keep you from rebuilding?" asked a blond woman with a pen in her hair. At least she stayed on topic.

"We put up a heck of a fight. We'll see."

"But aren't you Logan Cole? Isn't Lorne Cole your father?"

Logan's stomach clenched. Swedish Fish and coffee and Junior Mints fought with the tacos. She gripped the metal frame of the padded chair and leaned forward in her seat. What was the daughter of a disgraced former billionaire and current felon supposed to do anyway? Wave a magic wand? For one thing, she didn't have to sit through the predictable slaughter, their inexorable ridicule. Not everything in life was inevitable.

Logan spun to Kath. "I think we're done." She stood, pushed her chair back and skirted the shocked man at her side, and walked to the door. Cell phones raised as reporters took their last shots, and Kath scrambled to shift the questioning and salvage the event with grace.

Grey shuffled by the door, behind a stunned woman in a pencil skirt. Logan grabbed his sleeve as she pushed through, and he stumbled behind her into the hall. "Are you allowed to just walk out like that?"

She spun to him and spat her words. "I'm not going to sit there and let them destroy me because I'm related to my father."

"Then prove them wrong. Don't assume they'll vilify you. You didn't do anything wrong. When you get up and leave like that you look guilty. It's all public perception. Isn't that what you said?"

Logan held up a hand. She shook like a leaf at the end of a fragile branch. "I can't go back in there. I've lost control of this. They have all the power now, just like they always have. Can we just go back to the hotel?" She'd rather sit in that room and watch the sunset over the dumpsters than face the press for a moment more.

Grey walked Logan around the corner, out of sight of the door.

"You're making a big mistake. What if you talked to *one* of them? One of the nice ones. That guy from the local channel. They never air anything complicated. It's all fishing tournaments and when will the ice melt. Tell *him* your story."

"Controlling the narrative." Logan shoved her hands in her back pockets, her back against the wall.

"If that's what you want to call it."

"I made myself look guilty. Shit. How could I be so stupid?" She kicked at a pull in the carpet with the toe of her shoe. "Okay. I can fix this. I'll talk to that local guy. Give him just enough of the juicy details people want to hear, how I left with nothing and life is hard. Then I'll refocus the story on the bar. Okay. I'll talk to him."

"You want me to go get him?" Grey pointed his thumb toward the end of the hall. "It'll just take a second. I mean, what's he gonna say? No?"

There'd be no turning back.

"Yeah." Logan wiped her palms on her jeans. "It's long overdue."

Grey slipped down the hall. She rubbed at a knot in her neck. She'd have to look small. Vulnerable. People would take her seriously if she didn't look defiant. She didn't need the world's compassion or their pity. She needed them to leave her alone. Letting them think they'd already won would give her back her life. And if the universe would let her have it, she could get the bar back.

When Grey returned, he brought the man in the cheap sports jacket. Logan stepped forward and accepted his shake.

"It's an honor to get to tell your story. Your friend says you want to do an exclusive? I've got a camera guy. If you give us a second, we can—"

"Yeah. Can we find somewhere else to stand though? I'd rather not be interviewed in front of a bathroom."

"We could go the fancy route, set something up in a suite with the right lighting."

"Nah. That'll take too long." Down the hall, a group of teens stumbled off an elevator. Laughing. Clutching purple tote bags. "Let's get this over with, if that's okay."

"There's a little alcove down there." Harold pointed down the hall in the direction of the elevators. "Around that corner. A few chairs and a little table with some fake flowers on it."

After all the running and hiding, deleting apps and avoiding newspapers. After being spit on in doorways and hissed at on the street, it came down to an interview in a convention center hallway next to a plastic plant. Whatever it took to control the narrative.

"You guys go ahead." Grey grabbed Logan's arm. "I'm beat. I'm gonna sneak back in this room and take a nap. Find me when you're done?"

"Yeah." Logan cracked her neck. She straightened her back and lifted her chin. "Let's do it."

CHAPTER TWENTY-EIGHT

The shadows of wiry tree limbs scraped across the ceiling of the little hotel room, backlit by the never-ending stream of New York traffic. Grey snored, but Logan was awake. Still. Rehashing every word she said to Harold. Every empathetic furrowed brow, every *tell me more about that* had dragged more of Logan's past out of her and into the camera. She'd said plenty worth regretting. From her father's crimes to the hints she missed until they were in the crosshairs of hindsight. And the threats. From people on the street, on the internet. From the news. All the way up to the bus ride to Ramsbolt.

Arvil got the worst of it. Her words played back at her again and again, like a game-losing fumble replayed for the fans.

Men like Arvil are the ultimate consumers. They take and take. Only he's not smart enough to realize that once he has it all, there won't be anyone to share it with, because he's destroyed everyone along the way. Greed is like that. There isn't a person in Ramsbolt who doesn't hate that man for the way he treats people, what he's done to that bar...

Her words smoldered in her chest like a molten cannonball. She couldn't get comfortable. Tossing and turning made the bed frame creak, so she lay flat, beneath the shadows of tree branches pointing their skeletal fingers, and waited for the dawn.

When the sun arrived without circumstance, Grey stirred in its rays.

"You said last night you wanted to hit the road early." Logan rolled onto her side. Grey fumbled for his phone on the nightstand. "What time you want to get moving?"

A blue glow lit Grey's face when he unlocked his phone. "It's seven. Soon?"

"All I have to do is hop in the shower and brush my teeth. You want first dibs?"

"You're more awake than me. Go for it."

The water was warm, though the pressure was lacking, and Logan was happy to make it a short one. Grey must have felt the same because his shower took less than two minutes, and their bags were packed before the steam dissipated.

"This thing never would have survived a flight." Logan placed the trophy back in its box. She set it on the bed, next to her duffle bag and did one last scan of the hotel room.

Grey zipped his bag shut and plopped it next to hers. "Even if it survived, I wouldn't."

"You don't like to fly?"

"No. I like my feet on the ground where the good Lord put 'em. If he wanted me to fly, he'd have made me a bird."

"That's a really beautiful thought. Also, it's a cop out. You can see amazing things from up there."

"There are amazing things down here, too."

Logan looked away. Sometimes Grey said things in a certain tone, and his eyes lingered a little too long. She wasn't ready to encourage anything he might feel. Once his expectations were on the table, she'd have no choice but to let him down, and it could destroy the only friendship she had.

Logan paid for their hotel stay with the prepaid Visa that came with her winnings. They tossed their bags into the back of his truck and aimed for Maine, the trophy safe on Logan's lap. Eight hours of riding in the truck, of recounting everything she told Harold. How, when he asked about Arvil and the fight to save the bar, she'd been so relieved to focus on something other than the past that she forgot about the present and the future. It felt good at the time to let it all fall out of her, to let the words gush out and take with them all the anger and hurt. But in the release, she forgot that Arvil had loosened his grip on the bar's fate. She forgot to mention Arvil's promise to let them rebuild. But Arvil wouldn't forget. He would read the article, call her words slanderous, and refuse to let them rebuild out of spite.

She pretended to sleep, her eyes squeezed shut, as miles and miles passed, bringing her closer to Helen. She would have to explain. To Arvil, who would want another confrontation. And to the town. She owed them an apology for throwing it all away.

She opened a browser window on her phone and typed in *Logan Cole*. Reception was spotty, the results slow to load. And there it was. "Exclusive: Disgraced Billionaire Logan Cole Found Destitute in Maine."

It was the death of her former self that she hadn't grieved. The loss of it all. The ornaments and Christmas gifts. The birthday cake toppers. The stuffed sheep Marta gave her when she got the chicken pox. It wasn't just that she'd lost it all. It was that she walked away, as if it never meant anything to her at all. What hadn't been taken she'd given away to become someone new, but she never stopped to say goodbye.

The article was short, a teaser for the interview that had aired the night before, while Logan and Grey ate Chinese takeout in their hotel room. "Then the dive bar where she worked in Ramsbolt burned down, leaving some to ask...*is there really such a thing as the Cole Curse?* In our exclusive interview she slams the owner of the land, calling him a greedy coward."

"Are you crying?" Grey shouted over the sound of the engine.

Logan wiped her cheek with her sleeve. "Maybe. A little."

"What happened?" He shot a quick glance at her phone in her lap. "What does it say?"

"The truth. Just the truth this time."

She couldn't bring herself to tell Grey what she'd done, that she'd ruined the bar's future by slamming Arvil in front of the world. She wanted that last moment with a friend before the whole world hated her. Before he hated her, too.

When they pulled into town, plenty of daylight still shined on the Welcome Home banner strung across the burned-out remnants of Helen's bar.

"I didn't even know anyone knew." Logan craned her neck as they turned the corner. The banner waved in a slight breeze. Ramsbolt must not have watched the news. She'd have to break it to them herself.

"Helen knew we went. She probably told everyone." Grey steered them around the circle. They passed through the shadow of the stoic sailor.

"Right. I bet Riley noticed I wasn't around and asked her. I hope they don't make a big scene."

The truck crunched to a stop outside her apartment.

"Thank you for coming with me," Logan rolled the window down and reached for the door handle. Ramsbolt was an easy fifteen degrees cooler than New York, and the icy air didn't encourage her to stick around outside. "And thanks for booking the room and everything. I probably would have had a meltdown if I'd had to go through that alone."

"Nah. You would have been great. You did it all yourself. I had nothing to do with it."

Logan stepped onto the curb and grabbed her bag from the back of the truck. She reached back into the truck for the trophy box. "Who am I kidding. You're probably right. I kick ass that way. Lunch soon?"

"You bet. Text me. I really do want to hang out. We need to celebrate this."

"It's on me this time." Logan wound up the window. She still hadn't mastered the art of winding up a window using a crank and looking graceful doing it. She rested the trophy box on her hip. "I need a huge nap, then I have to figure out how to handle this money stuff with Helen and Arvil. Tomorrow's another day."

She closed the door and waved to Grey as he pulled away from the curb, then shoved her key into the lock of the door that led to her apartment. The street fell quiet. The bell from the newsstand rang out when Warren stepped onto the street. His voice boomed and echoed off the buildings.

"Saw you on the news last night. Good job sticking up for yourself and the town against Arvil."

The last of the warmth drained from her face, and she fought to return even half of his smile. With a quick wave, she turned her back on Warren. There was nothing to say. Once her interview got out, once news people showed up to dig into her life and make an example of her, to laugh at her misfortune, it would only get worse for the whole town. The world would show up to mock her, and she would have to contend with that, too.

She took the stairs two at a time, the last surge of energy from her weary body and leaden feet. She issued her own verdict and locked the door to her own prison. She'd been so stupid, so careless, her own worst enemy. And she was more like her father than she ever thought. It was so easy to destroy someone else to get what she wanted. How could she recover from this? Arvil would never believe she made a simple mistake and misspoke. He would never believe the truth, that she panicked and missed the chance to elaborate or clarify and vilified him instead. It was as if the instinct to hurt people were a part of her. She would always be a fighter, and she would always fight dirty.

Her father had been right all along when he said that only the strong get what they want, and the only way to get what you want is to take it. If she hadn't been so vulnerable, if she hadn't told the truth, if she'd lied to protect herself, she would be celebrating. Not sitting on the edge of her bed in a one-room apartment wondering how to tell a whole town that she destroyed their bar. She lost her chance to save her job, her apartment, everything she'd built. And she let Helen down. She clutched her phone in her hand wondering what to say to Helen, whose name lit up when her cell phone rang.

CHAPTER TWENTY-NINE

She ignored Helen's call. Then she ignored Riley, who yelled up from the street to her open window. Warren's call was followed by two from unknown callers. She turned off her phone and let the last of the day creep up the wall until it burned orange and faded to black and she slept.

She woke to a bird outside her window and the first hint of pink to light the sky. The old instinct to grab her phone took hold and she retreated beneath the blankets with it, hiding from the world in the warmth of her bed. The phone rested on her pillow, and the screen went from black to blue as she turned it on. The red notification bubble appeared beneath her voicemail app, and the pain in her chest sharpened as dozens of messages showed up. She turned the volume off. The last thing her heart needed was the shrill ring of a phone.

As the world passed beneath her frosty window, she listened to the newest voicemails first. "Oh my God. Logan? This is Margo from middle school. I moved before high school, but we were in the same class for years. I can't believe you're working in a bar." The voice didn't strike a chord, and the emphasis on *bar* said the woman was no old friend. "I followed all the news when it was happening, and I was *so shocked.* How could he leave you with nothing? You must be destitute. How do you even eat? Call me if you want to chat. I'd love to hear all about it."

Of course, she would. A call from someone named Caitlin followed. Then Michael, the son of her father's old business partner, lamenting that she hadn't called and begged for help. After all, they'd been through so much together. None of it was memorable to her.

Then a message from a Florida area code. Expecting a journalist or random harassment, she pressed the play button and hovered over delete.

"Hey. It's Joanne. You probably don't remember me, and I'm not sure if this is even your real number. Our mothers used to go to things together. You were a few years older than me, and we never hung out. Anyway, I saw you were doxxed online. I know you deleted all your social media stuff a while ago, so I figured you might not know, and if it was me, I'd want to know. Maybe you have some security or something? Someone you can tell? Anyway, the whole thing sounds horrid. I have no idea what I would do, you know? But you look really good. You looked happy on TV, and I hope you really are. Call me if you ever wanna talk."

That explained her sudden popularity. At least there were still a few good people out there. People who could fake it, at least. Not that she had any intention of trusting them.

"It's Ian again. Long time, right? Last time I called, your dad was just being charged. We didn't get a chance to chat back then, but I'm still doing cable news and wondered if you'd be willing to sit down for an interview. It's a slow news week and your story is *huge.* I could come to you. I'm thinking a walkaround through Ramsburg—"

Ramsbolt. She deleted the message and went on to the next.

"Logan, it's Helen. I'm so happy for you, and I can't wait to wrap you up in a big hug, but I won't even try to make it up your stairs. Look how far you've come! I hope you're enjoying this night with Grey. Come see me as soon as you can and tell me all about it. And bring that trophy. I need to sample those drinks you made! I'm so impressed and so excited for you."

The text messages were less sincere. "Don't even have the guts to face the press. Guilty!" "You shuld be in jail w him." "Thief. U burn that bar down for the $$? U should of burned wth it."

As disgusted with the grammar as the sentiments, Logan shoved her phone beneath her pillow, suffocating her connection to the rest of the world. If she knew then what she knew now, she would have wasted the money and changed her name. Got a new cell phone plan with a new number and a new contract. What if her address leaked, too? How could she walk into Helen's house, show off the trophy and make her a drink, then tell her she'd destroyed the bar by slamming Arvil to the press? Oh, and the world was on its way to make sure she burned along with all their plans. How could she walk through town? What if some crazy person rolled through the circle and knocked on her door? She ran down the stairs to check the deadbolt, just in case. In case someone found out where she lived. In case someone out there thought she hadn't suffered enough.

She settled at her little table with a cup of coffee and her notebook, focusing on the future to cut through the distraction. After paying Grey back for the boots and coat, and after setting money aside for taxes, there would be plenty to pay the lot rent Helen owed, and a little left to help with construction. If Arvil still agreed. As much as that man gravitated to bad news, there was no way he missed it.

She checked her bank balance, and the money was there. She hadn't seen more than one digit before a comma in so long that the sum felt huge, but it didn't make her whole. It didn't fill the ache. She'd dreamed of setting aside a little for a decent dinner, a slab of meat she didn't have to cook herself. But money wasn't infinite like it once was. She couldn't splurge on a trip to Prague. She didn't deserve to splurge on anything. She owed it all to Helen and Grey.

And then she'd have to go.

Logan dragged a chair to the window. The shadows retreated as the sun rose high, making puddles below the lifeless trees. Soon there would be buds and spring would come. Nothing she could do would stop it, and with it, she would leave. Find a new job in a new town. The passing of time was an inevitable truth, and as gracefully as it came, one gentle day at a time, it delivered sharp blows and severed her, time and again, from the things that she knew and loved. But this time she wasn't leaving before she put up a fight.

Everything hinged on throwing the truth at Arvil's feet. He had every right to deal her one final blow after what she'd done to him, and the only shot at surviving it was to stand before him, willing to take it.

"Logan!" Grey's voice called up from the street. She cracked her neck and tugged on the window. It clung to the frame as she shimmied it open the rest of the way. He stood on the sidewalk below with a plate held high like a religious offering. "I have food."

"I like food. Do you want to come up?"

"Yes, please. It's cold out here, and you're not answering your phone."

Her phone was still on silent, tucked beneath her pillow on her unmade bed. "I'll come down. I need a second, okay?"

"Okay. I might eat this chicken, though."

The window closed easier than it opened. She changed into jeans and a T-shirt, threw her pajamas under her comforter, and threw the covers over her bed before bounding down the stairs to unlock the door.

"Where's the food from?" She closed the door behind Grey and followed him back up the stairs.

"It's from your party."

"No." It came out more of a whine than she expected. "I don't want a party. Don't they know how horrible this is? I haven't figure out how to fix it yet."

"It's not horrible. It's delicious. It's grilled chicken and potato salad. People brought it outside in forty-three-degree weather. They're out there at the bar with tables and food and punch with ice in it that won't melt for another three months. What's there to fix?"

Logan dragged her chair from the window back to the little table. She took the aluminum foil from the chicken and bit into a leg. It was still warm, but barely. "The mess I made of everything when I talked shit about Arvil."

Grey opened a drawer in the kitchen and grabbed two forks and a stack of flimsy takeout napkins. "There is no mess with Arvil. People are happy. They want to see you and celebrate for a while. Things like this don't happen in Ramsbolt. A couple journalists stopped by, too, asking questions and talking to people."

"Great. That'll end well. I've been doxxed. All morning it's been emails and calls and texts saying how horrible I am."

Grey dropped the napkins and silverware on the table. "So what. A few internet trolls are upset. That's in your phone. These are real people. Outside. Where you live. And they're not pissed at you."

Logan sat. She pulled the Styrofoam tray close and stabbed a chunk of potato with a fork. "What about Arvil?"

"What about him?" Grey fell into the chair next to her.

"Has anyone seen him?"

He grabbed a fork and pulled at a piece of chicken. "No one's seen Arvil. Not that I know of. But everybody thinks what you said was perfect. He's such an asshole. Look." He took his phone from his back pocket and opened Facebook. He scrolled past lost pets and complaints about the weather and stopped on a news post. "Here's one. They're everywhere. The internet is going crazy about this little bar that had the best drinks in the country until it burned down, and the angry man who owns the land won't let them rebuild."

"Look at these comments. This isn't good, Grey." Logan pushed his phone across the table. "Arvil is going to see this, and he's gonna take it back. He'll find a way to keep us from rebuilding out of spite. We don't have enough money to pay for a big legal fight to make him honor the contract. And I don't have a lot of time to spare. I have to figure out how to fix this fast, so I can pay my rent. And I'm not taking anybody's charity."

"Well, let's figure it out fast, then. Because everybody is down at the charcoal pit where the bar used to be, and they want to see you."

Across the room, her cell phone buzzed beneath her pillow. Another text. Another hostile message or hateful accusation. Another person looking to pick the last of the meat from her bones. She went for it, shoved her hand beneath her pillow, unlocked the screen and threw it on the table.

"Look. This has been going on all day. Messages and texts. People from my past with more money than God who pretend to feel sorry for me for being reduced to working in a bar. A guy from high school who has a news show and wants me to take him on a tour of town so I can boost his ratings. This has been going on all day." The phone buzzed with a call. "There's another one."

She spun the phone around. She didn't recognize the number, but she knew the area code.

The Dominican Republic. What if?

"I'm gonna take this one." Logan slid her finger across the screen and held the phone to her ear. She gestured Grey to stay and slipped into the bathroom, closing the door.

"Hello?"

"Logan. I'm so glad this is your real number. My brother saw it on the internet, and I had to see if it was real." Marta's voice was an instant balm. She could have said anything, read the side of a cereal box for all Logan cared. Hearing Marta's voice on the phone was like being picked up after scraping her knee as a kid.

Logan sat on the toilet lid and cringed when it creaked. "I miss you so much. I never got to say goodbye to you."

"I wish we could have stayed in touch." Why did Marta have to be a million miles away? "I'm so proud of you for standing on your own two feet. I would never expect less from you. Do you feel freedom from that world? That's what matters. That you carry the best of it with you, and feel free from what constrained you."

Logan laughed. "Thanks. There is a freedom to it. I wish it came with more money, but we all start somewhere, I guess."

"Where are you? In Maine? I haven't been to Maine since I went with you to Bar Harbor when you were little."

Logan sat on the toilet seat, her knees nearly touching the tub. "It's this little place called Ramsbolt. The whole town would fit inside Central

Park, and its population is about the same as a condo building. Everyone is nice here."

"Sounds like you have a nice little town to live in where everybody looks out for you and nobody begging you for things, following you around and taking your picture. You can trust your neighbors. That sounds like a perfect life."

It would be perfect, if she could think of a way to fix it. "It's a pretty awesome town. The biggest scandal here is that Warren might change the window display in the newsstand next year to something less classic for Christmas. I'll be devastated."

Marta laughed. "Remember sneaking into the city to look at the Barney's windows?"

"I miss doing that. And eating Easter cookies in a pillow fort. I had the best childhood." Logan pulled her towel off the rod and laid it across her lap. It was thin and scratchy, and the binding was unraveling.

"I enjoyed spending it with you. You sound happy there. Are you?"

"I'm terrified I'm going to lose it all. I messed up. That guy who owns the land? I had him wrapped around my little finger. He was going to let us rebuild, and then I said all that stuff, and now I'm not so sure." She couldn't keep the urgency from her voice.

"Well, now he knows you're one of *those* Coles. He's probably not going to mess with you." Through the phone Logan heard a rustling. "My brother has come with our lunch. I have to run. We're having a big lunch for my dad who turned eighty-five this week. But we will talk again soon. I'm glad I found you again."

"I didn't know how to find you. For a long time I thought you left. I asked, and no one would say. Then one of the drivers said you were fired." She pushed the towel back around the rod again and left it in a bunched-up mess.

"It wasn't anything bad. Your parents disagreed with the way I spoke to you. They are right to raise their daughter as they see fit. I was sad and angry for a while, but it all worked out."

"Maybe I would have been different if I hadn't had you. If you hadn't taught me things instead of taking orders from a child."

"Does that matter? Who you may have been?"

"I guess not. What matters is who I became."

"You became a good person. You would have become a good person no matter what." The voices of Marta's family mixed with the clanging of plates and glasses and the tinkle of silverware. Logan wanted that kind of loud, messy life. Maybe if it didn't work out in Ramsbolt, she could buy a one-way ticket and live with Marta. A comforting thought, but it would be like running home to Mom instead of cleaning up after herself.

Marta laughed, spoke to someone in Spanish. "I have to go. Stay in touch okay? Call me. Send me texts."

"I will. I'm sorry we lost touch. I'm sorry about all of it."

"There's nothing to be sorry for. I'm glad you found a great place there."

"Me, too. Thanks for everything. I still love you like a mom."

"I love you, too, Bug. I'm glad your number was spread on the internet so I could find you again. If you change it, tell me."

Logan ended the call. In the short time they had talked, more text messages came through. She skimmed, blocking numbers as she went, then paused.

It's Jill! If this is u please text or call! I was so bummed when we lost touch. I never wanted us to grow apart. Hope you're happy in Maine! Let's get together for hot dogs sometime. :)

Jill. After all those years she still knew what to say. Logan returned the text.

I miss you so much. Yes, I'm happy here. Hope you are too! I think about you all the time. Will call you tomorrow to chat.

Water was running in the kitchen, Grey cleaning up. She straightened her ragged towel and stepped from the bathroom to find him washing her coffee cup.

"You don't have to do that." She leaned against the counter next to him.

"Gave me something to do." He placed the clean mug on her drying mat, turned off the water, and flicked his hands dry. "That was an old friend? None of my business. You just never mentioned anybody from before you moved here."

"That was Marta. She raised me. Sort of. She was my nanny, but my dad fired her, and we lost touch. She said Ramsbolt sounds nice, and she's glad I found a happy place to live. I wish I became the kind of person she thinks I did, though."

"You *are* the person she thinks you are. You just made a mistake. It'll all blow over, and you'll go back to being anonymous. It's like this whole thing was inevitable, and you had to let your real identity out, you know? Come down to the bar. Nobody gives a shit. There's chicken and boozy punch." Grey pointed to the table, and Logan declined the offer of more. He covered it and put the plate in the fridge.

"I have to put this right. God knows Arvil won't let it blow over. He doesn't deserve to be treated like that. I can't go down there and see everybody with this feeling of dread. I need to talk to him."

"Now?"

"Now. I have to do the right thing. I have to tell him the truth, and that I was wrong. And then I have to give him money." There was one language Arvil and Logan had in common and only one way to be sure he heard her apology. She had to speak with cash.

"Then we can go down to the party?"

"Then we'll go to the party."

Grey took off his hat. He ran his hand through his hair, eyes fixed on his shoes. For all his urging to get her out of the apartment, now he wanted to stall?

"Lo, I know you'll say no, and I'm okay with that. It's just that if I don't ask you this, I'll never really know, and I don't wanna not know anymore. See, I don't wanna be one of those guys who misses their chance only because they were bad at reading signals and too scared to lose a friend to make a move."

"Yes." Logan grabbed his hand and squeezed. Harder than she should have, but enough to feel his warmth. "This one can be a date."

CHAPTER THIRTY

"Wait. Don't go out there yet." Logan grabbed the back of Grey's jacket and brought him to a halt in the narrow stairway. "I gotta think."

"There's barely enough room to turn around in here. This is where you want to think?" Grey's shoulder brushed the wall as he spun on the narrow step to face her.

"Helen. We should take Helen with us." If Arvil was going to say no, he was going to do it to Helen's face. Besides, she owed an explanation to both of them.

"She's not at the bar. She must be home. We could go get her. Take her to Arvil's and then what?"

"Talk."

"Okay. To Helen's it is." Grey used his weight to open the door, and Logan locked it behind them. She climbed into his truck and turned her face against the assault of hot air from the vents when he turned the key.

Grey turned knobs, a frantic adjusting. "I had the heat on to keep the chicken warm."

"The chicken made it, but I don't know how you did."

He pulled away from the curb and took the roundabout. The truck handled like a log flowing downstream, and she let herself be tossed from side to side. At Helen's house, she wound down the window and opened the truck door, beating Grey to the doorbell.

"Logan!" Helen waved them in.

"We can't stay. I need you to come with us. We're going to Arvil's. I can tell you everything there."

"But I just sat down with tea."

"I'll make you more tea when we get back." Logan waved a hand. "Come on. Get your keys."

Helen shuffled down the hall. "Alright. They're in my purse. I just need a minute."

"Hurry."

"Goodness, kids. I'm old. What's with the rush?"

Logan needed to get the weight off her chest. "Trust me. It's important. I don't know if Arvil's seen the news or not, but every second matters. I can't let him think I slammed him on purpose. And it's too hard to tell you one at a time." She'd rather not face the fury of either of them. She'd always been the type to rip off a Band-Aid.

Grey situated Helen in the truck, and they rounded the circle again, Logan in the middle, listing toward Helen to avoid touching Grey. Her mind was on the fight with Arvil, and she couldn't afford to be distracted. She ran through what she could say, what words could possibly make him understand, but it was useless to prepare a statement. The truth was best when it was allowed to spill out.

Grey stopped in Arvil's patchwork driveway and pulled the keys from the ignition. "Look at it this way, Lo. If it doesn't work out, you'll have the small satisfaction of knowing that you left an oil stain in his driveway."

"What do you mean, if it doesn't work out?" Helen tugged on the door handle, but the door wouldn't budge.

"You'll see. Here." Logan reached across and wound the window down. "If all this works out, I'm going to pay to fix that handle. You have to open it from outside. Damn truck doesn't want anyone to leave."

Together, the three of them stood on Arvil's porch, facing the broken mortar and faded door that belonged to the man who could be their undoing. Like every horror story, fear of the thing was made worse by the waiting, so Logan opened the screen door and knocked.

The door flung open and a wave of warm, stale air smacked her in the face.

"What do the three of you want?"

Logan took slow, shallow breaths. "We have to talk to you. *I* have to talk to you."

"Well get in here. You're letting the heat out." He looked smaller somehow, as if he'd shrunk in the dryer. And he moved slower. He fell into his recliner and grasped his remote.

Behind Logan, Helen closed the door. Anxious energy bristled off Grey. He fidgeted, twisting his cap in his hands. Logan patted his shoulder to put him at ease. "Arvil, I need... I want to apologize to you. Have you seen the news?"

The man shook his head, his chin grazing his chest. "I don't watch all that fussing anymore."

He hadn't seen. He didn't know. It would have been easier to counter his rage than to build the case against herself from scratch. "It's not good. I made a mistake. Remember that bar competition? Well, I won. I have you to thank for that. Partly. But I did an interview after, and I got carried away. I said the wrong thing. Instead of being clear that you're letting Helen rebuild, I made it sound like you're standing in the way. And it'll be twisted, the way the news does. I hope you know what matters most is the truth between people, and we can fix this. I'm sorry."

"There's nothing to fix." Arvil's voice was firm.

Logan's heart sank. "No, there is. I am trying to apologize. To tell you I was wrong. I should have put the emphasis on the town. I should have cleared your name and said that you were totally willing to work with us—"

"Why do you have to make this so hard on me?" Arvil raised his eyes to her, and she saw, in the deep creases and lines, in the hang of the skin beneath his eyes, that he was preoccupied with something bigger than her scant apology.

"I don't. I'm sorry. Whatever you're going through—"

"My wife died years ago, and my kids moved away. I see them once a year at most. Funny, how that happens. You spend all those years doing everything for your kids, and they grow up, too busy to care. But they cared when they saw the news. They both called here, screaming and ranting at me for being an asshole and tearing down the one thing the town loves."

"I'll call them. I'll tell them the truth."

Arvil clutched the arm of his chair, his knuckles white. "Why don't you tell the *whole* truth?"

"That I lied to get the job? I did. That I'm the daughter of a man who's in prison in disgrace? I am. I didn't tell you I'm Lorne Cole's daughter because I wanted to make my own way in the world. I don't want to be my father's crimes. That's not fair to put that on me. But I messed this up. I made this mess, and I own it. I can't get forgiveness unless I ask."

Arvil let go of the remote. His fingers drummed the binding on the arm of his chair. Logan could feel Helen beside her, the questions sizzling off her like heat from the pavement on a hot summer day.

"Helen, I'm sorry I lied to you. I had the best of intentions. You know I sucked at the job, so I'm sure it's no surprise, but I couldn't tell anyone who I was because I was afraid the threats that drove me from New York would follow me here. I was safe from rogue internet trolls as long as nobody knew."

Helen clutched her purse at her side, her eyes wide and darting between Arvil and Logan.

"No wonder you can't get it together." A wry grin spread across Arvil's face and Logan returned it.

"Sure. Imagine going from housekeepers and private jets and multimillion dollar bank accounts to living in the apartment above the post office. I'm not looking for pity for what I lost. I'm asking for respect for what I made."

Grey shuffled his weight. "Fake it till you make it. That's what my dad always said. Doesn't work out well in plumbing, but it worked for her and bartending. She won."

Logan took her phone from her back pocket. "You pushed me, Arvil. You made me better at this. When you challenged me, I think a part of me mistook you for my father. And when I stood up to you, I was standing up to the kind of power and influence he had, the kind that crushes people for the thrill of it. Now we can both prove me wrong. I can wire you the money right now, and we can all move forward together, in a better place."

Late winter wind pushed down the street and rattled Arvil's ancient windows. The first time she passed his house it had been autumn. She'd been terrified when she stepped off the bus, marking time, certain that things would turn around, and she'd be back in her old life. There was no defining moment when she knew it was gone forever. But there had been several that told her she belonged in Ramsbolt.

"I fought dirty for a while because that's what I knew." Logan unlocked her phone and touched her banking app. "I'm sorry. Please forgive me and accept the payment so Helen can get back on her feet, and we can rebuild this bar. Don't do it for me, do it with me. It might not make you rich, and it won't bring my old life back, but we never wanted those things anyway, did we? It'll set things right with your sons, too. Save the bar with us?"

"What happens then?" Helen asked. "What happens with the bar?"

"We take the insurance money and a little of this, and we rebuild it like it was. Maybe with a few more windows. Place was dark. It won't be a five-star night club, but it never was. It'll be perfect for Ramsbolt. Arvil has to take this money first. The two of you sign an agreement. Then we'll craft an announcement that says Arvil saved the bar, that there was a legal paperwork delay, which is the honest truth."

Arvil ran a hand over his chin. "What if you end up in default again?"

"They won't." Grey tilted his head back and sighed at the ceiling. "Dude, half the town is at the old place waiting to celebrate. It's not even open, and it's crowded."

Arvil pushed up from his chair. It creaked when he stood and rocked in his absence. His face twisted in wrath and exhaustion.

"Please." Logan begged. "Please help the bar. The whole town, really. It all comes down to you."

A slow smile spread across his face. Not the kind he shot at her when he was full of complaints and ire. A smile Logan had never seen before.

"I'll get the account information. But I'm going to give you one piece of advice, Helen. You should make her your partner. She might be a shitty bartender, but at least she has the guts to keep the place open. Makes me think you didn't really need to sacrifice anything to learn a lesson either, Logan Cole. You just had to work for it."

CHAPTER THIRTY-ONE

Logan parked her Jeep behind the bar. The forecast called for rain. She zipped the windows back in place, secured the soft top, and stopped at the potted herb garden outside the back door. With her pocket tool, she snipped some garnish for the night's drinks—mint and a few sprigs of rosemary.

She walked along the side of the building, its bricks still smooth like new, and fought her key into the deadbolt to unlock the bar. She never tired of seeing the sign lit up. Cole's Tavern.

Eight years, ten months, and a few days had passed since she transferred money to Arvil's bank account. And it was two years, almost to the day, since she bought Helen out and made the bar her own.

She dropped her bag to the floor in the lobby, flipped a switch, and the light buzzed and flickered. Down to the last detail, the entrance had been recreated with a few exceptions for function, like sturdy coat hooks. The wood paneling had been salvaged from a restaurant in Bangor, and the cigarette machine, the ironic sole survivor of the devastating fire, had been restored by a man in town. It was empty now. A reminder of how far the town had come.

It would be a busy night, like most. Monday night football would bring in a crowd. Guided by the light from the coolers behind the bar, she crossed the room, opened blinds, letting what remained of the sun creep through the row of windows. Summer was ending, the days growing shorter.

Behind the bar, she flipped the row of switches. Streaming radio and lights came to life. With a quick glance at the walk-in cooler in the back and the stock at the bar, she decided that tonight would be one dollar cold Coronas. Someone had to drink them eventually. There would be few takers, mostly the drunks at the end of the night convinced they should have one more. Logan tied her hair back, dug her work shoes from her bag, grabbed a knife and cutting board, and sliced lemons into wedges and wheels.

She looked up when the door slammed. Arvil was on time. He wobbled on his cane to the edge of the bar, to the seat closest to the door. Shuffling into the bar chair that no one dare touch, he waved a hand and propped his cane on the hook below the bar top.

"Evening, Arvil." With Arvil's bad hearing, Logan had to shout to be heard. "What'll it be tonight?"

He leaned forward and squinted to hear, as if focusing his eyesight would give help to his ears. He waved a hand. "Nothing yet. Too early to drink. You'll have the game on?"

"Always. I'd never deprive you of football or hockey." Logan slid the remote down the bar. She hated sports but loved the customers. "Here. You're in charge."

He lifted his glasses from his nose and smashed the buttons until the television came on. The radio gave way to a pregame show, and he sat back, a satisfied lump. The room filled with chatter as the hours passed, and Arvil went from listening to reading the bottom of the screen.

People arrived in clusters. Groups of two and three. Men and women fresh from work in shops and fields. Logan popped the caps off brown bottles and filled frosty glasses with craft beer from the taps. There were few cocktails to be made on football nights, but the work was easier with fewer dishes to wash.

She didn't notice when Grey came in and slid onto his usual seat in the shadowed corner, but when he caught her eye, she tugged the bar towel from her shoulder and gave him her full attention. At least for a minute.

"Hey, babe. How's the night going?" He reached across the bar and stole a cherry from the garnish tray.

She gave him a playful swat. "Pretty good. A little busier than usual, but it's football."

"Ever miss...days...dead in here?"

Logan leaned across the bar. "What? I can't hear you."

"Do you ever miss the days when it was quiet in here?"

"Oh! No. Sometimes I miss the peace, but I don't miss being that poor." She rubbed at a spot on the bar with her towel.

"Can I get an Oxbow? The Loretta?"

"Sure." Logan filled a cold glass at the tap. Her phone buzzed in her back pocket. She placed the beer before her husband as she turned her back to the bar and pulled out her phone. The number wasn't familiar, but caller ID gave it away. The only person she knew at a Central Detention Facility in a Washington, DC area code was her father.

"Gotta take this," she yelled to Grey. "I'll be right back."

"I'll hold down the fort."

She swung the office door open with her hip. The room was hot. She flipped a switch on the back of the small metal fan, and it whirred on her desk. She fell into the office chair she'd scavenged from the antique shop and slid the toggle to accept the call.

"You have a collect call from an inmate at—"

She listened to the prompts and accepted the charges.

"Father. Hello." The last time she heard his voice, he was on the other side of bulletproof glass. It was the week before she married Grey, and she'd been proud to introduce to her father a man who was nothing like him. He'd told her never to visit again. He didn't like to be seen in orange.

"Peanut! You still have the same number. Of course, you do."

"I'm at work."

"You work at night?"

Logan tapped a pen on her desk. She wasn't giving him a single thing to use against her. Whatever he wanted, she couldn't relent. "I know calls from prison are timed, so you probably don't have long. What do you need? Money? Did you run out of quarters for the commissary?"

A snort or a snarf came through. It may have been a laugh.

"It won't hit the news until tomorrow, but I've been pardoned. I'll need a place to go. Tell me where you're living now, and they will see to it that I get there."

"Go to Mom."

"She divorced me. You know that. And she lives in Europe. I'm not *allowed* to have a passport. I can't leave the country." If he tried to conceal his condescension, he didn't put much effort into it. That anyone would allow Lorne Cole to do anything was still an abhorrent thought. You could lead a narcissistic felon to prison, but you couldn't force him to drink the redemption. "I'll stay with you and your plumber until I can get back into the ring. A few good suits and a long weekend in New York, and I'll be back."

"It's not a good idea that you come here." Logan took the cap from a pen and scribbled little pinwheel flowers on the back of the electric bill. No matter how many times she signed up for paperless billing, the bills kept coming. "There's gotta be some program that will help you get settled somewhere, but I can assure you that this place, where I live, is not a stepping stone to anything you'd want."

Silence fell on the battlefield between them, a verbal weapon they both possessed. She pictured him in his prison uniform, sitting at a desk in a small concrete room with a battered rotary phone to his ear, his chin lifted against her will. His silence wouldn't work this time. Not on his daughter. Maybe he still played his games of intimidation with his fellow inmates, who stepped aside and bowed to his whims. Perhaps they made room for him at their tables hunching over their trays of slop, afraid of the consequences of crossing Lorne Cole, but Logan lived in the real world, and she owed him nothing.

On the wall next to her desk, hanging next to a calendar she never changed on time, was a framed picture from the cocktail competition nearly a decade before. Her father would not have been proud of the woman she was then, and he wouldn't be proud of her now. He would never be content to sit in her bar and talk to the people of Ramsbolt, and he wouldn't respect them for making room for him.

"You ungrateful child. Billions of dollars I spent on you, that education you threw away, and all those lavish clothes and trinkets so you could fit into your skin. And now you don't have room for your father. You and that plumber. You're still a Cole. Remember that."

"You know what? You're right. You didn't want me in your life when it mattered to me, and I never forgot that. So I changed what it meant to be a Cole. I didn't take Grey's name because I'll always be a Cole. While you were in prison not learning your lesson, I was out here earning my integrity with hard work. Every penny and every ounce of respect I have I earned. It's not about shiny things and tainted money anymore. This town respects me. They don't care one bit about the money you lost or the influence you wish you still had. Life is different here, and if you think you're gonna stage a comeback from my home, forget it. I wish you the best, but you won't find a warm welcome here. Not with me."

"I have no intention of staying in that dump forever—"

"Exactly. No matter where you go, no one will respect you. They never really did."

"How fucking dare you."

"You know how? With the balls I earned with hard work. You'll figure it out."

"Don't come to me for help getting out of there. Whatever shithole apartment you live in with rats and cockroaches and human filth. I won't give you a dime."

"I live in an adorable Cape Cod that Grey and I pay for on time, every month, with money we make from the businesses we own. Give me a dime of what? You made ninety-two cents an hour in prison." And then it hit her, the way the earliest light of morning makes shapes of the dark. "You hid money, didn't you? In Cyprus."

"No, I did not."

"You did. You won't admit it because these calls are recorded, but I know you. The second you get out of there, you'll start the cycle again, flinging money through accounts, using the interest to build your powerhouse. Don't you get it? It's all fake. Until you hit rock bottom and have to pull yourself up, you won't know what integrity is. It's not being a bully with a bank account. I gotta go. I gotta get back to work, but you take care, okay? Good luck."

She held the phone away from her ear, and her finger hovered over the *end* button. She couldn't hear his words, but the rage came through loud and clear. She pressed the red circle in a quiet victory. There would be pictures in the news of an older Lorne Cole dressed in jeans and a sweatshirt, being ushered into a hotel by undercover agents. It would have been better optics to ride in an SUV to the cottage in Maine his daughter shared with her husband. She couldn't blame the man for trying.

There was a sense of peace that came from saying no. Her father had taught her that. The beggars will come knocking, he always said. Say yes once, and they'll never leave. It was a crude lesson, meant to protect the social class. She hadn't taken it to heart until now, when wealth had a different meaning.

Logan shoved her phone back into her pocket, adjusted her ponytail, and pulled the door open. She stepped into a crowd screaming about a fumble and waved a hand at Grey. The crowd meant everything to her. She couldn't care less what they wore when they walked through her door, what team they cheered for, who won or lost. It only mattered that Ramsbolt showed up. That was all the validation she needed.

"It was my dad." She yelled over the chatter. "He's getting a pardon. I'll tell you about it at home. Refill?"

"Sure. You okay?"

She gave a nonchalant shrug and pulled an empty glass from the cooler. "Yeah. Means nothing to me. I mean, I wish him well. He'll figure it out." A stream of beer filled the glass, and Grey gave her a wink. She never kept secret how she felt about her dad, though she never said a word about how thankful she was that he taught her well. She placed the beer before Grey, raising a hand to acknowledge Arvil as he flagged her down. There was a time he would have railed at her for stepping away from the bar, and her heart would be in her throat, waiting for the rebuke. Whether one or both of them had tempered with age, or she'd earned his trust, she no longer expected his criticism. Now she expected his drink order.

"What can I do for ya?"

"Drink," he said and pushed his empty glass in her direction.

She placed his glass upside down in the tray. No drip of golden liquid ran from it. Whatever dredges he'd left had gone dry. Arvil squinted at the rows of bottles behind the bar as if searching for one that called to him.

"You want a minute? I can come back."

"I don't know what I want."

"Straight? You want a cocktail?"

"That. A cocktail. Nothing too girly. Nothing cold. I don't want to get hit in the face with ice."

It had been years since he stumped her, but he still tried sometimes, in this softer way. He kept her on her toes, and he was twice the man her father was. Sometimes blood wasn't thicker than water.

"How about cherry and blood orange?" Logan took a cocktail glass from a rack beneath the bar.

Arvil pounded the bar in agreement. "Perfect. You make the best Blood and Sand."

ABOUT THE AUTHOR

A Maryland native and Pennsylvanian at heart, Jennifer M. Lane holds a bachelor's degree in philosophy from Barton College and a master's in liberal arts with a focus on museum studies from the University of Delaware, where she wrote her thesis on the material culture of roadside memorials. She resides with her partner Matt and a tuxedo cat named Penny.

Receive free prequel stories, news about upcoming releases and more by signing up for the author newsletter at
jennifermlanewrites.com

OTHER WORKS BY THE AUTHOR INCLUDE

Of Metal and Earth
Stick Figures from Rockport
And The Collected Stories of Ramsbolt Books:
Blood and Sand
Penny's Loft
Hope for Us Yet

ENJOY THIS SPECIAL PREVIEW CHAPTER

Penny's Loft

The Collected Stories of Ramsbolt, Book Two

"How many LEGOs did you eat?" Penny put her pen light back in the pocket of her lab coat and nudged the boy's chin, closing his mouth. She held up a hand to count backward from five and tucked in her thumb. "Was it this many?"

The three-year-old boy shook his head and blond curls bounced. "Free," he said.

"Three. That's not many. Were they the big green sheets or the little tiny onesies?" Penny pinched her fingers together and wrinkled her nose. The boy giggled. Kids who weren't really injured were the second-best part of being in medical school, right after the ones who were that she could mend with a lollipop.

"Little blocks. Like blueberries."

The boy's mother clutched her purse in both hands and perched on the edge of the padded chair. "His sister was building food out of them. That must have been where he got the idea. I turned my back for one minute to take a call. Another one of those telemarketers. My parents are older, and I have to answer the phone, you know?"

Penny had seen it before, the guilt of a parent and leaving a child unattended and returning to find the unimaginable. She'd bandage the wound, and they'd show signs of relief, yet the fear of things far worse would stick with them for days.

She removed her gloves and dropped them into the trashcan by the sink. "Kids are sneaky. It's not your fault. It should pass through him in three or four days, and he'll be fine."

The woman didn't look relieved, though. Her knuckles were white, her fingers digging into the tan leather of her purse. "Larry's going to kill me."

"Is Larry his father?" The woman wore no rings.

Her nod was small. Almost imperceptible. "He's on his way." It sounded like a threat.

Penny had been trained to see the signs. A woman whose fear was disproportionate to the situation. Certain scrapes and bruises on a child. Little Bobby seemed unharmed, except for the assault on his esophagus from a LEGO or two. But something about the woman's demeanor said she wanted to be gone when Larry arrived.

"I had to call him. Last time..." she trailed off, white lines appearing on her leather bag as her nails went against the grain.

The hospital had an officer trained to deal with abuse, and Penny was obligated to report it, but she needed a little more confirmation of her suspicion before she called in the big guns. Starting a spiral of paperwork could throw a child into a system that he didn't belong in, and it could damage a woman's reputation if all she had was a nervous tic.

Sometimes it was better to be upfront about things. "I'm not a full-fledged surgeon yet, but I do have a duty to report if I think there might be something going on. Is there anything you want to say?"

The woman was still looking at her bag when the curtain yanked to the side, and a man Penny assumed was Larry stormed into the room, nearly tripped over the trash can, and hovered over Miss Hopkins. She looked like a puppy who peed on the floor, assuming a stance of ridicule and shame.

He spit his words loud and fast. Accusations about terrible parenting and neglect.

Penny clapped her hands to get his attention. She knew better than touch him or raise her voice and make things worse, but at the clap of her hands, Bobby began to cry. Miss Hopkins raised her hands to cover her ears, which seemed to cause a demon to rise within Larry. He swung into the stainless-steel tray that sat atop a cart. Metal forceps and scissors hurled into the air and Penny lunged, covering the boy with her body.

The boy's primal fear unleashed, and he screamed into her chest. She held him close.

"Shh. It's okay. People are coming. It's okay."

They had to be. There was no way all that racket went ignored by the nurse's station. It was only twenty feet away.

Her back was to the curtain. The sound of it ripping from the rail and falling to the floor was a welcome one. Peeking at the floor, she saw the shoes of a police officer. One was always stationed at the hospital. Orderlies in their white slacks rushed in behind him. As they wrestled with Larry and calmed Miss Hopkins, Penny lifted Bobby and carried him to the nurse's desk. His little form trembled, and he settled on her lap as she fell into an old office chair that had lost its seat padding years before.

"Do you like lollipops? I always keep a magic stash back here. They're really good for soaking up the tears."

She tugged open a drawer, and candy slid against the front. She plucked a green one with a looped paper handle and ripped off the wrapper. "Here you go. Can you tell me a story? Do you have a kitty at home? Or a doggie?"

Bobby clutched the popsicle in his little fist. Between gulps of air that wretched his body, he said, "I had a kitty, but Larry took it."

That man really is a monster. She wanted to curse but knew better than to say it out loud.

Penny never had a pet as a kid. The security deposit cost too much, and her mother couldn't afford it on a single mother's income. But she'd always wanted something to cuddle that relied on her. And this man was destroying everything in this boy's life.

"Penny? Is this Bobby Hopkins?"

She straightened her back and lifted her chin to see over the high counter. In the background, the emergency suite was empty. Instruments strewn across the floor, the cart on its side. Blood splattered on the torn curtain where Larry must have put up a fight on his escort to a police car. Someone ran a piece of yellow tape across the entrance. It would be photographed before it was cleaned. And before her was Rebecca from child services, her arms out ready to take the boy.

Penny cleared her throat. "This is Bobby. He was just about to tell me if green was his favorite flavor or not. Bobby, this is Rebecca."

In a sea of doctors and nurses in pastel scrubs, Rebecca wore yellow scrubs covered in puppies. Her hair was pulled back in a curly ribbon barrette, and she wore a wide expression like a Broadway musical cast member. She held out her arms.

"I know where your mom is. Do you want to go see her?"

Bobby nodded and slipped off Penny's lap to the floor. He walked around the counter to the bubbly child protective services work.

"Someone will be by for your statement, Penny. Hang tight."

"Will do. Carry him if you can. He wants to be close, and he's really

315

scared."

And just like that, the little boy was gone.

"You did good in there." Cassie wheeled next to her. "Nice instinct, protecting the kid."

"Thanks. What else was I supposed to do?" Knock Larry upside the head with the tray, for starters?

"More paperwork. Aren't you overjoyed?"

"Poor little boy is full of LEGOs and tears, and all this place is worried about is paperwork." Penny pulled her ink pen from her lab coat pocket and stuck the cap in her mouth.

Cassie scowled and turned back to her computer. "That's a disgusting habit. Really."

"As if you don't look at a thousand bowel movements a day."

"Lee says he thinks you have one of those stress-related oral fixation things."

"Yeah, well if Lee saved his diagnosis for his patients, I wouldn't have a Lee problem on top of my stress problem."

"You know he has a crush on you, right?" The corner of Cassie's mouth curled into a smile.

"Ever the matchmaker. Thanks, but no thanks. I have one goal. Surgeon. Anything else is a distraction." Anything else would break the promise she made to her mother in her dying days, that she would get a good education and become a surgeon, to keep more kids from losing their parents. Many years had gone by since then, but she'd never lost sight of that goal.

"You look exhausted." Cassie nudged a drawer with her knee. "We've got energy drinks stashed in there."

She stifled a yawn. "I hate those things. It's gonna take a lot more than an energy drink anyway."

"Maybe you need a vacation. Some place warm. A little long-weekend fling? Or a long little-weekend fling?"

"Funny. But no." Penny shook her head, and red curls came loose from her hair tie.

"You have been doing a lot of doubles lately."

"I wouldn't have to if Lunsford had put me on rotation at the start of the semester instead of giving me a week off for no reason. Then my grandmother died, and I had to make that up. I didn't even know her. I said I only wanted one day off, but they gave me the week anyway for bereavement. Now here I am. Doubles forever."

"Sorry, Penn. It's been a rough semester for you. It'll all work out. Maybe you can find a way to sneak in a little calm. Some aromatherapy. Tracey swears by a hot bath at the end of the day with lavender in it."

Penny rolled her eyes. "Hard to find peace in an apartment with neighbors like mine. I just have to get through school, be a surgeon, save my pennies. Someday I'll be able to afford a penthouse condo. I've never lived in one, but I hear it's the American dream."

"Well, I'm gonna have to leave you to your dream. This ER is full of patients, I'm down a room, short two nurses, and all this paperwork doesn't file itself." Cassie spun in her wheelie chair and scooted across the tile. If it weren't for Cassie keeping an eye on the residents, helping them avoid mistakes and route paperwork in the right direction and for stepping in to defend them and take the blame when they made simple mistakes, Penny would have found herself on Lunsford's bad side twice as often. And if not for Cassie's banter, Penny would probably lose her sanity.

Her phone buzzed in her pocket. "Shit." She dug for it past the pens and her stethoscope. It was forbidden on the floor, but she'd forgotten to leave it in her locker.

New email. Fifteen new notifications on top of the sixty-three she hadn't read yet. She scrolled through them, deleting the spam. It was a gratifying purge, watching spam from shoe retailers and life insurance scammers fly out of her inbox. The only things left were from school, a few memos from the hospital about medical errors and needlestick procedures. And the email that had been sitting in her inbox for ten days now from some guy she didn't know with the subject line "Eliza's Will—Info about Ramsbolt Antique Shop."

The subject line glared up at her like the kind of unfinished business that gets worse the longer it's ignored. The kind that would take forever to unravel and stress her out for days. It was her favorite kind to ignore, in fact. But now that she'd opened it, there was no going back. At least she could get a sense of what she was up against while she waited to give her statement about the psychotic dad who'd scared that little boy, abused her instrument tray, and caused her a ream of paperwork.

A few files were attached to the email. A scanned letter from her grandmother. A copy of the will.

What was I just saying about distractions?

Her face grew hot with anger. Her mom had always kept her from Ramsbolt. Said the town was small and junky, and her grandmother's antique shop was nothing but a hoarding store, that the woman never sold anything. If her mom was right, it was probably packed to the gills with crap.

I'm so sorry for your loss, the email said. *Everyone here loved her, and she's been missed the last two months.*

Months. Had it been that long since her grandmother died? Since she drove to Ramsbolt in the rain just in time for the burial, hid beneath an umbrella while people she never met put the grandmother she never knew to rest? She'd been ashamed of running off so soon, rushing back to the city and back to work. Like she turned her back on some ancient mourning ritual that was supposed to make her feel something about the loss. But the truth was, she only saw the woman once, and she had no interest in Ramsbolt.

She opened the second attachment first, the letter from her grandmother. A black and white scan of a missive in ink, in the shaky scrawl of an aging hand. Still more legible than half of what she saw from fellow doctors. The edges were blotchy, and the thin lines of her writing were broken up by the scanner, but her name was clear at the top of the page.

Dearest Penny,

It shall probably come as a surprise to find yourself in the possession of a cluttered antique store. But with your aunt and mother both gone, you—as Arvil tells me—are the rightful heir. I'm ashamed to have left you with so much jumble and debt to dispose of.

Who was Arvil? How much debt? A wave of heat washed over her, and anger rose with it. She had enough debt of her own between school and that stupid credit card she almost maxed out when she was young and hungry. As if she wasn't still young and hungry.

My hope is that you'll be able to sell the stuff, sell the store, and make a tiny profit to put toward school. Wherever you are, whatever you're doing with your life, may it be some small help to you.

Some small help? Penny swiped the apps closed and turned off the screen. Who did this woman think she was, throwing herself into Penny's life after not being a part of it? This was more than a distraction.

It was a disaster. She stuck the cap of the pen in her mouth and squeezed it tight between her molars.

"That can't taste better than tater tots. Wanna go get lunch with me?" Lee leaned across the counter and peered down at her. "Whoa, you look like someone just handed you an accreditation visit and a massive pile of complicated medical histories to read."

"Yes, and worse." She nodded toward the cordoned-off room. "A guy flipped out on his ex in front of his kid."

"That's not so bad. Happens all the time. Come eat with me. I hate eating alone. You can tell me about the worst part." His puppy dog eyes would have given him away if she wasn't already aware of his sentiments. He didn't care one bit about eating alone. "Besides, you look like you could use a break."

"Can't. I have to stick around until the cops take my statement. The worst part is this email I just opened that I got two weeks ago. My grandmother left me some store full of junk and a lot of debt, and now I have to figure out what to do about it. I've been pulling a string of doubles. I'm tired. I just need more than a break. I need like a month off."

"You got an email from a lawyer two weeks ago and didn't open it until now? Christ. I know you've been exhausted and working a lot, but you've gotta read your email more often."

"I still haven't read the will. Just the email. And it wasn't from a lawyer. Some guy who lives in town. Anyway, how's the world of addiction counseling?"

Lee shrugged. "Fixating. Pun intended. But don't deflect. You do that. You like to avoid things. You really should read that will and take care of that."

She feigned a dramatic collapse on the desk. "It can wait. I'm really ticked off though. Who the hell just gives somebody a store without asking? Like I don't have enough on my plate to be dealing with the end of her life. It's like revenge for my mother not wanting to be a part of hers, and now I have to go up there to that god-awful town and dig through all her trash."

"Where is it, the store?" Lee's beeper went off, and he dug it from his pocket.

"North. Much north. Little town called Ramsbolt."

"Never heard of it. Guess you'll be up to your elbows in a rural vacation, then."

"Lord, no." Penny waved at Officer Wilson as he approached the desk to take her statement. "Hell will freeze over before I step foot in Ramsbolt, Maine."